Lincolnshire
COUNTY COUNCIL

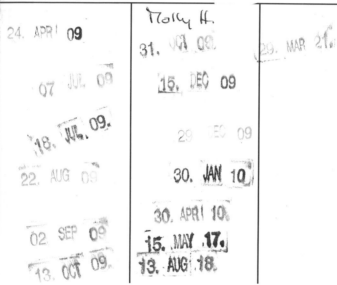

A Hanging Matter

A Hanging Matter

MARGARET DUFFY

First published in Great Britain in 2002 by
Allison & Busby Limited
Bon Marche Centre
241-251 Ferndale Road
Brixton, London SW9 8BJ
http://www.allisonandbusby.ltd.uk

A catalogue record for this book is available from the British Library

ISBN 0 7490 0562 9

Printed and bound by Creative Print & Design,
Ebbw Vale, Wales

MARGARET DUFFY was born in Woodford, Essex and has worked for the Inland Revenue and the Ministry of Defence. She now lives in Devon in a one-time crossing-keeper's cottage with her husband and two cats. She divides her time between writing and garden design.

To Mike and The Wednesday Walkers

Lydtor, Devon, Friday 4th August 5.45 pm

'One day, if I'm alive and in honest employment, will you consider me for general tidying up and emptying your wastepaper basket?'

'Yes, I'll have you to grace my heart and my hearth even if you're broken and old and just out of prison.'

Those words, Patrick's second proposal of marriage - we have been married twice - and my reply, returned to haunt me the day he was arrested.

The Inspector from Special Branch, who arrived with a quite staggering amount of back-up, appeared to be aware of the uniqueness of the situation: for after all it is not very often that the Co-ordinator of Defence Studies at Army Staff College, Camberley is taken into custody and charged with murder. That the suspect had also worked for MI5 and, before that, for a Special Forces unit and was in possession of an awesome, if not downright scary, reputation for self-preservation was no doubt the reason for the van loaded with armed men from the Territorial Support Group, the brace of dog-handlers and a rather sinister individual whose role remained unclear and who was wearing an outfit that can only be described as a black leather wet-suit *sans* flippers.

None of them was needed of course, Patrick's only response to the Inspector's stiff little oration being a curt nod. On his way out however, having been permitted to change his clothes and pack a bag, he did smile, or rather bared his teeth fleetingly, at the leather-clad one as one might flash a knife.

A certain amount of awkwardness had possibly been averted by the presence of the children, all keen on that Friday afternoon to welcome Patrick home for the beginning of his summer leave. This had also no doubt accounted for the sheepish look on the arresting officer's face when he first beheld the dangerous suspect in his Lieutenant-Colonel's uniform with his own offspring, Justin and Victoria, in his arms, and our adopted pair, Matthew and Katie, who are older and too big to be thus casually scooped from the floor, bouncing delightedly by his side, all four talking at the tops of their shrill young voices.

I kept quiet and firmly in the background. There were important reasons for this, the main one being that my first responsibility was to the children, especially right now as their nanny, Carrie, was on holiday. Also, I was far more use to Patrick in possession of my freedom, although it would be foolish to assume that I would not be questioned at some stage. I had worked closely with him in his MI5 days and between us we probably knew more about the case in question than all branches, special or otherwise. So I had acknowledged Patrick's warning glance with what I hoped was a calm smile, even though inwardly in turmoil, and concentrated on damage control with regard to the devastated youngsters watching the vehicle bearing him away.

Chapter One

Much later, when all the children but Matthew, who is twelve, were in bed, I had a chance to sit down in order to think things through. Life with Patrick has been full of surprises, not all of them pleasant, but this latest development had left me numbed. His briefcase was still where he had put it down in the hall - I don't think he and I had actually had time to greet one another such was the pell-mell haste of the police on his tail. I had an idea they had concealed themselves in one of the village's ancient and overgrown lanes - some now used as bridleways - and Patrick, for once, had not spotted their presence. It would have made no difference if he had for I imagine his conscience was clear and he little expected after all this time to be enmeshed with the death of that particular Commander in the Anti-terrorist Branch.

Before coming indoors I had wandered in the garden for a while, not enjoying my latest project, a patio, as I usually did, in fact hardly seeing it. It was shock, I supposed, that made me feel like this, as though I was in a vacuum. All the bad memories were returning, things I thought I had forgotten about that I had earlier promised myself I would put in a novel to exorcise them. But I have never been able to and now know that turning your worst nightmares into print does not mean they lose their power over you. Shivering, even though the early evening was very warm, I had returned to the cottage.

Matthew came looking for me. He has a very grown-up head on his shoulders and I felt that the explanation I had given the others - that Patrick was not actually under arrest but was helping the police with an investigation - for him simply wouldn't do. Unnervingly, he looks very much like Patrick did at that age - he and Katie are actually the children of Patrick's dead brother Larry - and right now as he entered the room I found myself subjected to his uncle's searching gaze.

I patted the settee cushion next to me and he came and sat down.

'Once upon a time,' I began with a wry smile, knowing that he would understand and appreciate the irony of my tone, 'Two or three very senior policemen put their heads together and came up with an idea to catch the world's most wanted terrorists. They created a new identity for one of their number, in short they turned him into a criminal. Then they set up a survival school in the Brecon Beacons in Wales where people were taught outdoor skills and so forth. But that was just a front for another kind of enterprise entirely, a school for terrorists. The idea was that foreign criminals would be lured into this country and then arrested at the end of the course after as much as possible had been found out about them, who their partners in crime were and what they planned to do next.'

'And they fell for it?' Matthew asked in amazement.

'The underworld credentials of the man running it were very, very good and he employed real criminals as instructors,' I told him. 'Police forces abroad had allowed him to commit a few crimes like killing other crooks and he'd been deliberately blamed for things no one knew who was really responsible for.'

'I think it's a terrible idea,' Matthew said.

Patrick had thought so too.

'It gets worse,' I continued. 'The man in charge realised that these people would have to be asked to hand over large fees for their tuition, otherwise they would begin to suspect a trap. He and a friend of his decided, after the first couple of courses had taken place as rehearsals, with policemen taking the part of students, to keep the money and arrange quite a large "accident" to befall their real customers. So no mention of fees would ever reach the ears of their superiors, of course.'

'I suppose Uncle Patrick found out about it.'

'Only by chance. Your Dad had a pot-shot taken at him when he was leading a group from his school on an activity weekend in the area. They were deemed to be too close to the survival school's HQ in old mine workings. Quite a few youth groups suffered damage to their kit and other interference as the so-called survival school people tried to scare them out of the area. Your father told Patrick about it and he investigated.'

'But to run something like that where lots of people go on holiday!'

Patrick, of course, had added quite a few imaginative epithets to his own comments.

'And surely trying to scare people away only drew attention to themselves?'

'There were a lot of things that weren't thought through properly, Matthew.'

'You're very calm about this, Auntie,' he observed.

The children have never been told of my role as Patrick's working partner. And now I was probably, in an effort to help him, going to have to cast off what I had come to regard as my normal way of life; that of successful author living on the fringe of Dartmoor with four children, a horse and a cat, not to mention the army officer husband in a highly paid job who until three hours previously had been as safe as houses - albeit bored out of his skull.

'There's no use flying into a panic,' I said rather lamely. In truth I was half expecting the phone to ring at any minute and to hear Patrick's voice telling me that it was all a mistake and he was on his way home.

'But he went and sorted it out, didn't he? He must have done. And someone was killed. Now he's in trouble for it.'

I could hardly reveal that quite a few people had been killed. The final showdown, Operation Rookshoot, had actually finished up as a small war in a natural cavern deep inside the mine workings. Yes, we had sorted it out together, although my part had been a small one. But only after the

15

man in charge had captured us and, even though he knew who we were, forced us to reveal quite a lot of classified information about our department, mostly to boost his own image and ego.

'It wasn't quite that simple,' I said. 'But in a nutshell, yes, you're right.' I didn't tell Matthew that the reason Patrick had sworn to personally close the place down was that two children had been killed by one of the men on the first of the real 'courses', deliberately knocked down by the car he was behind the wheel of for no other reason than they had been walking on the side of the road on which he wished to drive.

'Uncle Patrick might go to prison.'

'That would be the worst thing that could happen,' I agreed. Especially now he was no longer working for MI5 and therefore under that organisation's protection.

The truth was perfectly straightforward. Commander 'X', as he had been referred to, had survived the 'war' and, still in his role of international criminal Anton Lyndberne, had given himself up to the local police. Those in the know at the Home Office - it was only much later that the Home Secretary had been forced to resign - had come to the conclusion that even though a small department of MI5, taking direct orders from the Prime Minister, had put an end to the operation at Brecon it would be set up again, for one last time, somewhere else. The problem of bringing Lyndberne to 'trial' was overcome by the neat arrangement of having him extradited to Germany, ostensibly to answer for crimes he had committed there and the entire episode had faded from public memory.

Commander X had returned to the UK using his own passport and shortly afterwards gone on holiday, fishing in Scotland, where his rowing-boat had capsized on a loch. He couldn't swim.

Although it was not strictly true to say that Patrick had organised the killing he had definitely been an accessory to murder; a conversation with an old friend, a one-time Brigadier in the Tank Regiment who had become a mercenary and eventually died fighting for the Croats in Bosnia, had resulted in that colourful but dangerously irrepressible man drawing his finger meaningfully across his throat and departing to hunt down his prey, never to be seen in this country again.

'Is there much evidence, do you know?' Matthew ventured cautiously, divining my own thoughts.

I shook my head. 'Only insofar as your uncle told two detectives in Bath what had happened.'

'When Dad died?' All the hurt had returned to his eyes.

I had to be careful here as I had no wish to resurrect unhappy memories. Larry had been murdered by a colleague of Commander X who had been involved with Brecon, although not actually present. That man was now in prison, serving a life sentence.

'There was a connection,' I replied and left it at that. The fact that Superintendent Buller and Detective Chief Inspector James Carrick were not the kind of men to lie under oath could not be ignored. But the case against Patrick could hardly hinge on their evidence alone, evidence it must be said that, to my knowledge, had never been committed to writing or recorded on tape. Surely that made it inadmissible in any British law-court.

I gave him my best smile. 'Patrick has been in all kinds of trouble in the past for slaying dragons and rescuing damsels in distress. Don't worry, I'm sure he'll soon be home.'

'But he didn't actually kill this man himself, did he?'

'No, of course not,' I told him, cursing my stupid choice of words. 'We were in the States when it happened.'

Matthew went away, still looking unhappy.

Was I being complacent? Was the fact that the man in my life had always in the past got himself out of trouble - and often in contentious cases been proved right - clouding my judgement of the situation? Soldiers, of course, do kill people. But he had never been arrested before, never strayed too far outside his Queen and Country guidelines or made me feel any the less of him. Did one though become innured to it, in effect become brainwashed?

I made myself examine what my own feelings would be if in fact Patrick *had* swum out to that boat, capsized it and held the man who had been sitting in it under the water until he was dead. Commander X, in his role as Lyndberne, had been very dangerous, prepared to do anything in a frenzied quest to catch the most wanted men in the world. He had been driven by ambition, hoping to persuade the Home Secretary to allow him to set up an outside-the-law unit along the lines of the Secret Police forces of the most repressive countries on Earth.

Yes, he had certainly been more than slightly mad and influential, equally ambitious politicians had allowed him his way.

How else do you stop people like that?

Later still I went to bed but could not sleep. What had occurred not two minutes after Patrick had walked through the door didn't actually make a lot of sense even if one discounted the fact that the police had now discovered that a verdict of Death by Misadventure should have been Unlawful Killing by Person or Persons Unknown. Naturally, they would want to catch the murderer of a senior colleague. But what new evidence had emerged? Patrick had met his friend in a pub in Soho and they had been seated outside, alone. It had not been an arranged meeting, they had literally bumped into one another. There was no question of Patrick's thirsting for revenge, after what had been done to us and finding himself a contract killer for he was perfectly capable of doing the job himself.

There was one possible lead that might have been followed up and used against him. The drowned body of Commander X had been washed up or, more likely, dragged onto the shore *and there had been a dead rook by its side.* A bizarre coincidence one might say except that, as already indicated, Patrick had called the final showdown at Brecon Operation Rookshoot. Not many people - who had lived to tell the tale, that is - had been aware of this. Patrick, I think, had been surprised when he had heard about the discovery of the dead bird because unprofessional and dramatic gestures had not been one of his friend's failings. He had put it down to his famed eccentricity and forgotten all about it.

Now it looked as though chickens, not rooks, were coming home to roost.

D12, the small department in MI5 that Patrick had headed, had been disbanded when he left, the reasons for this complex and nothing to do with dead policemen. Colonel Richard Daws, Patrick's boss, had retired to his castle in his better known capacity as the 14th Earl of Hartwood, married his old friend Pamela Westfield and settled down to write letters to the *The Times* and grow roses. Other members of the group were now scattered far and wide, relieved, probably, that that hair-raising part of their lives was behind them. It was beginning to look as though I would have to do any investigating on my own.

Two days passed - I forced myself to be patient - but then, having heard nothing from Patrick, I decided to take action. First of all I would go and talk to Daws.

I was in sober mood as I regarded myself in the mirror that morning to behold a fairly tall, slim woman still the right side of forty with dark hair cut into a long bob. My green eyes stared back at me as I asked myself if I was really fit for more excitement - and this latest development held every promise of living up to all the others - or whether I should simply find Patrick a good lawyer and concentrate on staying safely at home, writing, for my family's sake?

I collected the short-barrelled Smith and Wesson and ammunition from the wall-safe behind the print of Cadell's *Interior - The Orange Blind* in our bedroom and put it in my bag. (All the bags I have had for some time smell of gun oil.)

Never mind being fit, this woman was angry, and quite prepared to create a little awkwardness of her own if necessary.

Carrie had not gone abroad on holiday, she was just staying at her boyfriend's flat in Plymouth. It is written into her contract with us that she will forgo leave in an emergency but until now I had never had to take advantage of it. She seemed not to mind returning to Lydtor, in fact I thought I had detected relief in her voice when I had rung and wondered if the relationship was on the rocks again.

I had decided not to use the phone for further arrangements in case it was being tapped, although my trained ear had not detected any strange clicks or other sounds on the line that would have aroused suspicion. And all the while, my mind relentlessly churning out just about everything relevant I had been taught while working for D12, I was still half expecting Patrick to come breezing in, grinning widely, and take me in his arms in a bear hug.

We have known one another for almost always, or to be more precise since he was eighteen and Head Boy at the school we both went to. Although our lives had brushed a couple of times beforehand it was not until the day that he arrived at my home to help me with my physics homework - our respective fathers had made the arrangement but not thought to consult us beforehand - that this had been on a one-to-one basis. Patrick had made it perfectly clear from the start and without saying a word that girls were always lousy at physics anyway and he was wasting what would otherwise have been a pleasant evening. But soon, after a little point-scoring, we became involved with not physics but chemistry and I decided that here was the man I wanted for ever and ever.

We rode our bikes, took the dogs for long walks on Dartmoor and picnicked with a bottle of white wine chilling in a stream and I discovered that Patrick's main attraction was his ability to make me laugh. Then one day we laughed until we cried, hugging each other under the hot summer sun. We

20

were both quite innocent until that moment when I felt the warm skin of his back beneath the material of his shirt and the way the sinews of his body flowed beneath my fingers. Innocents one moment, we had not even kissed before, and the next as close as two human beings can become.

For a whole week of that long, hot summer we escaped to the empty open moor and extracted every possible moment of pleasure from our young bodies. We both knew we were doing wrong, our upbringing had seen to that. Then Patrick, openly suffering from a severe bout of conscience, had offered to marry me. My reply that I was only fifteen had caused him to attain a shade of paleness that I had previously thought humanly impossible but he had repeated the proposal, come hell, high-water, horsewhips and jail adding, as an afterthought, that he was crazy about me. I accepted but we did not marry until I was twenty-one and Patrick simply not the marrying sort by then; too many places to visit, too much to do, a real professional soldier.

Carrie arrived, breaking into my memories, full of concern for us and assurances that she had been thinking of coming back anyway as indeed there had been a big bust-up. I took my leave quickly having already told the children that I intended to visit Patrick and find out what was going on. This was perfectly true but I wasn't optimistic as to my success.

I had again considered getting a solicitor but then told myself that if everything was legal and above board Patrick would have the opportunity to do so, someone of his own choosing. It was only when, appalled, I analysed that thought and wondered why the doubt involving those four simple words 'legal and above board' had even entered my head that I realised that, subconsciously, I had called the whole thing into question right from the start. The gun was in my bag but really no more than as a morale-booster, a kind of declaration of preparedness.

I decided first to contact our old liaison officer, John Brinkley at Scotland Yard, and make enquires about the credentials of the man from Special Branch. I had remembered his name even though he had only given me a very quick glimpse of his warrant card.

Brinkley, now that D12 was no more, had been promoted and transferred to the Fraud Squad. It had been of vital importance to have someone with an overall view of surveillance operations. Otherwise, to have operatives deployed by various organisations involved with crime and national security blundering into one another's set-ups would have resulted in chaos.

But, as Patrick had remarked crisply to Daws afterwards, referring to Brecon, 'The last thing I think I'd do if that happened would be to string them up from the ceiling and plug them in to the mains.'

Brinkley hadn't been monitoring that one, no one this side of madness had.

John's deep voice was reassuring as he answered the re-directed call that I had made after walking to the call-box by the village post office. 'Lovely to hear from you, Ingrid. How's life in deepest Devon?'

'Complicated,' I told him, in the mood to get right to the point and also aware that people in his position are too busy to indulge in small talk during working hours. I related what had happened.

'I take it you want me to check the *bona fides* of this bloke.'

'Please - in view of what we both know has gone on before.'

'It'll take a couple of minutes. Do you want to ring back?' He gave me his new extension number.

I gave him five.

'Gold plated,' Brinkley reported briskly.

'But not twenty-four carat?' I queried.

'No, he worked his way up through Traffic and Complaints.' He laughed.

I have always found the snobbery attached to certain police departments utterly impenetrable.

'Do look me up if you're in town,' he went on to say. 'And

don't worry about the governor - I'm sure it's one of the complete balls-ups that Special Branch are prone to making when there's a full moon.'

'There was another man wearing bike-leathers who sort of lurked in the bushes.'

John laughed again. 'Well, you said they arrived with everyone but the Mounted Branch. Perhaps he was from Diplomatic Protection.'

'Have you any idea where Patrick might be being held?'

'Sorry, can't help you there. Could be at any one of several places.'

I thanked him but was not feeling particularly grateful. His tone had been light, disinterested even. The days of D12 were in the past and he was no longer involved.

I had not expected to be tailed but was prepared if it did happen. It did. Thinking it about time the Gillards chalked up a few points I decided to lose them and having recently completed an off-road driving course - with an Advanced Driver's One already under my belt - was keen to see exactly what our new Lichfield conversion Range Rover could do. It more than lived up to expectations and on one of the more scenic and interesting moorland routes to Hexworthy I caught a last glimpse in the mirror of my followers as they headed, at speed, shedding trim and other more important bits and pieces down a steep boulder-strewn slope towards the River Dart at the bottom.

Hartwood Castle is in West Sussex, in a fold of the South Downs. It guards the top of a narrow wooded valley and the closer you get to it the bigger it looks. This is partly an illusion, deliberate intimidation, for the moated keep at one end was built, like another at Arundel Castle not far away, on a high mound. The keep houses an armoury with ancient dungeons and store rooms below, deep inside the mound. Later additions to the structure, constructed over four centuries and in several architectural styles have been rationalised by the latest in the line of noblemen living there - Victorian and Edwardian additions were demolished - to leave today, in effect, a large adjoining country house.

When, towards late afternoon, I turned into the long curving drive lined with chestnut trees I soon realised that some kind of house-party was in progress. Vehicles with a good sprinkling of the Aston-Martin, Bentley and Porsche variety were parked with the careless aplomb of the wealthy. I manoeuvred into a space within half an inch of a Rolls, to enter into the spirit of the thing, and made my way to the main entrance.

There was still the feeling that I had rushed off into the blue too precipitantly. But Patrick had memorised my mobile phone number and hadn't rung. Nor had Carrie contacted me from home during my journey with any news. There had been nothing about the arrest in the papers and I was at the stage by now where national defamation heaped on his head would have been almost preferable to this utter silence.

There was no wish on my part to gate-crash a private social occasion. I just wanted a quiet word with 'our Richard' as we had referred to him, hopefully receive advice and a promise of help, and then depart. It seemed a shame to have to leave so soon as the Hartwood estate is extensive and very beautiful, the roses growing on the walls of the house included a breathtaking *Kiftsgate* and showed every sign of enjoying their retired owner's care and attention.

As I went by one of the open diamond-paned windows I was a little dismayed to hear the discreet but distinct sounds of the upper-class at tea; a murmur of conversation against a background of the chink of silver cutlery on fine bone china. I racked my brain. Was it in fact Daws' birthday?

There was no choice now but to brazen it out.

The butler answered my press of the large bell-push on the imposing oak front door. Jordon, whom I had met before, is one of the new breed of well-connected and highly paid young butlers who double as chauffeur and, in view of his employer's one-time career, was also his bodyguard.

He smiled. 'Miss Langley. Good to see you.'

'I know I'm barging in,' I said. 'But it's important I have a word with his lordship.'

He opened the door wide. 'I'm sure he'll be delighted. It's her ladyship's bash - she's hosting the AGM of the South of England Arabian Horse Society and he's been banished for the afternoon.'

With exactly the right mix of deference, friendliness and good-humour he led the way to the library, quite a long walk, where Daws was watching cricket on television. Morosely watching cricket on television. He switched it off with alacrity and every sign of relief when my presence was announced.

'Lousy match,' was his comment after greeting me.

I refrained from enquiring further in case I really spoiled his afternoon.

'Tea for Miss Langley, if you please, Jordon,' he ordered and went on to fuss as to which chair I should occupy and whether there were too many cushions in them.

I wasn't fooled by this. Daws does his old-duffer routine automatically while his shark's teeth wits give him a quick résumé of where he last saw you, what was said, what gossip he's heard about you in the meantime - probably from at least half a dozen different grapevines on both sides of the law - and whether he ought to mention anything that he's learned. It was from one of these sources that he originally heard the commander's death had been no accident.

He looked well, marriage suited him. I wondered if he was missing the buzz of D12 as much as Patrick. I also wondered whether he had already heard my news and if he had I was inwardly promising him that I would blow my top.

Daws - after all the years of not knowing about it I still couldn't think of him with a title - raked his greying fair hair from his forehead with the fingers of his right hand, a lifetime's mannerism, and regarded me with his steel-blue gaze. 'You're going to be very annoyed with me,' he said.

I took a deep breath. 'You know then.'

'That's not why you're going to be angry, Ingrid. I expected this. I always have done. I hinted as much to him on more than one occasion. The only course he has, and it's the right one, is to plead guilty and hope for the leniency of the court.'

For a moment, such was my shock, I couldn't breathe.

'From whichever way you look at it - and I'm just as aware as you are that the man who died was a monster - members of the security services can't arrange the death of a policeman and hope to get away with it.'

'Who told them? Was it you?'

'It's not in my interest to dig up the past like that,' he replied quietly, not seeming to be offended by my aggressive stance.

'Well, I can't see James Carrick or Superintendent Buller in Bath doing it. Buller said the case was closed as far as he was concerned and James is a friend of ours.'

'Several of the criminals taking part in the Brecon scheme survived and were either deported to face charges in their own countries or were jailed over here. One or two might be out of prison by now.' Daws shrugged. 'Quite a lot of potential for tale-telling.'

'But a trial will rake up all over again the resulting political scandal when the Home Secretary was forced to resign and...'

'That was a previous administration,' he reminded me grimly.

'You means it's really political?' I said. 'The government's using Patrick in some cheap point-scoring exercise as part of their election campaign?'

'I meant nothing. And I can't really be expected to comment.'

'I rather think you've just put the idea into my head,' I retorted.

'I must point out that there's no question, if he's found

guilty, of the Lieutenant-Colonel being led out and hanged from the nearest lamp-post. The judge *will* be lenient when all the evidence emerges of how you were treated at that damned set-up. As you know there's actual evidence of that.'

'The videos they made?' I gasped. 'They've been found? Of us naked and hanging up and...' Words failed me.

'It has to be admitted that it will also act as a reminder to certain people that the Home Office can't take on the Cabinet Office and prevail.'

Lots of birds, it appeared, were about to be slaughtered with one stone. I suddenly realised the real reason he had expected my fury. 'You've been acting as adviser on this.'

'Yes, but as a completely independent one.'

Just then Jorden entered with my tea.

When he had gone I said, 'It's a really despicable way to treat a man who's served his country so well for over twenty years.' I found myself gazing around the book-lined room, seeing the long-case clock that had stood in his office in Whitehall, the display cabinet housing his jade collection and the Wedgwood 'Black Astbury' china. All from the past, from that other lifetime.

'There was no question of revenge,' I said quietly. 'And from what I understood from Patrick when he related what had happened to the man who went away and did the deed, there was no stopping him.'

'No, Tim Shandy was always a hot-head. But in spite of it he was a very good tank commander.'

It was the first time I had heard a name mentioned - Patrick had never revealed who it was to me - but I let it go for a moment. I said, 'Be so good as to clarify one point for me; *this* time the scam isn't with Patrick's knowledge and co-opera-tion. Right now someone's really dropped him in it.'

A couple of years ago Patrick had been carpeted in a ploy to catch a top civil servant who had been serving his own ends. It had worked and an even bigger fish had been netted.

'Nothing like that at all,' was all Daws said, pouring the tea for me and placing cup and saucer before me, a plate of small fancy home-made cakes within easy reach.

I had no intention of wingeing on my own behalf. But the hurt was awful, it was a complete betrayal. All I could think about were the times Patrick and I had reached rock-bottom during various difficult assignments and somehow, somehow, picked ourselves up and seen the job through. Brecon had been like that.

I wanted to scream all this at Daws, rant and rave but instead merely put a level spoonful of sugar into my tea and stirred slowly. I don't take sugar.

'If he goes to prison I promise you it won't be for very long,' Daws said.

'No, they'll let him out for good behaviour,' I murmured. 'He'll have lost his job of course but it won't matter a bit because most of my books have either been made into films or dramatised for television so we're actually rather well off. I shall just have to decide what I'm going to tell the children.' Automatically, I sipped my tea and there was a short silence. Then I said, 'I never thought you'd support a scheme that would do this to Patrick.'

'As I said just now, I'm in an independent advisory position. The job demands that I remain impartial. And by his own admission he discussed with Shandy putting an end to this man's life. You were actually present when he said to *me* that had he known Lyndberne's true identity he would have put a bullet in him when he had the opportunity. And please let us stick to reality. You know as well as I do that if he so wishes Patrick Gillard has the strength of character to stop *anyone* doing *anything*.'

It seemed useless and petty to point out that people say all kinds of things in the heat of the moment. The irony of the thing was that Patrick had really refrained from shooting Lyndberne when he had the chance because he had then thought him a criminal.

'Where is he being held?' I asked.

'I'm not at liberty to give you that information.'

'D'you think I'm daft enough to try and break him out? So, no visits from his wife at whichever secure remand centre or police station it is, no legal representation, no...'

'Of course there will be legal representation,' Daws interrupted.

'But any lawyer worth his salt will sink such a case with all hands! Even the Director of Public Prosecutions will be made a laughing stock.'

Daws shook his head slowly and meaningfully.

'Fine,' I said, getting to my feet. 'You've just told me everything I want to know. It's a copper-bottomed stitch-up, one with Number 10's seal of approval.'

Daws also rose. 'It will only complicate matters if you start making a fuss.'

'That sounds just a little bit like a threat.'

'No, it's advice,' he said, quite kindly. 'You have my word that things won't go badly for him if everyone involved keeps their head. He might even be acquitted.'

'Thank you for the tea,' I said, making for the door.

'Ingrid...'

I butted in with, 'I thought it was only countries like the old Soviet Union where people could be pawns in show trials.'

His only response was to smile at me sadly.

I found my own way out.

Chapter Two

Absolutely the worst part of all this was knowing that Daws was probably right. People who were involved with stratagems to murder others should not be allowed to get away with it even if their part was only a minor one. I wondered exactly how much influence Daws had had on the decisions that had been made. Enough to have prevented Patrick's arrest? Possibly not. But Daws hadn't been at Brecon. He had not tried to give Claire, one of the children who had been killed, the kiss of life as she lay horribly injured in the road, the boy already dead in a nearby ditch. He hadn't tried to comfort their grieving parents. Daws was childless.

So was this 'trial' a price worth paying to remind the country yet again that the police should never be given virtually unlimited powers? That would be a by-product of the event even if the real purpose of those at present in government was to discredit a political party which might soon be voted back into office. The answer to the question, surely, was no, the reason being that if faceless civil servants in a police monitoring department were going to cook up 'evidence' in order to make a prosecution viable - and it would have to be pretty conclusive - then the same methods the trial was ostensibly concerned with presenting for public condemnation were being utilised.

In that case, in short, it stank.

I went home, there was nothing to be gained in blindly rushing about. Until I knew more I would give every appearance of meekly accepting the inevitable.

Whether Daws had pulled a few strings I was never able to discover but early the following morning I received a phone call from a solicitor, one Auguste DeKrille, inviting me to visit him in his London office at a time entirely at my own convenience. I did not press him for any details, just told him that I would fly up and be with him at three that afternoon. Then I changed my mind and said I would drive. He gave me the relevant directions of how to find him just off the Bayswater Road.

I had remembered just in time that the Smith and Wesson, still residing darkly at the bottom of my bag, and most emphatically going to stay there, would have been revealed by the airport's security X-Ray machine.

The traffic was bad so I left the car in a friend's driveway in Kensington, put a note through her letterbox saying that I would explain later, and took a taxi.

DeKrille did not look the kind of man to take part in anything dubious. But I had learned to ignore first impressions and rely on what my father had called my 'cats' whiskers', a certain sensitivity to vibes that has even, over the years, impressed Patrick. In appearance DeKrille was unremarkable; short and slightly tubby - a fact not concealed by an extremely well-cut suit - with dark curly hair, large brown and quite kindly heavily-lidded eyes and a somewhat lugubrious expression. He was, I supposed, around forty-five years of age.

I was waved to a leather chair in his surprisingly magnificent office and used the time while he gathered some papers together on his desk, bundled them up and tossed them into a tray on the top of a nearby cabinet to assimilate my surroundings. The soft furnishings; deep plum-coloured curtains and matching sofa, were the same shade as discreet stripes in the ivory-tinted wallpaper. The pictures, chosen, I felt, because the colours were right for the room rather than for any artistic merit, were the kind of soft-focus photographs of fruit and flowers that I have always found rather pointless and boring. You can tell a lot about people's characters by the pictures on their walls.

'Your husband asked me if I was small fry,' he said, seating himself behind the desk and donning gold-framed half-moon glasses. 'I told him only to basking sharks.' He gazed at me and I suppose the small upturn at each end of his mouth could be described as representing a smile.

'That was really rude of him,' I remarked, thinking that, for Patrick, the comment was actually quite polite.

'Ah, but we were both joking.'

'Was he really in joking mood?'

'But yes. Someone's crazy if they think they can make this stick.'

'So he's not going to plead guilty?'

'Of course not!'

'Wouldn't it be sensible if he did?'

He steepled his fingers and assumed a judicial expression. 'No, it wouldn't be at all sensible. Guilt has to be proved.'

I experienced a lift of spirits until I realised that if Patrick pleaded guilty the prosecution would then be denied the full song and dance act. Also, I was on difficult ground. For right now I was in possession of more insider information than even the accused, let alone his legal representative. How much of a farce was this trial really going to be? What exactly had Patrick told this man? If Daws was to be believed, and surely there was no reason for him to lie, *no one* was on our side.

'Can I offer you some coffee?'

'No, thank you. Will I be prevented from seeing him?'

'Under the circumstances you can't be denied access.' He paused in reaching for a thin file with a red cover. 'Don't worry, you probably won't be called to give evidence.'

'Ye gods!' I exploded. 'I was there. Too right I'm going to give evidence. We're talking about something that up until a comparatively short time ago was a state secret. But for Patrick and I hardly anyone knows anything about it.'

His small mouth pursed. 'Oh, you mean what happened in Wales. I don't think we ought to touch on that too much, do you? I mean, what went on there gives the Lieutenant-Colonel a real motive for murder.'

'Excuse me, I was under the impression that the prosecution

were in possession of video tapes showing the late-lamented commander taking my husband and me apart.'

'You've just confirmed what someone told me earlier today. Tell me, why were these videos made? There was always a danger that they would fall into their superior officers' hands.'

'It was a school for terrorists. They were to be used for training purposes.'

DeKrille's face expressed distaste. 'And possibly for other things one can't help but think. But what you must remember is that there is no point in continually emphasising the perfidy of the deceased, although obviously the man was a complete bastard, if you'll forgive the expression. That only points to the likelihood of revenge on the accused's part.'

'Okay,' I said briskly. 'What actual evidence is there against him?'

'Other than the secretly filmed meeting of him and the man who was alleged to have carried out the drowning, you mean? It would appear there's very little.'

'But that's impossible! Patrick bumped into him completely by accident in Soho and they went and had a beer at The Sun and Thirteen Cantons.'

Again the pursed lips. 'Is that what he told you?'

'Mr DeKrille, when my husband tells me something, I believe him.'

'Who was this man?'

I pulled myself up short and then said, 'Patrick hasn't told me. And for what possible reason could he have been under surveillance?'

DeKrille looked embarrassed, probably because he could not answer the question. 'Umm. Er - look, Miss Langley, I'm sure you realise how vital it is that everyone representing his defence speaks with one voice. There *is* a film. I haven't seen it but I gather that the two men are sitting in what appears to be an hotel room, talking. The conversation is clearly a plan to murder the commander - although no names are mentioned - and your husband is suggesting methods. Now there's every chance that this film is not genuine and the men are actors. Either that or the other man may not, indeed, be the alleged killer - he has his back to the camera and of course is dead now so cannot be...'

'Hang on a minute,' I interrupted, doubting that any actor could take Patrick's part well enough to fool an entire court-room, especially in view of the fact that they would have the genuine article right there in front of them. 'If the other man in the film may not be the one who's supposed to have done it then how the hell can this hang together as *evidence*?'

DeKrille shrugged dismissively. 'The snooping was done another time, perhaps? The meeting was in connection with something else entirely?'

Sarcastically, I said, 'So he makes a weekly habit of plotting to do away with people and there might be confusion as to which victim we're talking about this time?'

The solicitor smiled thinly. 'Whichever way it is, it doesn't make too good an impression on a jury, does it?'

I was starting to see exactly what I was up against. It was much easier to blacken a man's name than I had previously thought.

'And then there's the matter of the gillie...'

'Gillie?'

'Jamie Kirkland, the man who had been in the boat with the commander. Or, at least, he had made an arrangement to row him out onto the lake that morning. The conversation was overheard by several people. He disappeared. No one saw them leave, you understand, as they went very early and the loch is a large one with bays, small islands and overhanging trees - all kinds of places where a rowing boat wouldn't be noticed.'

'Up until now no one has said anything about missing gillies,' I said angrily. 'All the evidence at the inquest pointed to the commander having gone out in the boat alone.'

'It would seem not. The problem was that Kirkland had had a row with his wife and said he was leaving her. When he

34

failed to return home she assumed he'd meant it and gone. And as she had a boyfriend in Inverness and was all ready to move in with him anyway she said not a word to anyone, just packed her bags and left. They had lived in local authority housing so there was no property to sell.'

'And?' I prompted when he paused.

'Last week the loch yielded another body, or what was left of one. It was entangled in tree roots on the shore of one of the islands. Some boys found it when they were out in their father's dinghy, exploring. Dental records have identified the body as that of Kirkland. Cause of death indeterminate after all this time but probably by drowning.'

'That doesn't point to foul play any more than the post-mortem on Commander 'X' did.'

'Yes, there were the remains of a piece of rope around the neck. It's thought likely that the body had been tethered to something underwater by it.'

'Question. If Kirkland's wife thought he'd left her what about his clothes and other belongings?'

'I haven't had time yet to go into this fully,' DeKrille said huffily.

'Patrick wasn't charged with being involved in this death.'

'No, and I should hope not. But, as I'm sure you appreciate, it doesn't *help* matters.'

I took a risk. 'Is there the slightest suspicion in your mind that this whole thing might be purely political - the spin-doctors reminding the country in the run-up to the election what a mess the previous government's Home Secretary got himself into?'

'That kind of thing doesn't go on in Britain,' DeKrille replied, obviously angry. 'What on earth should give you that idea?'

I gave him a crooked smile. My cats' whiskers told me that the question had hit home. 'Perhaps it's my writer's imagination.'

'Well, I think it would be extremely damaging to the

Lieutenant-Colonel's case if I were to even hint at such a possibility in court.'

'Why?' I asked baldly. I had just realised that Daws had probably as good as told me the real state of affairs because his conscience was giving him hell.

DeKrille appeared to go into some kind of state of suspended animation, like a computer that has just crashed.

I leaned forward. 'Why?' I asked again. 'Or is it that more dangerous fish than basking sharks have got you by the short hairs?'

'Your husband has chosen me to represent him,' DeKrille reminded me, finding his voice.

'From a list he was shown, no doubt. Knowing him he just picked the one with the most idiotic name. *Then* you got a phone call and were invited to go and have a little chat with someone connected with the Cabinet Office.'

'I... I deny it utterly.'

'What I really want to know is where Patrick's being held.'

'I'm afraid I can't give you that information in advance of arranging a visit. When I shall accompany you, of course.'

I removed the Smith and Wesson from my bag and showed him what the business end of it looked like.

'Hopefully the safety catch is on,' DeKrille said, eyeing it, his forehead having acquired a sheen of sweat.

'It doesn't have one,' I told him sweetly. 'You just have to pull the trigger quite hard.'

Slowly, dragging his gaze from the gun, he drew a pen and pad towards him and wrote. Tearing off a sheet he folded it in half and pushed it across the gilded leather desk-top towards me.

'One squeak about this and I shall talk to the papers and blow your whole shabby little scam wide open,' I said, glancing at what he had written. 'I might just do it anyway. And if this address is a load of rubbish and Patrick's somewhere else...' I left the rest to his imagination, rammed the weapon - which anyone with a modicum of sense could see had no ammunition in it - back in my bag, got up and walked out. Behind me, I was aware that he had half risen to his feet flapping his hands and was making odd little twittering noises.

I felt I had not only made a bonfire of my boats but was now endeavouring to set sail in the charred remains.

There was every chance, of course, that DeKrille had immediately picked up the phone and called the police. If not then surely he would still report what had happened to the person I suspected was pulling all his strings. Some kind of welcoming committee *had* to be waiting for me when I arrived at the secure remand centre in downtown Oxford, the name of which he had written down. If it was indeed the police then I would be charged with several offences, all of which are punishable by a prison sentence. Threatening him with the gun had been a bad mistake and I was very much regretting losing my temper with him. But if faced with stalemate and obstruction, Patrick had always taught, make things happen.

It had also occurred to me that if political capital was the name of the game then with such high stakes a certain amount of bumping around off-stage by aggrieved parties would be tolerated. Thought about along those lines it was also fairly obvious that people about to drag stinking fish into a court of law, where presumably those giving evidence for the defence would not have a knife held to their throats, were actually at a disadvantage. This conclusion gave me no cheer at all for then I immediately realised that any manipulation of witnesses, plaintiffs and so forth would be done well away from the public gaze.

The business of the secret filming of a meeting bothered me the most. No one, *no one*, has ever succeeded in carrying out this kind of surveillance on Patrick for the simple reason that he has never in his entire career, both working for MI5 or in his 14th Intelligence days, arranged to meet people in hotel bedrooms. It's too risky. He was far more likely to be the malodorous wino slouching on a street corner or the down-at-heel plumber's mate playing darts in the public bar in the pub. He has also done stints as fencing man, gardener, bodyguard and, infamously as far as his clergyman father was concerned, Hell's Angel.

The remand centre was one of those modern buildings that look like a cross between an Albanian slaughterhouse and a multi-storey car park. It was exactly the opposite of what I had imagined for I had pictured him being held in one of several establishments I know of that have at one time been barracks or military establishments, thus ensuring that he felt slightly at home. Not so, not in this concrete misery factory.

There were no police cars parked in the vicinity and I checked, driving all the way around the block before entering a small Pay and Display car park not far from the entrance gates that seemed to have been created for the use of visitors. I could see no other reason why anyone should want to come to the place, the entire area seemed to consist of flyovers and litter-strewn underpasses, the only other building in sight a boarded-up and heavily vandalised warehouse of some kind. All I could hear was the ceaseless roar of traffic on the nearby motorway, the air pollution so marked I could taste it.

I glanced up at the building. So, the man who had helped with investitures at the Palace was now banged up in this hell-hole. On the other hand DeKrille might have had the last laugh and Patrick was actually in Birmingham, or Manchester, or anywhere east of Nempnett Thrubwell. There was no guarantee that I would be permitted to see him either, wherever he was.

One of the security guards on duty at the gatehouse asked only for proof of my identity - making me wonder if I was expected - the other escorted me across the small open space fronting the main doors and rang a bell on a smaller door set within one of them. It whirred aside and I was handed over to a female warder who was standing ready, facing us in somewhat unsettling fashion just inside it as though she stood there all the time, like an android. The door hummed closed and clicked shut behind us as we walked down a short passageway towards another similar door which the woman activated by pressing numbered buttons on a panel. We entered a reception area decorated in a fetching shade of battleship grey.

'Name?' said one of the men in prison officer's uniform behind the desk, a beefy individual with no discernable hair situated north of his eyebrows.

I refrained from mentioning that I had given it already. 'Ingrid Langley.'

'Nature of business?'

'I wish to see my husband.'

'Name?'

'Lieutenant-Colonel Patrick Gillard.'

He looked up from the computer keyboard with which he was obviously having an all-fingers-and-thumbs work-out. 'Common law wife then are you?'

I wondered which charm school they all attended before taking up duties. 'No, Langley is my maiden and professional name. I'm a writer.'

'But you *are* Mrs Gillard.'

I gave him my best scathing stare. 'Of course.'

'Then why didn't you say so?'

No answer was expected and I wasn't about to give him one.

'It says here that you were at one time Mrs Clyde.'

I had just recollected that the place was run by a private security company. 'Oh, so you have it in front of you after all,' I said. 'Yes, that's right.'

'So was that an assumed name?'

'No, I married a policeman called Peter Clyde. He was killed in a shooting incident in Plymouth. And in case you run screaming from the next bit as well I'll tell you now that I married him during the time I was divorced from my present husband whom I remarried four years after we split up. And the cat's name is Pirate.'

'Don't get funny with me,' he said in a low voice through his crooked yellow teeth.

'I'm actually a crime writer,' I told him in chummy fashion. 'And also a member of the Howard League for Prison Reform. They just love feed-back. You know, little snippets of information that tell it how it really is.'

When the warder and one of her colleagues - a woman of reckless, if not suicidal proportions whom I immediately christened Tirpitz - marched me away and strip-searched me I made no further comment. Not being a particularly naive sort of person I had expected it. They didn't find anything as I'm not particularly stupid either.

Finally, after quite a journey along a maze of high, wide corridors, all of which looked exactly the same, I was shown into a room. It contained three cheap-looking armchairs, a low table upon which there was a small foil dish - the kind that factory jam tarts are made in - in lieu of an ashtray and that was all. There was one other door opposite that by which I had entered but no windows, harsh artificial illumination being provided by strip lights above and coming through a large glass screen that took up one entire wall. Another warder sat behind a table in the small room beyond. He indicated that I should sit in one of the chairs, got up and went away. After a twenty minute wait the other door of the room I was in opened and Patrick entered.

I forced myself to be very objective and watched him carefully - this man whom to me was still the boy I had first made love with on a hot summer afternoon - as he came across and seated himself in the vacant chair.

'Do you know if we can we talk freely?' I asked with a glance in the direction of the glass screen. There was no one on the other side of it.

'No idea.' He smiled, despite the fact that his normally vibrant grey eyes were dull, his thick wavy hair tousled, despite the pain. 'How are the kids taking it?'

'They're obviously very disappointed you're not at home. Katie's doing a special drawing for you.'

'One of her famous dragons?'

'It's going to be coloured like camouflage gear so no one can see it.'

Patrick chuckled and then, alarmingly, coughed, arms holding his chest.

'Are you all right?'

He nodded but I wasn't fooled. 'Have Special Branch been questioning you?'

'Yes, here.' Clearly, he wished to say no more about it.

'You look as though you fell down the stairs.'

'I did - an iron staircase a bit like the one at Justin's school.'

In our own personal code the telling of small deliberate lies - nursery schools do not usually boast such potential hazards for toddlers - indicates that the meaning of the whole statement is also a lie. So in other words, he had been beaten up. Carefully. There was only one small grazed bruise on his face but from the way he moved I knew that a good percentage of the rest of him was black and blue.

'How careless of you,' I said, gazing around the room and hoping desperately to convey to him by my apparent disinterest that I knew something he didn't. In actual fact I felt dreadfully guilty in not showing any sympathy but then again he's as allergic to wifely 'there there' and 'diddums' treatment as the next man. I concentrated on wondering if a closed circuit television camera was concealed in what appeared to be a hole in one wall near the ceiling and said, 'What on earth do people do all day here?'

'Speaking personally I've started helping a young suspected post office raider with his reading and writing.'

I gave him a big 'I really love you' smile. 'You know, I hadn't expected to be able to talk to you face to face like this in a private room.'

'This part of the building is reserved for the Ministry of Defence as a holding place for senior military personnel who shoot each other up, hold up trains and things like that so perhaps there are a few perks. I don't think it's been used until now since the centre opened. Did you see DeKrille?'

That little yarn sounded a tall story too but I couldn't quite see the purpose behind it. 'Yes - I sort of gave him the sack.'

Patrick's eyes opened wide. 'Why?'

'No *chi* in his office at all, all negative energy,' I said. 'His aura was lousy too.'

Patrick nodded sagely but was looking at me in strange fashion.

'I went to see Daws.' It was safe to mention his name now he had retired. Well from MI5, anyway.

'How is he?'

'Old,' I said shortly. 'Going a bit cuckoo, if you ask me.' Another code word.

'That's really sad.' No emotion had accompanied the remark though: this wasn't about Daws at all.

I came over all brisk and impatient. 'So when do you get out of here then?'

'After I've found myself another brief, been tried, found not guilty and phoned for a taxi,' Patrick replied with laboured patience, scratching his chin to let me know he understood I thought he ought to try to escape.

Why had he been beaten up? Was it part of a softening-up process to weaken him so that he accepted what was happening to him? Was he refraining from telling me about it because he had been told to or knew I would guess something was wrong and was hoping thereby to warn me?

'Several people heard me say I wished I'd shot the bastard,' Patrick went on gloomily, no doubt thinking that by making a few natural-sounding remarks he would convey to anyone listening that we did not suspect hidden surveillance.

'Hindsight isn't a hanging offence,' I told him.

'I'm really glad I never told you who tipped the commander out of his boat.'

I forced myself to look casual, shrugged. 'He's dead now though.'

'He had a family.'

So that was it. To strengthen the somewhat weak case they had against him, or more likely, to prevent themselves being laughed out of court, the authors of all this needed as many facts as they could lay their hands on. Wives and even children of the dead man would be questioned at length about what they might know. His name would be all over the gutter press and the media would camp on perfectly innocent people's doorsteps. I now knew that name they wanted. Had Daws given it to me deliberately so I could spare Patrick any further pressure? Daws would have no particular sympathy for a brother officer who resigned his commission, left his family and sallied off to fight for money in one of the nastiest wars in recent history.

I changed the subject. 'You were filmed talking to whoever it was in a hotel bedroom.'

Patrick's response to this was unprintable, the gist being that the learned gentlemen of the prosecution had made a grievous error.

'And now there's the business of the gillie.'

'What bloody gillie?' he growled.

'No, DeKrille wouldn't have known about it when you saw him, come to think of it, the body's only just been identified.' I told him what DeKrille had said about the body in the loch.

'Jamie Kirkland,' Patrick said softly and reflectively when I had finished.

'Does the name mean anything to you?'

'No. Did you bring the BMW or the Ford?'

The almost certain presence of snooping devices successfully strangling any really constructive conversation, we continued to chat in general fashion for a little while and then Patrick was taken away. Now, at least though, we both knew there was something underhand going on. I thought I had conveyed to him that Daws had hinted it and made it plain that I thought he ought to escape. And as we had sold the BMW and the Ford some months previously it was obvious that the name of the dead gillie meant something to him. Of most significance to me was his failure to kiss me, not even a peck on the cheek when he left, another of our little devices, a signal that life was very rough indeed.

It was a horrible dilemma to have the kind of information that would probably prevent Patrick being badly treated. But he had been used far worse at Brecon without cracking. How long though could I sacrifice his health and safety for the sake of people whom I had never met and was never likely to?

But surely, a small inner nagging voice was saying while all this was going through my head, this was happening in Great Britain in a new century. Was England's green and pleasant land *really* host to a grubby quasi-legal pantomime that belonged in the era of Stalin? That Daws appeared to be playing a part in it was a real shock. Impartial or devious? I was forced to admit that I had had experience of the latter.

The only possible explanation if my faith in Daws was to remain intact was that the wily old campaigner had been given more intelligence by one of his sources than he was at present revealing.

I drove home, the Smith and Wesson back in my bag after its short stay in a special and very well-concealed locked cubby box that would not be revealed to the nosey short of stripping the Range Rover back to the chassis. Once back at Lydtor I replaced it in the safe and then made arrangements for Carrie to take the children, who still had several weeks left of the summer holiday, away. This, understandably, took quite a lot of organising but I wanted them a good distance from Devon, London and all places associated with what was going on. At last, I waved them all off in their hired camper-van at seven thirty the following morning, driving behind them at some distance for a few miles to make sure they were not followed. Neither of us was.

The cottage seemed very empty when I returned bringing it home strongly to me that Patrick and I had been planning on taking the children on holiday ourselves. How much longer was my life going to be ruled by a past job in the security services? Forever?

And did I, although strictly speaking he was on three week's leave and nothing had appeared in the newspapers, telephone the Army Staff College and report that Patrick was under arrest? I decided to wait.

Two hours later the phone rang.

'I realise our parting was a little acrimonious,' said Auguste DeKrille's voice unctuously. 'But I've now had a chance to look at this covert film.'

Were lawyers for the defence permitted to examine this kind of evidence produced by the prosecution prior to a trial, I wondered.

'There's no doubt that the man doing most of the talking *is* the Lieutenant-Colonel. He has a manner about him and way of speaking that would actually be very hard to mimic. But it's anyone's guess who the other man is. I advised him to reveal his accomplice's name when I saw him first thing this morning to enable a little light to be shed on the matter but he is obdurate.'

I said, 'I don't *think* this person can be described as Patrick's accomplice. And I can't see how his saying who it was will help him at all.'

'Only insofar as the other party actually committed the murder.'

'And can therefore take all the blame? Aren't you forgetting something? No one knows if he actually did it.'

'A man died,' the solicitor said heavily.

'And the inquest returned a verdict of Death by Misadventure. Mr DeKrille, rowing boats capsize very easily, the presence of gillies or no. I think you would be far better employed, if in

45

fact you *are* working on my husband's behalf - something I'm actually beginning to doubt - in examining the legality of this whole wretched business.'

I put the phone down very, very gently.

I went up to my writing room in my empty home and shed a few tears. Patrick is not the kind of person to easily acclimatise to being cooped up. Although he works in an office for most of the time these days he can escape sometimes, in his lunch break or when things are quiet, to nearby wide open spaces for fresh air and spiritual refreshment. He is not an indoor animal and seems to blend naturally and gracefully into what for simplicity's sake I'll call landscapes. That is why he was such a good undercover soldier. Sometimes I'll look from an upstairs window and only after a moment or so I'll spot him standing at the top of the garden, gazing out over the moor, quite motionless but for perhaps his hair ruffling in the breeze.

By the time we married the Gillards had moved to Hinton Littlemoor in Somerset and the ceremony was performed by the Bishop of Bath and Wells. It was every bride's idea of a dream wedding; a horse-drawn carriage, a military guard of honour, the ancient village church aglow with flowers. All went well with us to start with but then we began to have rows; about his long absences from home (my fault, I had known what I was marrying into), his holier than thou attitude when he *was* around (all of a sudden he had turned into his own idea of the perfect man), everything culminating in total war when he discovered I had been taking birth-control pills without telling him.

Why such a normally articulate man had been silent on the subject of children I have never discovered. We had simply not discussed the matter. I had started writing by then and the last thing I wanted was a brain blown from lack of sleep and biscuit crumbs and sticky fingers all over the typewriter. One night there had been one final, terrible row where I had thrown his guitar down the stairs, smashing it, and then shown him the door. Yes, it was my cottage, bought entirely with my earnings. Looking back I cannot really understand my anger towards him; there had been no other women, no heavy drinking- well, perhaps sometimes- no violence towards me. Just his insufferable arrogance.

The divorce papers had come through at a time when I had had five novels published and was beginning to make a name for myself. Patrick, in command of a small undercover unit, was living in sheep-pens near Port Stanley in the thick of the Falklands War. I met an old friend of ours Peter Clyde, by now a detective sergeant working for Plymouth CID. He had been wonderfully supportive. We married and probably because I had been quite successful in blotting Patrick from my mind I really loved him. Then Peter was killed, shot by hitmen in connection with a case he was working on.

In the aftermath of this Patrick came to see me. There had been an accident with a grenade during his assignment in the South Atlantic and he had been terribly injured, his legs smashed and damage to the genital region. He was still recovering, limping, in constant pain and the arrogance had gone as if it had never existed. Offered a job with a new department of MI5 he had been told to look for a working partner, at that time someone, preferably a woman, to act as part of his cover. He was offering this job to me but what he really wanted was for me to take him back.

To see him like this, suffering, like a whipped dog that has been thrown out into the rain, was simply more than could be borne. Whatever we had had together, the magic, the special something from all those years before, was still there and I think I knew, in that moment when I invited him inside my house again that whatever it was would eventually restore him. It had.

I dried my tears eventually and started to make a list. I could remember the names, unfortunately mostly either aliases or nicknames, of just about all those who had been present

47

at that school for terrorists at Brecon. Part of the reason for this knowledge was that, under threat, I had been given the task of lecturing the "students" on what I knew about British intelligence. I had made it my business to find out as much as possible about everyone else.

Top of the list of course was the man whose real name I still remained in ignorance, the Commander who had been re-created as Anton Lyndberne. His secretary-cum-floozy at the centre had been Rhona. She had run away before the final showdown finally proving that she had not been as stupid as she looked. The four tutors had been Adjit, an Egyptian who Patrick killed in self-defence, McFie, a red-haired Scotsman, taken into custody by the local police having spent the finale locked in a cupboard and two other men whose names I had never discovered, one of whom I had shot in the leg. The fate of the fourth was unknown to me.

Of the eleven "students" on the course I had initially recognised four as internationally wanted criminals. A Lebanese man, referred to confusingly as The Greek and actually in the pay of Syria, had had with him two younger men he had called his brothers but who were actually rumoured to be his nephews; Jubeil and Batrun. The Greek had been shot and killed by Lyndberne himself, the other two had been injured in the fighting. John Murphy, an ex-IRA man wanted for murder had also died and his compatriot Regan, first name unknown, had died on a night exercise. Another man, surname King, had also died in the course of an exercise, shot by Adjit after he broke his leg. Of the five remaining, Harvo from Estonia had been killed, Jake, who had looked like an Ethopian long-distance runner with dreadlocks, had survived along with three others from the Middle East who had always refused to give me their names even after I had christened them Shadrach, Meshach and Abed-Nego.

There had been other sundry helpers; a cook and several menials - I had never known the exact number - two of whom had lost their lives after taking up weapons on Lyndbern's behalf and one wounded. The rest, probably recruited locally, had run off and given themselves up to the approaching police.

There was every possibility that a file existed containing more accurate and up-to-date information: I could not believe that in the aftermath of the violent demise of the Brecon project no further research had been undertaken. Patrick, no doubt, would know.

I decided to postpone that line of enquiry and concentrate instead on what had happened to Jamie Kirkland. Surely the two deaths were connected. It seemed an odd coincidence though that someone should make the decision to re-open the case of the policeman's demise and then, shortly afterwards, the body of the gillie had been found. The whole thing cried out for further investigation.

I would investigate. The following day I would go and see what the police had discovered in the case of the tethered gillie.

Chapter Three

In the night, I heard a sound. I lay for a moment, listening and trying to define exactly what had woken me. There are all kinds of noises in the countryside at night and you hear them because it is otherwise so quiet. Nocturnal wildlife can be amazingly noisy; a hedgehog can sound like a much larger animal as it roots around looking for slugs and snails. Foxes examine dustbins and knock off the lids, owls walk around on rooftops.

This sound had somehow been different and I was sure that it had not been made by something indoors. Pirate, the tortoiseshell cat, was on her blanket at the foot of the bed so it was not her playing with a mouse in the courtyard. She too, had woken and now jumped down and then up again, on to the window ledge. The window was open just a little, the curtains with a gap just sufficient to allow a cat to pass between them. I got out of bed without putting on a light, soundlessly opened the window wider and peeped out.

The sky was overcast but only lightly so with hazy cloud, the moon's glow dim but providing sufficient illumination for me to see clearly everything below. Across the courtyard was the converted barn where Patrick and I live when the children are at home: even with a new kitchen extension at the rear the cottage is simply too small for everyone. Behind the barn is the garden, sloping up with fine views of Dartmoor from the top. To the right of the courtyard is the drive, with a double garage halfway along it. It curves up towards the entrance gate, to the right of that again there is a gentle grassy slope down to the river. To the left of my viewpoint at the courtyard's limit is a wide hedge, more of a thicket really, that marks our boundary. It has a narrow gated path through it, one of the remnants of an ancient public right of way through the village and which nowadays leads into our neighbour's garden. Patrick has never been at all happy with the lack of security that this path represents and with our neighbour's permission has allowed the thorn hedge to grow tall and put a padlock on the gate.

As though mocking me, an owl hooted.

There was no sign of disturbance and nothing moved. Again, I tried to analyse the sound I had heard. A kind of thump and a shuffling sound. Then, Pirate growled deep in her throat, eyes wide. She only does this when she sees a strange person or animal approach the cottage. I stroked her and her fur had bushed. Her tail thrashed from side to side.

The man who came into view carrying what appeared to be crowbar in one hand, a backpack in the other could not be Patrick although the height and build was similar. By the time I had returned with the Smith and Wesson he was examining the door of the barn by the light of a small torch. It was then switched off and he wandered over in the direction of the cottage. There was nothing particularly covert in his movements, they were more like those of a security guard checking that all was safely secured. This did not prevent me from opening the window as wide as it would go and training the gun in his direction.

'That's far enough,' I called.

He came to a stand but seemingly was not alarmed. 'I'm unarmed,' he said, after looking up and noting the gun in my hands. The voice was quite deep and pleasantly modulated.

'That isn't really relevant at two thirty in the morning,' I pointed out. 'Were you trying to break in?'

'No, the noise you heard was me apprehending the other fella. I kicked his backside. He was the one trying to get in to your barn.'

'Tell me who you are.'

'The name's Shandy.'

'Tim Shandy?'

'That's right.'

I took a fresh grip on the gun. 'Try again. Shandy's dead.'

'I thought I was dead too. But I was sent back to be in hell for a while until they let me in the place upstairs.'

My skin was still crawling. 'I think I'd prefer a bit more proof before I let you in.'

'I'm not asking for admittance. I was hoping to look up an old chum and heard he's in a spot of bother. I came down straight away and was about to pitch my tent somewhere nearby when I saw a man acting suspiciously. His ID card says he's Special Branch but as they don't usually carry crowbars and have every appearance of being prepared to clout a member of the public who wants to know what they're about...' He broke off and I saw the white of his teeth as he smiled. 'I know you're Ingrid. We've never met but Patrick said you could shoot the spots off a ladybird.'

'Wait,' I said.

'One thing...'

'Yes?'

'The Serbs made a good job of almost killing me and afterwards their doctors had even more success. I look...' He broke off, shrugged and stared at the ground.

I let him in.

It was apparent, immediately, that what I had been able to see from above, the right hand side of his face, was comparatively normal. The other side was a nightmare, a blinded, lividly burned travesty, his features as though smeared, the mouth pulled up in something that approached a leer. But I did not focus my gaze on him at all just then for he was wincing as the bright light revealed his disfigurement like someone receiving small but painful electric shocks.

He left his heavy backpack and the acquired crowbar in the porch and I led the way into the sitting room and switched on a couple of small table lamps, inviting him to seat himself in what was actually the dimmest corner. The reward for this was that he ceased to want to hide and answered quite warmly in the affirmative when I asked him if he would like a drink. It transpired that he had not eaten since seven in the

52

morning and I finally persuaded him to have a mug of coffee and some fruit cake, with a tot of single malt first.

I gave him the whisky and then took my time brewing proper coffee - I needed some myself - giving him time to relax. When I returned with it and the cake Pirate had seated herself on his lap and he was stroking her with tender concentration. He consumed the refreshments with every sign of enjoyment and it occurred to me that a very close brush with death had had the effect of making this man deliberately relish every pleasant moment of his resurrection in case it was his last. Although brimming with questions I wanted to ask him I quietly drank my coffee, waiting until he had finished. I guessed he was in his middle to late fifties and had once probably been very good looking. His hair was a sandy sort of colour, but greying, his one good eye bright blue and he had the kind of fair complexion that would immediately redden when exposed to the sun.

'I'd be interested to know how you found out about Patrick's predicament,' I said when every crumb of cake had gone.

He gave me his ready but twisted smile. 'Let's just say that someone in Special Branch mentioned it to an acquaintance of a chum of mine.' He added, 'He and I belong to a club that not many people know about for army bods who have had bits of themselves shot off. He railroaded me into joining when I got back to the UK. You can live there if you want to, you see. I do.'

I recollected the family Shandy had left behind, one of Patrick's reasons for remaining silent, but said nothing.

'I was going to look the old warrior up anyway,' Shandy went on. 'This makes it imperative.'

'You're putting yourself at risk,' I said.

'From creeping Johnnies armed with crowbars? Not a chance.'

'Didn't your chum tell you why Patrick's been arrested?'

'The actual details were vague but I assume we're talking

about a bent copper who met a nasty end when his boat turned over on a Scottish loch.'

I nodded.

' "Tis double death to drown in ken of shore", wrote the Bard. I hope the bastard enjoyed his death twice over.'

'There's evidence,' I informed him. 'A secretly filmed meeting you had with Patrick in an hotel somewhere to discuss the matter.'

Shandy forgot for a moment to keep the injured side of his head turned slightly away from me and looked me straight in the eye. 'This is indeed a momentous success for Special Branch! I shall heap them with wreaths of laurel when I next see them. I didn't meet your husband in any kind of hotel. We spoke about it on a London pavement outside a pub.'

'That's what Patrick told me. Nevertheless, there's a film. Patrick's solicitor's seen it. It doesn't actually implicate you, as the man Patrick's talking to has his back to the camera. But according to the solicitor, DeKrille, the conversation is definitely about topping someone who remains nameless.'

'They can't use it as evidence if the victim's name isn't mentioned, surely?'

'DeKrille recognises that but said it still wouldn't give a very good impression of the defendant to the jury.'

'I know very little about the law but would have thought it was inadmissible.'

'Brigadier...'

'Tim, please.'

'Tim, I think I should tell you that Patrick's old MI5 boss gave me a very strong hint that this has all been cooked up as a pre-election ploy to remind the country what a mess the previous administration got into over additional and covert police powers.'

'But of course it's a load of old cobblers! It can't be anything else. That's why I'm here. I shall go into the nearest police station and tell them that Patrick and I had absolutely nothing to do with it. We sat and had a beer, several actually, sharpened our fangs as we spoke of this now wonderfully deceased piece of shit - if you'll excuse my language - plotted, raved, loaded our cannon with grapeshot, had several more beers and finally I blundered off, pissed to the gills and with a knife between my teeth, swearing vengeance.'

Ye gods, I could picture it, frame by frame. 'It still isn't evidence though, is it? There's absolutely no need for you to be involved. Patrick won't reveal your name.'

'But he must!' Shandy's large hands made a series of movements in the air as though they were tying a knot in something. Then he wagged an index finger at me. 'Are you refraining from mentioning that he's been under some pressure to do so?'

'Only to give the prosecution's case some credence. It would be a good idea if he pleaded guilty to make the whole thing less of a three-ring circus.'

'I see. So if I try to explain and am also arrested it means you're on your own when it comes to finding out who actually killed this man - that's if the police don't follow up what I have to say.'

Dumbly, I stared at him and then dropped my gaze when I saw him wanting to hide again. Then I managed to get out, 'You *didn't*, you mean?'

'Sorry, I should have made that clearer. No, I had every intention to but someone got there just ahead of me. I found the body in the water and left it there.'

'And the boat was capsized?'

'Yes, in the lee of one of a pair of islands.'

'So obviously you didn't see it happen.'

'No. The island concealed the spot from the part of the shore I had swum out from. That was to my own advantage, you understand, and I waited until the boat went from my sight and then set off in my diving gear. Incidentally, it was also hidden from the hotel jetty from which he had rowed out from.'

'Are you sure?'

'Yes, I couldn't see the hotel when I arrived and surfaced. It's important, isn't it? The murderer could have been keeping watch from there and also waited until the dinghy went from view. Or more likely, as I didn't meet anyone, he set out shortly after the boat did.'

I was so elated I kept on firing questions at him. 'What about the gillie?'

'I saw no gillie.'

'No one was in the boat with him?'

'Only if they were lying in the bottom of it. The man I was after was rowing.'

'Only the body of a missing gillie's turned up with the remains of a piece of rope around the neck as though it had been tethered underwater.'

'Perhaps that's another crime.'

'Apparently before he disappeared he was heard talking to the commander arranging to row him out on to the loch. And then there's the business of the dead rook.'

Shandy eyed me gravely, a twinkle in his one eye. 'You have enough material for several novels already. What infernal rook?'

I flopped back in my chair. 'Sorry, I'm badgering you for information when you're tired.'

After a little pause Shandy observed, 'But nevertheless you're offended, Ingrid.'

'And you're bloody perceptive,' I retorted.

He carefully placed Pirate on the floor and stretched his legs. 'I apologise for mentioning books when you're obviously moving heaven and earth to get Patrick out of prison.'

'I was there,' I said dully. 'At Brecon. I don't suppose Patrick told you because he doesn't, more to protect me from questions than anything. And a man doesn't like to admit that his wife was tortured because he thinks he's blundered.'

Gently, Shandy said, 'The brave commander knew who you were too.'

'Oh, yes. The idea was that it would increase his standing with the students.'

'You mean the scum. Did it?'

'No. The course was all supposed to be about subversion. Patrick had subverted them. They liked him, respected him actually. Even bent minds...'

'Despise a man who uses a woman like that,' he finished for me. 'Yes. *Did* Patrick blunder?'

'Not really. He just tripped over a dead branch on a hillside and stunned himself hitting his head on a tree. That was how they succeeded in catching us.' There was another short silence which I broke by saying, 'There's a guest room in the barn. Please have some rest.'

He looked thoughtful. 'It would certainly be a good idea if someone was sleeping over there. I worry about this country of ours when policemen fail to get search warrants. What could he have been looking for, do you think?' His hands did a little more knot tying. 'No, first of all tell me about the significance of this bird.'

'The body must have been taken ashore by someone for it was found on a shingle bank with a dead rook alongside it. Patrick called the final act at Brecon Operation Rookshoot. So whoever did it knew about it or had been there.'

'And he thought I'd signed my work in fancy fashion.' Shandy shrugged, probably a little offended himself. 'No matter, he was not to know. There was no reason at the time why anyone should know. Obviously I had no wish to get involved in a murder inquiry even when I had played no active part in it, so I merely returned to my hired car, got changed and left. Left the country, left my life really.' The final few words were uttered in a whisper.

I thought it best at the moment to divert him from his memories. 'Could it have been an accident, do you think?'

'I suppose, forgetting about this dratted gillie for a moment, that it's possible. It must have taken me about ten to fifteen minutes to swim out to the island and then I surfaced quickly to get my bearings before circling round it to where the dinghy was. Anything could have happened in that time.'

'I was making a list earlier,' I said. 'Of all those present at Brecon. Most of the names are false or nicknames, though. We need to get hold of the official file.'

'I like your style,' Shandy said. 'Like needing to rob the Bank of England for a little cash or for Britain to win all the gold medals at the next Olympic Games.' But he was smiling as he spoke.

I smiled back, enigmatically.

Having come to the conclusion that Daws as likely as not undertook most of his advisory work from home I rang him from my friend Lynn's house at the top of our drive at eight thirty that morning. I used a well-committed-to-memory number from my D12 days but nevertheless expected, after all this time, to hear BT's electronic version of a raspberry. Not so. It rang for quite a long time and then he spoke, just giving his name.

'Good morning,' I said breezily. 'It's Ingrid. I hope this isn't an inconvenient moment.'

There was a strained sort of silence and then he said, 'I can't speak to you if you're on an open line.'

'I don't have any other variety available right now and this is an emergency,' I told him bluntly. 'But rest assured this isn't my phone. I'm sticking my neck out and trusting you. I'll come straight to the three points. Patrick's been beaten up, Shandy's alive, kicking and didn't rock the boat and I want the file on Brecon.'

There was a click and then silence and I thought he'd rung off. But he must have been pressing a scrambler button for after another few seconds he said, 'Is there any proof of the second?'

'Only that he's here, doesn't have to be and I believe him.'

'I'll meet you at Claridges at six.'

The line went dead.

'Everything all right?' asked Lynn, having stayed tactfully out of earshot.

'I think there are gremlins in my phone,' I said by way of a reply.

'Only I thought you said you and Patrick were going off somewhere with the children for a week.'

'Hiccups with his leave too.'

'That's a real shame. D'you want some coffee?'

I declined, thanked her warmly and congratulated myself that I hadn't actually told her any lies. Lynn is lovely but also a gossip.

Shandy was finishing off the breakfast I had cooked for him, basking - if that is the right word - in bacon, eggs, sausages and mushrooms. Expecting to have everybody at home for several days before our holiday I had filled the fridge with fresh food and I now set about parcelling up the rest to give to the elderly neighbour who feeds Pirate when we're away.

'He has expensive tastes?' Shandy enquired when I relayed Daws' instruction to him.

'No, old habits die hard,' I said.' "Claridges" is actually our old code word for an appalling pub on the outskirts of Shaftesbury. I'm afraid we have the longest drive.' I had been speaking from the kitchen but now berated my thoughtlessness and glanced quickly at him round the door. 'That's if you want to come.'

He remained silent and when I went into the dining room he was carefully mopping up egg yolk with a piece of bread. I didn't stand there gazing down at him, but busied myself tidily folding the previous day's newspaper prior to putting it in the recycling bag.

'I haven't been going anywhere but for walks when it's dark,' Shandy said at last. 'I don't think I could go to public places.'

'Colonel Daws wouldn't mind if we talked in the car.'

It was as if I had not spoken. 'And here's old big-mouth

saying that if the police decided to arrest me you'd have to find out what really happened to our dead cop all on your own. My mind has gone, obviously. I can't do it, Ingrid, not yet. I'm deeply sorry.' The knife and fork clattered onto the plate and he put his head in his hands.

I sat down at the table with him, on his good side. 'When Patrick came home from the Falklands and the pins in his right leg weren't really holding he had to take painkillers all the time in order to be able to function. He had nightmares of standing naked in the centre of a huge stadium with thousands of people shouting "Cripple!" at him. Then, when at last he had to have the lower part of that leg amputated below the knee and was fitted with the best artificial one in the world courtesy of Her Majesty's Government he thought all his troubles were over. They weren't, they still aren't and although no one looking at him unless he's wearing shorts would ever guess and he only limps a bit when he's very tired, every moment has to be worked at. I don't want you to think I'm lecturing you or tritely saying that your problem is the same as Patrick's: it isn't, it's worse. But however many startled and horrified looks you get from people it won't alter the truth.'

He removed a hand, leaving the other hiding the scarred side of his face and I was shocked to see that he had shed tears. 'What truth for God's sake?'

'Tim Shandy, you're a fine, commanding figure of a man. Anyone can see that whatever appalling disaster befell you it was in the course of your hurling thunderbolts, driving racing cars or flying planes.'

'Yes,' he said slowly. 'Or being on the receiving end of a Serb shell. I can appreciate that reasoning- hadn't really thought about it like that before.' After a long silence he continued,' I know of course that one day I shall have to give it a try. I will - but not yet. I can't.' Hopefully, he added, 'Under the circumstances it might be a good idea if I stayed here to hold the fort.'

'You're absolutely right,' I said and put all the food back in the fridge.

*

"Claridges" was very busy so had probably experienced a change of management since I had last visited the place. A little late due to having been held up at road works I left the Range Rover parked mostly on a pile of gravel left over from some building project as I had no intention of searching for a space and thereby being any later. I entered the building through a door still marked Smuggler's. Improved, obviously, but still unrelenting tacky and not too strong on apostrophes.

As might be expected Daws was in a less crowded and slightly up-market room entitled Captain's and, having erected around himself an impenetrable wall of icy aloofness, had a large table all to himself.

'Sorry I'm late,' I said, determined at least to start on the right footing.

He finished the last drops of his gin and tonic. 'What can I get you to drink?'

Not having Jordon out there somewhere with the Rolls I asked for a small glass of dry white wine.

'Were you followed?' he asked when he returned.

'Yes, but I left them in the middle of the Tavy.' When he looked puzzled I elaborated with, 'There's a ford which is fine as long as you notice how high the river's running and know how deep it has to get before your car drowns. Theirs drowned. And I feel I ought to mention that Special Branch tried to break into the barn last night.'

His eyebrows rose. 'Any idea what they might have been looking for?'

'Anything to use to incriminate him, I suppose. Or, more likely and for the same reason I'm being followed everywhere, to frighten me into not interfering. It crossed my mind that you might be behind it, actually.'

'I'm not and I'm sure I needn't ask you if the Lieutenant-Colonel's silly enough to keep diaries or other records there.'

'Patrick's never kept one.'

Eyeing with distaste the arrival of a noisy group Daws said, 'What have you done with Shandy?'

'He can't face public places,' I told him.

'Oh?'

'He's dreadfully disfigured.'

'He's genuine though? Given you proof of his identity?'

'I really can't think of an advantage to *anyone* if he were a plant,' I said acidly, angry because I had forgotten all about asking him for identification.

He fixed me with his steely gaze. 'Only to you. Especially as now you're telling me he didn't do it.'

I countered this with, 'He's one of those people you believe without question - actually I think he's incapable of lying. Are you quite sure you didn't bring a photograph of him with you so you could secretly check him out if I *had* brought him along?'

There was a pause and then Daws sighed and took a small envelope from his breast pocket. 'I did have time to do a little research before I came out. As I'm sure you know, the Red Cross and the Red Crescent did their best in Bosnia but huge parts of the country were made no-go areas by the Serbs. The business of finding out who had died, or been injured or captured, practically went to the wall for months. Shandy was listed as missing, presumed dead, after an almost direct hit by a Serb shell on a Croat bunker in the mountains. This was based on information from the Croats themselves. Nothing has ever been updated as far as he's concerned so one must assume he was found by another faction and patched up.'

'By the Serbs. They didn't make a very good job of it.'

Daws grunted sympathetically. 'His wife, his second actually, gave him up for dead. It would appear she sold the house and she and the two teenage sons are now living with a stud farm owner in Horsham.' He took a photograph from the envelope and slid it across the table to me.

Yes, Tim Shandy had been good-looking once, the smile, even though the photo was a semi-official one, was roguish. I wondered if he knew about the new life his family had made and immediately decided that he did. Was he bitterly aware that his wife would not want back a maimed, ugly man who now shrank from almost all contact with other people and who now would probably never be able to provide for her and their sons again?

'That AGM Pamela was hosting...' I murmured.

'AGM?' It was plain I had thrown him completely.

'The South of England Arabian Horse Society.'

'What of it?'

'There must be the usual grapevine.' I said, half to myself. 'Someone must know this person she's living with who has a stud farm in Horsham and could get a message to her - even if he doesn't breed Arabs.'

'I don't quite follow what it has to do with the matter in hand. Is that a picture of the man you've spoken to or not?'

'She might not be aware that he's still alive. Yes, of course it's Shandy.' I then told him what Shandy had said.

'It's interesting but there's still nothing in the way of proof,' was Daws's reaction. 'Get his version of the whole story though - something valuable might come from it.'

Emotion got the better of me. 'Colonel, how the hell am I going to get Patrick out of that hellish remand centre?'

He shook his head. 'I myself am quite helpless without a lot more evidence.'

'I still really don't know whose side you're on.'

'I'm on no one's side - as I told you when we met before. I have to admit though that I'm finding it increasingly difficult to remain neutral. If I advise you to tell Shandy to go to the police with his story - which you tell me he's more than willing to do - then there's every likelihood that he too will be arrested and have to prove his innocence in court. I'm afraid the people calling the tune on this have a far more powerful voice than mine.'

'You used to have the ear of those right at the top.'

'I still do.'

I said nothing in reply to this. There was no point. He had said it all. 'Well, I suppose I could spring Patrick out of there and we could go and live in Peru.'

'That would be madness!'

I finished my wine, surprised and also amused at the way his alarm had indicated a conviction that I was perfectly capable of having a go. 'And the file?'

'It's in the car.' Then the stiff formality softened. 'I've put everything in it that I think might prove useful, including some information recently forwarded to me by both MI6 and the International Intelligence Force to Combat Terrorism.'

I thanked him, privately quite amazed at this assistance. 'Have you any idea when this is going to hit the media?'

'On the morning of the leader of the opposition's speech at their party conference next week.'

Better and better, I thought. One had to admire these spin-doctors. I could imagine the scenario: following the emergence of new evidence, a dawn raid on our cottage would be reported and a murder investigation re-opened into the death of the senior police officer at the forefront of the scandal, several years previously...

I accompanied Daws to his car thinking that whatever Auguste DeKrille might say I had no doubt that the prosecution would expose everything that had gone on at Brecon. In the aftermath Patrick and I had concealed nothing, in fact we had given highly detailed reports to both the Welsh police and to Daws himself. Now that D12 was no more how had he got hold of the file and so quickly?

Jordon was listening to the radio but switched it off when he saw we were almost upon him, got out and at a sign from his employer opened one of the rear doors. I had already told myself that I would not be handed anything that was blatantly a folder in a public car park and this was proved correct for I was presented with a large arrangement of flowers; roses, carnations, and lilies in my favourite shades of cream, yellow and apricot.

'I'm sorry I doubted you,' I said to Daws.

'I believe I called your actions into question too,' he responded in an undertone. 'And I'm sure you're wondering why I'm not going into this more deeply myself. My present position *does* demand impartiality but show me good strong evidence and I can act.'

The big car purred away and, carefully carrying my slightly heavier than might be expected gift, I rescued the car from its miniature mountain and left. A couple of miles farther on I parked in an empty lay-by, removed the folder from where it had been tucked into the arrangement and locked it in the secret cubby box. Constantly now, the worry was dogging me that by leaving a second surveillance team disabled in my wake I had exhausted the patience of whoever was in charge of them, not to mention the one overseeing the entire wretched shooting match. If I was arrested I could do nothing.

It was very late when I got home. My cursed writer's imagination had promised all kinds of horrors awaiting me; Shandy being led away in handcuffs, the police on the doorstep with a warrant for *my* arrest, the grim individual in the tight black leather reach-me-downs lurking somewhere indoors, steeped in malice aforethought, having broken in. I turned off the ignition and silence and warm night air flowed in through the open driver's window and there was no sign of anyone, not even of Pirate. Forcing myself to be practical I admitted that this did not represent cause for alarm. I could hardly expect Shandy to leave a warm bed on my behalf. (Although I discovered afterwards that he used a sleeping bag on the floor of the room.) To pound on the door of the barn to make sure he was still safe and sound seemed a trifle over the top and hysterical. But several minutes later when, still jittery,

I had put the kettle on to make myself a drink to go with the quick snack I had prepared, there was a series of soft taps in the pattern we had arranged on the front door.

'Just checking everything's well with you,' he said. 'Is it?'

'As well as a second written-off unmarked police car can leave one,' I told him.

Shandy grinned and prepared to go back to bed.

'Tea?'

He visibly asked himself if he could bear being in the company of another person, even though he now knew her, who might look at him.

'Bruichladdich, ten years old?' I amended.

I let him choose his own lighting in the living room while I found the bottle and a glass. Two glasses, to hell with tea. It was time for more questions.

'Sorry about the pyjamas,' Shandy said from the same slightly gloomy corner that he had sat in when he first arrived. What he was referring to was actually a dark green track suit.

'No visitors while I was out?' I enquired.

'Not to my knowledge.'

To hell with pride too. 'Tim, I know it looks as though I've lured you in with whisky because I'm scared but would you be an angel and check upstairs? I'm being really pathetic and it's probably just tiredness on my part but there was a man here when Patrick was arrested who worried me a bit and...'

'Ah ha!' Shandy cried, electrically coming to life. He loped off to grab the crowbar, returned and thundered up the stairs. 'Where are you, you swine?' he yelled. 'Come out and be pulverised! I know you're here!' There was some scurrying around overhead and the sounds of doors, wardrobe and otherwise, being opened and closed and then a muffled scream, sounds of a struggle; gasps and grunts, and then ghastly strangling noises. These were followed by a loud thump and, after a pause, the upstairs toilet was flushed. By this time I was laughing so much I almost dropped the whisky bottle.

'That sorted him,' Shandy reported gleefully, coming down.

When we had both stopped giggling and were on our second tot of whisky I said,'I know it's late but can I ask you about what happened in Scotland?'

'Fire away.'

'How did you know Commander 'X' was there?'

'I didn't. Perhaps I'd better tell the tale from the beginning. But before I do, do we have a *name* for this character yet? He signed himself Keith Somerton in the hotel register.'

I had brought the file indoors with me and now fetched and opened it. The press report of the man's death had withheld the name on the grounds that his next of kin had not yet been informed and to my certain knowledge the story was never followed up.

'Yes,' I said. 'It's here in my old boss's own handwriting; Commander Keith Andrew Somerton.' There was a lot more about Somerton's career and background typed below which I decided to peruse later.

'The morning after I'd got drunk with Patrick,' Shandy began, 'and planning on flying out to offer my services to those poor devils fighting Milosevic's filthy hoards, I decided to keep my promise and wipe the smile off a bent cop's face on the way. God, Ingrid, you have no idea how bent cops disgust me! So when my hangover had abated a little and in possession of a photograph of Somerton- a mugshot of him in his role of Anton Lyndberne that Patrick had got hold of - I parked myself not far from his house for a couple of days to see what was what.'

I had been unaware that Patrick knew the address or had access to photographs, a fact that involved him - ignoring for a moment the assurances from Shandy that he hadn't carried out the killing - more than I liked.

Shandy continued,'Naturally, there was no question of my shooting this bloke in cold blood or involving his wife and twin daughters. I have to say that the existence of a family made it difficult for me. Somehow you imagine folk who carry out what amounts to atrocity as social misfits and loners, not family men. I fully intended to make whatever happened to him look like an accident and when he started putting fishing rods and stuff like that into his car one afternoon I nearly cheered. The family weren't going either which was even better, although the little ones obviously wanted to, standing like lost sheep on the pavement while he loaded the boot with top of the range luggage. The wife's face was like Chatham when there's an easterly blowing straight off the North Sea, I can tell you, and Old Suspicious here wondered if another woman would be baiting his hooks for him. In the end though the poor cow had to drive him to the station.

'I wasn't laughing either when I stood next but one to him in the queue at the ticket office and heard him book a return fare on an overnight train to Inverness. I'd thought the Lakes at the absolute worst. I had no gear with me to speak of, just my rucksack with a few useful things in it so the first thing I had to do when I arrived - I risked it when he was having his porridge the next morning in the small hotel he'd gone into for breakfast - was buy some clothes. Then he headed for a car-hire place. That was where it got a bit difficult as I could hardly eavesdrop to find out how long he planned to have it and discover if he mentioned where he was going, just had to wait my turn and make sure he didn't spot me. But it worked out very well, the Scots love to talk and it took me no time at all to find out that the best fishing and walking holidays thereabouts were to be had at the Garrochmuir Hotel on the shores of Loch Duncreggan, to the east of Loch Ness. Which was where the gentleman in front of me had said he was heading. "Fancy that now," I said.

'I've never been an undercover soldier like Patrick and I wasn't going to start skulking in the heather or in the hotel grounds. So I booked a room, established by a quite-by-accident overheard conversation that our friend was there for a long weekend and relaxed.'

68

I broke in with, 'Could you relax, knowing what you were going to do?'

'In the army you learn to use well the moments you have to call your own. I had already decided that he was the enemy after what Patrick had told me and I only had to look at him to know not only that his conscience was easy but that he was mighty pleased with himself. As you know he wasn't very tall or even moderately striking to look at but nevertheless strutted. He was rude to the charming young Scots who staffed the hotel, swore at a waiter and accused a barman of serving him short measure. Eyes were very dry when he got himself drowned.'

'Did he upset the other guests as well?'

'I think most were offended by his manner but there were no open rifts. No, that's wrong. I remember learning about an altercation he was involved in outside in the garden. If you remain quiet and unobtrusive you get to know all kinds of things. Intelligence is everything.'

'You overheard the staff talking about it?'

'I think so. My memory's not so good as it used to be. I suppose it could have been with this gillie you mentioned but I never saw hide nor hair of him - not knowingly anyway.'

'And yet according to Patrick's so-called solicitor several people heard the two men making arrangements for the next day's fishing on the loch.'

Shandy shrugged expansively. 'One can't be everywhere at once and I didn't want him to become suspicious by openly shadowing him. It's perfectly possible he had conversations with all kinds of people when I wasn't around. I was reading a newspaper in a small lounge just off the reception area when I heard him ordering a packed lunch and asking for the use of a dinghy the following day so that's how I knew he planned an outing.'

'Did you speak to him at all?'

'Oh, yes! Good morning and that kind of thing. He usually responded with a quirk of the mouth that he might have thought was a smile but it actually looked more like a nervous twitch.'

'I presume no women turned up.'

'None. Unless they were very discreet. As far as I know his final night was celibate.'

I refilled Shandy's glass. 'And on the day he died you hired diving equipment and went farther along the loch shore where you watched and waited.'

'That's right. And a beautiful morning it was too.'

'Wasn't it difficult to get hold of that kind of gear in the Highlands of Scotland?'

'Inverness and Fort Augustus, m'dear, are the centres for Nessie hunters. I could probably have borrowed a mini-sub if I'd had the funds.'

'It shouldn't be too difficult to trace who else hired an aqualung and wet-suit.'

'No, unless they had their own. But that suggests fore-knowledge of what the man intended to do and also good planning. The fact that Somerton hadn't bought his ticket in advance tells me that the trip was a last minute decision.'

'You said you found the body in the water. But bodies tend to sink at first and then float back to the surface after a few days when decomposition has started.'

'It was just about motionless about six feet down. There was an inflatable life jacket but it was only partly inflated. The murderer must have let the air out of it in order to drown him and then, knowing that he wanted to retrieve the body later, partially inflated it again. A trained diver would find that simple to achieve.'

'That implies military or police training - possibly a colleague,' I said. 'Or someone with money who could hire a hit-man. It doesn't sound as though his wife was thrilled to bits with him so perhaps she was having an affair with one of his chums. Tim, there are so many possible suspects. The criminal element at Brecon who were killed or deported or ended up in prison must have friends who swore revenge. Where do I start?'

'By reading that file.'

Chapter Four

The file, which I started on as soon as Shandy departed, contained some surprises. The three men from the Middle East whom I had christened Shadrach, Meshach and Abed-Nego had lost their lives after all, killed in the explosion that had torn through one of the downstairs rooms of the house adjacent to the mine entrance, the house that Somerton had been using as his own living quarters. Oddly, for I had had nightmares about it for months, I had forgotten all about it. It had been the real finale, Patrick's loading of a small, ostensibly ornamental, cannon with Semtex and just about everything else he could lay his hands on. Somerton had noticed the wiring, the device primed to detonate when the television was switched on. In the immediate aftermath of the gun-battle in the cave, before the arrival of the local police, he had led the disgruntled survivors to the house and, still in his role of terrorist, had encouraged them to use Teletext to plan their escape flights home. He had then quickly left the house. No survivors, no tale-telling, just carnage.

Of the rest, Jubeil and Batrun, who really had been The Greek's nephews, had been wounded and subsequently extradited to Canada where they were wanted in connection with an attack on a holidaying American Middle East peace negotiator. The outcome of that was not known. Jake of the dreadlocks... here I laughed out loud. Jake of the dreadlocks had been planted by the CIA following lurid rumours that the British Police had gone right off its collective head and started training terrorists. Good for Jake. In hindsight I realised that he had guessed what Patrick and I had been trying to achieve and he certainly had not got in our way, saved his own skin and probably not fired a shot.

Then I reached the final page. It consisted of an update of those who had been employed in minor roles. Three who insisted they had cleaned and acted as odd-job men - the underground complex had been extensive - had been deemed due to lack of evidence innocent of any crime and released. Another three, local hoodlums - how useful to Somerton to have had access to criminal records, I thought - had been employed in their capacity as armed thugs but had had no idea they were involved with a police operation. Two had been killed, possibly by Lyndberne himself when they started to run away as they had been shot in the back, a third who had been wounded was also released without charge because of lack of evidence and the questionable legality of the scheme.

The cook had been James Kirkland.

There was even an address listed in the village of Duncreggan, which was situated close to the northern shore of the loch of the same name.

I sat for a moment trying to remember him, a modern-day Swelter in his kitchen pitiably lacking in facilities. Surely it could not be a coincidence that Somerton had gone to the Garrochmuir Hotel. Or had the boss and his cook been on such good terms at Brecon they had chatted about good places to take a break and Kirkland had recommended somewhere near his home village? It seemed unlikely. As Lyndberne, Somerton had chatted to no one.

Kirkland had been present at the final shoot-out though, a fact that seemed to have been missed by the anonymous writer of the report. I could only recollect him vaguely; small and thin, one of the armed men standing waiting in dim corners of the cavern for the order to open fire. That was the last I had seen of him, lounging against one of the wood-battened walls holding a sub-machine gun. There was every likelihood that he had slipped away when all hell broke loose and made his escape with the odd-job men.

It occurred to me that blackmail might have been involved, Kirkland having found out what Somerton really did for a living and Somerton had gone to Scotland to pay him off in more ways than one. For the commander had had no wish to be exposed as one more operation along the lines of Brecon was planned. Afterwards, if it was decided not to create the covert unit that he so desired, Somerton was to have been given a new identity, including plastic surgery, to enable him to return to a normal life and a position in another, regional, police force. I wondered if that new beginning was to have included his wife and daughters.

Now Kirkland was dead and had possibly died the day before or on the same day as Somerton. I recollected the piece of rope around the neck of the corpse, thought of hanging and shuddered. Had Kirkland's body been in the bottom of the boat for disposal when Somerton had rowed out on to the loch? No, Somerton couldn't swim, lifejacket notwithstanding, and would hardly have risked capsizing the boat and losing all his fishing gear to get rid of a body in broad daylight. Unless he had intended to bury it on one of the islands.

It was natural for all my thinking to gravitate towards laying the blame on someone I knew not to have hesitated in carrying out murder. But Kirkland might have drowned Somerton, suffered remorse or some kind of mental unbalance, gone away and hanged himself then someone else could have disposed of his body. Or another person had killed them both. The possibilities were endless but I kept coming back to the business of the dead rook beside the body on the shore. Kirkland did not appear to have been the type to have indulged in dramatic gestures- and why go to all the trouble of retrieving the body and risk being spotted anyway? Instinct told me that whoever had done *that* had been one of the main participants at Brecon. Who else fitted that description who was unaccounted for?

No one that I knew of.

No one that is except for the occasionally flamboyant, highly-trained, bloody-minded, excellent swimmer (man-made foot or no) husband of mine who had been in the States with me at the time of Somerton's death. It was then that I remembered I had left Patrick in New York for four days while I visited friends in Washington. I dismissed the implications of this immediately but at the same time asked myself how he could have known that Somerton was in Scotland. That was easy; Daws, tender of all grapevines, could have told him.

At seven, after three hours sleep, I got up, packed a case, cooked Shandy a vast breakfast as I had a theory that part of his problem was malnutrition, made myself two slices of toast and honey and drank a large mug of black coffee.

'I think you ought to make yourself scarce,' I told him. 'If you go to the police there is a real risk they'll receive instructions to grab you to give more mileage to this court case. If they've somehow cooked up a filmed meeting they can do anything.' What chance would he stand if questioned by the ruthless after all he had suffered, when even entering a police station would take him to the limit of his present endurance? It would take little effort to force him into admitting killing Somerton having used information supplied by Patrick.

Shandy nodded sadly in agreement and then said, 'It beats me. Really beats me. I've thought about this long and hard but am damned if I can think of any occasion when Patrick and I have been alone together in any kind of room. We've been in open spaces and crowded rooms; pubs, clubs, messes, regimental dining rooms, private houses, and restaurants. Under what circumstances *could* he have been filmed discussing murder?'

I shook my head in bewilderment.

'Training films? Classified role-play sessions? Did your department do that kind of thing?'

I groaned. 'Oh, of course. How stupid of me not to have thought of it.' And latterly, when we had become involved with training those infiltrating both the IRA and the UFF, Patrick often took the part of a terrorist in training sessions as he has such a good selection of Irish accents. All this material

74

should have either been destroyed when D12 was disbanded or given to the other MI5 department that had taken over the work.

'It wouldn't be too difficult to play around with the sound-track of a film, you know - not with the technology that exists today. Chop a bit here, add a bit there.'

'What will you do?' I asked.

Shandy laid down his knife and folk with deliberation. 'Many thanks - that has set me up for a week. I'm not sure. I'm not of a mind just to walk away. Perhaps I shall go to the top of a tall hill and ask the wind.'

Perhaps though he felt that he had done all he could in coming to see me. Under the circumstances it would be unfair to expect more. As I had told Daws I was convinced that what he had told me was the truth. There were no reasons why he should lie, surely, and he had come forward not to clear himself but in an attempt to remove suspicion from Patrick. If only he had been able to provide some real evidence; photographs, witnesses, anything. No matter, I would have to go and try to find that myself.

This time the opposition enrolled with a Shogun. I had no intention of driving all the way to Scotland but I didn't particularly want to be followed to Plymouth station and then run the risk of being effortlessly tailed as soon as I stepped off the train. I couldn't for the life of me understand why I was being followed unless someone with a sad lack of evidence hoped I was going to lead them to some. Or, as I had first thought, it was in an effort to scare me into staying at home. Patrick won't tolerate people breathing down his neck and, just then, Japanese off-road vehicle firmly in view in my rear mirror like a two-fingered salute, I couldn't see why I should put up with it either.

It is not necessary to visit the defunct Bradtor Quarries in order to catch a train from where I live, but as I'm not the kind of person to put the rest of the travelling public at risk in order to escape unwanted surveillance, once again I headed for the open moor. Those behind me obviously expected it. Initially I utilised farm tracks and access lanes, following a route Patrick and I had worked out several years previously. It was impossible to travel as the crow flew because the high moor in this area is closed to the public, a designated military range. Not to mention the several treacherous and extensive mires.

My escort trailing somewhat I turned onto the main Tavistock to Princetown road and after passing the inn at Merrival swung into the private road that led to Bullseye Farm. Once past the farm I really let the Range Rover go and arrived in highly satisfactory clouds of dust on a section of the disused Yelverton to Princetown railway, the moorland's wonderful rolling downs in shades of olive green and buff all around me. The railway tracks were removed years ago and as no walkers or horse riders were in sight to annoy I once again put my foot down. This was all highly illegal, of course, but I reckoned that even if a Ranger spotted me he would fare little better than my pursuers.

The old railway bed does a marvellous swoop around King's Tor and then, the Shogun still in sight, I really played dirty, leading them cross-country into an area of bright green bog. My heart was in my mouth here for there had been a lot of rain and I could see water glinting between the course tussocks of grass. But there was a track of sorts, a section of one of the ancient monks' ways, I was just praying that I would be able to remember where it was. There was a lot of alarming pitching and tossing, muddy water going in all directions and then one truly heart-stopping moment when I thought I had hit a semi-submerged boulder and was about to stall. But no, car and I floundered out the other side, shedding dollops of mud, onto what I knew to be one of the one-time railway sidings at another old quarry, at Crazy Well Tor.

I hardly dared pause to see if the stratagem had worked and those following me had cut the corner in an effort to catch up. Male pride, I felt, was at stake here and this driver might have been fielded because he was a specialist and knew Dartmoor as well, or better, than I.

In the end I did pull up, shaking a little with excitement, or, if I was honest, terror, and saw that they had indeed fallen for it. Even better, the Shogun was stuck, wheels spinning. I drove on, wondering who would pull them out.

After Ingra Tor it was a fast downhill drive, along the old railway bed again, to another farm and then I turned down a boulder-strewn track that led in the direction of Walkhampton. There was one bad moment when I came to a gate that was shut and appeared to be padlocked but the padlock fell open at my touch. I was fairly sure that I had lost those tailing me but to be on the safe side changed my plan and cut across country again, heading north east and using the narrow lanes with high banks on either side for which Devon is famous. I would abandon catching the train from Exeter and drive to London, leaving the car at my friend's house again. I wanted to talk to Somerton's widow.

I had remembered, right at the last minute, to ask Shandy if he could recall the address and of course he had, senior army officers always have good memories as they are required to know so many people's names. So after Kensington I was heading for Wimbledon and was hoping that if the woman was no longer living there the neighbours would have a forwarding address.

I had felt really sad seeing Shandy trudging off up the drive. I had offered to give him a lift to the station or airport but it seemed that he had meant what he said and was going to walk and camp on the moor in peaceful solitude. It had given me some satisfaction though to see him content to set off in broad daylight, his worn backpack filled with provisions I had been only too glad to give him.

'And poor puss?' he had asked, indicating Pirate, who was giving herself a wash and brush up on the garden wall.

'I rang a neighbour while you were packing,' I had told him, touched by his concern. 'She looks after her for me. As soon as everyone leaves here Pirate simply moves in with her and comes home when she hears a car she recognises.'

'Cats are so organised,' he had sighed.

What would he really ask the wind as he stood on a high tor and what would it say to him?

After some agonising I had decided not to visit Patrick again, or at least, not yet. If we could not talk in private and I had nothing to convey to him, using our own code words, regarding any kind of progress I had made there seemed little point. In truth I was missing him dreadfully, missing his flair for investigation, and knew I would miss his almost uncanny ability to get the truth out of people.

Perhaps it is hypnotism, I simply don't know and I have never been able to fathom how the air of brooding menace is achieved. Merely to occupy the same room, even though you know you are not the person under scrutiny, is uncomfortable. You think of small acts of unselfishness and bad temper of which you've been guilty over the past few hours and long to unburden yourself. I may be Patrick's wife but on those occasions he is too close, too strong and too damned dangerous.

It had already occurred to me that my description might have been circulated to the Transport Police at all UK stations and airports in which case the mud-bath on Dartmoor would have been a complete waste of time. Now, surely, I had exhausted the patience of those orchestrating what was happening. Perhaps he of the tight leathers - presumably also from Special Branch - would put in another appearance. I don't tend to scare very easily so why was I frightened of this man?

The journey to Kensington was uneventful and my friend was not at home again so it had to be another note through the letterbox. For all I knew she was abroad and the note would join the first one on the doormat. I then walked to a taxi-rank and asked to be set down at the nearest high street to the Wimbledon address. Having had very little to eat the day before I was light-headed from hunger. Also, unless surprise is the name of the game it is always preferable to approach a targeted house quietly on foot in order to be able to observe and take stock.

I was doing as Tim Shandy did, travelling light; cotton trousers and top with more of the same, together with underwear, thin and thick zip-together waterproofs and a few other things including one good dress in a small rucksack on my back. The last thing I needed was to lug around a handbag and suitcase. I felt that as a backpacker I blended well into the general London summer scene and such an identity would also serve me well in Scotland.

After soup and a salad roll in a *brasserie*, where I had consulted my London A to Z, I found the street I was looking for and strolled along it, in no hurry at all, looking for number ninety-seven. It was easy as I approached to count along the detached houses and see the one for which I was looking. The first impression was of conformity; black paintwork, white walls, net curtains upstairs, slatted vertical blinds down. The front lawn, I saw when I arrived, was smoothly trimmed, a tidy green rectangle surrounded by shrubs, some of which had been recently and inexpertly pruned. The driveway was of tarmac and between it and the lawn was a narrow border containing the only summer flowers in the entire garden; crimson pelargoniums, a few African marigolds, the colours jarring horribly, and some plants with dull purple flowers I didn't know the name of.

I rang the bell, having already planned what I was going to say, a ruse I had used before.

When she opened the door I knew, instinctively, that this was Julia Somerton. In some indefinable way that I cannot explain she completed the circle, represented the missing part of what I knew about her husband. He had been physically unremarkable; of medium height, thin pale brown hair that had been almost down to his shoulders when I had last seen him, very pale blue eyes, a pasty complexion. This woman was virtually a female mirror image of him. Then in the next moment the thought crossed my mind that I could be mistaken and she might be not his wife but his sister.

'Mrs Somerton?'

'Yes.'

'I'm sorry not to have telephoned or written to you first. My name's Ingrid Langley and my publisher has asked me if I'd like to write your husband's biography. Obviously, I need your permission and co-operation for that.'

Her eyes widened. 'His biography?' she echoed and I could hardly blame her for looking a bit nonplussed.

'May I come in?'

Wordlessly she backed away from the doorway and I took this to mean an affirmative. She had an odd flat-footed, slightly rolling gait I noticed as she led the way to a sitting room that overlooked the rear garden, a repeat version, from what I could see of it, of the garden at the front.

'I can't give you very long, I've got an appointment at the hairdressers.'

I sat down without being invited to, glad that my skin was as thick as ever. I needed it, for when she had seated herself she went on, 'Can't say as I've heard of you.'

No, you wouldn't if you stick to Mills and Boon, duckie, I thought savagely, seeing a whole row of them on a shelf, but said, 'In principle, would you be in agreement?'

'I wouldn't have thought he was interesting enough to write about.'

I went in at the deep end. 'People are always keen to know about covert police operations. It's like spy stories, they get to know about a side of life that's not normally open to them. And when a highly placed officer masterminds something like that...' I broke off, giving her what I hoped was a mysterious smile.

'I really haven't the faintest idea what you're talking about.'

'He didn't tell you?' I asked. 'Oh dear.' This was crunch

time. She would now either furiously tell me to leave or cancel her hair appointment and put the kettle on.

'My husband drowned,' she said as though that explained her ignorance.

I was prepared to risk everything rather than make suitable regretful noises. 'Yes, he did, didn't he?'

For several seconds longer she stared at me with her pale, very pale, blue eyes. 'Would you like some tea?'

'That would be lovely,' I said, making myself more comfortable.

After she had left the room I found the notebook and pen I had brought with me, still feeling a bit shaken that I was actually in the company of the wife of the man I knew to have been a sadist, was sitting in his living room in a chair that surely he himself must have sat in. For the first time since Brecon it was brought home to me that my nerve was not what it used to be and I had to take a very strong line with my imagination, telling myself that, no, he would not come walking into the room at any moment.

The room was decorated mostly in various shades of mushroom and beige; Dralon curtains, ditto three-piece suite, a plastic-looking reproduction fireplace-surround with a gas-fire, fitted cupboards and shelving of the kind that comes flat-packed from DIY stores. The hall had been beige too and I had an idea that the kitchen and bedrooms would not provide any huge surprises. And because I can also be horribly flippant sometimes- it does tend to save me from brooding too much over my *bêtes noires* - I asked myself if Keith Somerton had been driven to turn himself into a terrorist in order to get away from the dreariness of life at home. Though most men find relaxation and fulfilment in things like fishing or growing dahlias.

Patrick finds fishing so relaxing that as soon as he sits on the riverbank and casts he falls asleep. Quite a good proportion of the brown trout he has caught in our stretch of the Lyd have been discovered when he's reeled in the line, causing me to call a recipe I invented for them Grilled Snores. I was thinking about this and the fisherman when Julia returned with two mugs of tea and this was the only reason there was a smile on my face.

'Although I'll try I don't really know that I can help you seeing as you seem to want to know about things that he didn't talk about,' she said. 'Keith never said a word about his work.'

I was sure he hadn't told her about Rhona either. 'It's all right, I can get access to police files,' I lied briskly. 'I'd really like to try to clear up the mystery that surrounds his death - that's if you don't mind talking about it, of course.'

'Mystery? What mystery?'

I drank some tea, making her wait. 'It's not public knowledge yet,' I said, speaking slowly. 'But a man is shortly to be arrested in connection with his murder.'

The woman literally gaped and her hand jerked so violently that she spilt some of her tea.

'I'm sorry if that comes as a shock,' I said. I wasn't remotely sorry for she had had a good think in the kitchen and what I had seen on her face when she returned was avarice - a good handout from the publisher if she could supply useful information - and this had been replaced, in a split second, by fear. Equally swiftly, she controlled her expression to one of mere concern.

'Scotland, wasn't it? I asked lightly.

'That's right,' she said after a short pause, her voice a little hoarse. 'Loch Duncreggan.'

'Had your husband been there before?'

'Murder though,' Julia muttered, not seeming to hear the question, mopping up the tea with a tissue. 'Are you sure?'

'It appears there's some evidence. And the body of the gillie's been found.'

'Who, Jamie?'

'You knew him then?'

'Keith did. He came here once. I didn't like him much - he

82

looked a bit rough. You don't suppose it was him who did it, do you?'

'What makes you think that? Did they fall out?'

'I heard raised voices when I left the room, that's all. But I couldn't hear what was being said.'

I remembered to make some notes. 'Do you know if there was an arrangement that they would meet up and Jamie would act as gillie for him?'

'Keith didn't say. He just went off.'

Sometimes it's best to make no response and thereby virtually force the other person to keep talking.

'We'd had a bit of a row, actually,' Julia continued. She fixed me with her slightly disturbing gaze. 'I don't want this in the book, mind!'

'No, of course not,' I agreed, making a note to that effect in case she demanded to see what I had written. She would have to be able to read shorthand though.

'He just went off after the row. Said he needed to get away. The kids were really upset - it wasn't their fault, poor little mites.'

'From the point of view of my need to have an overall picture, would you mind telling me what the row was about?'

She hesitated.

'Off the record,' I prompted.

'I was under the impression he was seeing someone else,' Julia responded stiffly. 'I now know that it was a mistake on my part. I can only put it down to the fact, my mistake that is, that I was going through a bad patch at that time. My mother was very ill, Dad had had a car accident.'

'Stress can affect your mental state,' I agreed. 'It must have been a real relief when he told you there was no one else.'

'Yes,' she muttered, dropping her gaze.

She was lying. 'Ah,' I said. 'You thought his lady friend was going to Scotland with him - hence the row.'

Julia nodded.

'And of course no other women turned up.'

'That's right.'

I pounced. 'How do you know that?'

She was overcome with confusion. 'Well, no, I - I don't actually *know*, do I? I - I just realised I was being silly.'

I gave her one of Patrick's *Jaws* smiles. 'I thought for a minute that you were going to tell me that you'd hired a private detective.'

'Oh, no, nothing like that.'

'Look, if you do know something that would throw some light on this I can work it so that your name's not mentioned in connection with it - authors do it all the time. I'll just put it down as coming from an undisclosed source.' Would she fall for this load of eyewash?

When Julia sat back in her chair and once again regarded me I thought I had failed but then I saw that her eyes were not actually focused on me and she was weighing up the pros and cons of saying any more. Then she ventured,'This man you said is going to be arrested... '

'I told you that in complete confidence,' I interrupted.

'He must have been there then, either staying at the hotel, or nearby. D'you know what he looks like? I'm a bit worried now. I mean, he won't come after me, will he? You hear of people with grudges against the police and their families.'

Patrick almost certainly wouldn't have been staying at the hotel and if he had been nearby it would have been very unlikely that anyone would have noticed him. I was about to reply in the negative and then had the truly mind-boggling thought that he could well have behaved openly and confronted Somerton with no attempt at concealment. Hadn't Tim Shandy mentioned some kind of argument in the hotel garden?

'I don't think you need worry,' I said, having no desire to frighten her. 'Were you at the hotel?'

'No, a friend of mine was. I'd asked him to go to check up on Keith for me.'

I decided to come back to that in a moment. 'The suspect's

in his early forties, is six feet two inches in height, slim, has grey eyes and wavy black hair with a bit of grey in it.'

Julia slowly shook her head and I discovered that I felt quite weak. 'I can't remember my friend mentioning anyone who looked like that. Obviously, he was really only interested in the women, although he made a note about everyone. I didn't tell you the truth just now. I was actually thinking of divorcing Keith. He was a pretty lousy husband and father in several ways and was always away on account of the job, sometimes for weeks at a time. I think he volunteered for all the overtime possible but it seemed to make no difference to his pay and that's what made me think he had someone else.'

Yes, quite. He was in Brecon. 'Is your friend in the job too?' I hazarded.

'He was then. He worked with Keith but didn't get on with him.'

It seemed there was now yet another suspect. And someone in this ill-fated covert unit had tipped off the Bath police in connection with the investigation into Patrick's brother's murder. I said, 'Do you think this friend of yours would talk to me?'

She must have read my mind for she said sharply, 'He didn't kill him!'

'You're probably right. But as a one-time policeman he might have a good idea who did if I tell him the Death by Misadventure verdict has been found to be unsafe. Do you know if he saw Jamie Kirkland while he was there?'

'Yes, he did. But only the once, on the day before Keith drowned. He'd come to the hotel looking for him, I think, but whether it was anything to do with being his gillie...' Julia broke off with a little shrug.

'It will be dreadful if the police arrest the wrong man, won't it?'

'All right,' she said reluctantly. 'I'll give you Dave's phone number. It's up to him what he does and he can always refuse. Oh, I've just remembered! That description. There was a clergyman staying at the hotel who Dave mentioned who could have looked a bit like that. They chatted and Dave said his name made him laugh. I've forgotten what he said it was now but I don't think we need suspect him, do you?'

Yes, I thought, we do. Like hell we do.

Chapter Five

I was fairly convinced that Julia Somerton could tell me a lot more than she was admitting she knew but only after I had asked if I could use her phone to try to contact her friend Dave, and succeeded, did I leave. With, it must be said, great relief. She had given me the impression that she and Dave were no longer close, a notion fortified by his off-hand reaction when I spoke to him and mentioned her name. I had expected reluctance on his part to talk to me but he agreed to meet me a couple of hours later in his local, The Running Deer in Roehampton. As all that lay between me and the meeting place were a couple of housing estates and Putney Heath, I decided to walk.

The day was sunny and hot and I was in need of fresh air and exercise after the deadliness of the Somerton household. Drinking in the colour and scent of pink and white verbenas in hanging baskets outside a cafe, I mulled over what I had learned, working on the principle that what little had emerged was not the whole truth. Had Julia, in fact, left the two girls with a relative and gone to Scotland with Dave but kept right out of the way? I suppose some women might not blush at having what amounted to an extended dirty weekend while endeavouring at the same time to expose a cheating husband but I couldn't say that it was my style. Was it Julia's? The answer, without being a real bitch, had to be yes.

My mind was not at rest as to any part that Patrick might have played in Somerton's demise. Julia, who as I was leaving had seemed to recollect more about the clergyman than might have merely been conveyed to her by a third party, had suddenly remembered the name that had made Dave laugh: The Reverend Norman Archways. It had been noticed that he sometimes limped slightly.

'Oh, God,' I said with feeling to the warm breeze. 'Please tell me that he's one of yours.'

Yes, of course, one could go into the nearest large reference library and look him up in a copy of *Crockford's Directory.* Or phone John Gillard, Patrick's father, and ask him if he had one. I was heading away from the town centre but there was a phone box just along the road. Five minutes later I knew that John's copy was eight years old and the Reverend Archways-'Who?' John had asked, chuckling,'That sounds like one of Patrick's' - wasn't listed.

'Oh, God,' I whispered again.

Surely though, Tim Shandy would have recognised him. If their paths had crossed, that is.

I had told Patrick's parents the same as the younger children; that his leave had been cancelled and he had gone to London to help with an important investigation. Much as I hated not giving them the full story it was better than causing them day after day of worry. They would have to know the truth soon, however.

Heartwarmingly, Dave was manifestly not yet another Somerton clone but a big, burly Welshman. For the reason of his appearance alone I had hesitated approaching the only man sitting on his own at one of the wooden picnic tables in the garden of The Running Deer but he had turned, seen me and waved me over.

'Julia rang me back,' he reported with a wide grin that revealed perfect white teeth. 'To tell me what you look like and that you're writing a book about dear-departed Keith. You aren't really, are you?'

'No,' I said, sitting down.

'Well, she hadn't heard of you but I have. I've read most of your books. What can I get you to drink? Something long with ice in it? You look a bit warm.'

'Yes, please. Orange juice and lemonade.'

When he came back with the drink and another pint of

bitter for himself he said, 'I won't play if you write anything down, lady, and the name's just Dave. And as much as I enjoy being in the company of famous novelists you'll have to put your cards right on the table before I say one word.'

'Fine,' I said. 'I'm indebted to you for giving me your time.' With a big smile I added, 'I hope you'll be straight down the line with me.'

He held out a hand. 'It's a deal.'

We shook and then, using Patrick's technique of charm, retreat and then pounce I said, 'First tell me if you killed Keith Somerton.'

Dave's eyes screwed up in astonishment. 'Killed him? The stupid bugger fell out of a rowing boat. Julia didn't say anything about *murder*.'

'Perhaps she suspected you might have had something to do with it and was content for me to spring it on you,' I countered.

'No, I didn't. But probably only because it didn't actually occur to me at the time,' he said frankly.

'Exactly how I tell my side of the story depends on whether you were at Brecon.'

'You mean that crazy scheme MI5 blew out of the water on the personal orders of the PM? Too right I was. I helped set it up and we did a couple of dummy runs with members of several TSGs.' He smiled wryly. 'It was reckoned that they were the only guys tough enough to withstand the pace of the live-firing. I have to say though that I was bloody glad not to have been there for the final raid.'

'Somerton was the only cop there at the end,' I said. 'You may or may not know that by then he was relying almost entirely on criminals to run the place. And what happened wasn't strictly speaking a raid - he'd planned to finish everyone off and claim his students had rumbled him and broken into the weapon store. The local police had no idea what was going on there and were only alerted by MI5.'

'So where do you fit into all this? What's your angle?'

89

'I used to work for MI5 with my husband. We closed the place down. He subverted the so-called students and started what amounted to an underground war before Somerton's lot could begin shooting. Now he's in the frame for Somerton's murder on account of a political dirty-tricks campaign on the run-up to the next general election.'

Dave whistled and there was a short silence while he assimilated it all. Then he said, 'Sounds as though someone's spun a yarn and set it all rolling. Or is there evidence?'

'A bit of both, by the look of it. A highly dubious filmed meeting. And the very convenient discovery of the gillie's body this week with a piece of rope tied around the neck.'

'Jamie's *dead*?'

I nodded. 'He was found in the loch.'

'Bloody hell. Somerton knew him. That's how he got the job at Brecon.'

'And presumably not because he'd been trained by the Roux brothers.'

'No, but his bacon butties were the best I've ever had. Jamie had been a cook in the army but God knows how Keith met him. Keith had come up from the Porn Squad so perhaps Jamie was his snout.'

That fitted in rather neatly with what little I had been able to remember of Kirkland; thin, weasel-faced and with shifty eyes. 'Julia said you saw them talking the day before Somerton's death.'

'Only from a distance. I didn't really take any notice.'

'Do you reckon Somerton *was* just on a fishing holiday? Or was there more to it than that?'

'Heaven only knows. I can't help you there. It would be worth looking into Jamie's death - it might provide a few answers to Keith's.'

'I intend to. Chief Inspector, were you?' I enquired, judging I was erring slightly on the side of flattery.

'No, just plain inspector. I came outside altogether after that fiasco - I didn't join the police, never mind the Anti-Terrorist

Branch, to do that kind of thing. I didn't join up to turn one of my beautiful country's National Parks into a rat-run for the scum of the Earth either but I don't say too much about that or I'm accused of being jingoistic. It was in the wind Somerton's cronies intended to have another go, only dropping employing anyone with a record.'

'They did. On Mendip. It was after MI5 put a stop to that one as well that the political storm broke.'

Dave uttered a few expletives under his breath. Then he said, 'Now your old man's in the slammer. I don't see how I can help you.'

'Somerton's crony, Commander Christopher was in charge of that one. He shot and killed Patrick's brother and was arrested after one of his own men pulled the plug on him. I was wondering if you knew anything about that.'

'Nothing,' said Dave. 'Not one thing.'

'Okay,' I said, noting the way he had dropped his gaze. 'Then please tell me everything you can remember about that weekend at the Garrochmuir Hotel. It might be a long shot but I'm working on the theory that his killer was staying there too.' When he did not reply immediately I continued, 'Julia said that you went there following a request from her as she needed evidence that Somerton was having an affair with another woman.'

'Yes, she did. She wanted to come with me but I told her that would have been far too risky.'

'I'm actually finding it very difficult to believe that Julia was your kind of woman and my nasty suspicious mind is asking if you're going to be reluctant to talk about it because you tacked yourself on to her as you needed to know her husband's movements.'

'And what the hell would that have been in aid of?' Dave retorted.

'Because you wanted to get even with a complete bastard who had turned part of your beautiful country into a rat-run for the scum of the Earth.'

He just stared at me.

Quietly, I continued,'So shall we get that out of the way for a start? Writers watch people when they're speaking and I saw you almost choking with anger when you said that just now. I think I believe you when you said you didn't kill him and you're the second person I've talked to this week who said someone else got there just before them. I'm writing nothing down and your name's whatever the hell you want it to be. Just give me some leads.'

Dave rubbed the palms of his hands over his face, shook his head and then had a large gulp of beer. 'You don't mince your words, do you?'

'You did agree to talk to me,' I reminded him.

'Yeah,' he sighed. 'Perhaps I didn't think you knew so much.'

'And while you're sitting there shilly-shallying some nerds from Special Branch are putting the boot into my husband.'

I must have spoken more forcefully than I had intended for Dave looked a little alarmed. 'Yes, I suppose I did go up there to make life uncomfortable for him - spoil his fishing a bit. I knew Julia long before she married him and she was a different girl then, clever too with her own party-catering and wedding cake business. Keith made her give it up. He was one of those people who find out what makes people happy and then put a stop to it. She didn't know about Rhona, a right little tart who was supposedly his secretary at the survival centre they used as a front, nor about the other women he played around with. She got depressed - all the fun had gone out of her life - and started drinking too much. Yeah, I went to Scotland to let him know I thought he was a real shit. But you didn't faze Keith easily, he looked a bit surprised when he first saw me but then ignored me completely. I failed in what I'd set out to do too as, unless he had a women hidden in his suitcase, he slept alone.'

'I was told he had a row with someone in the garden.'

'I think that was with the Reverend Archways - God, what

a name - but don't ask me what it was about. It could have been in connection with his language, he'd sworn at the barman.'

Yes, I mustn't forget the hotel staff, I thought. It would be a complete anti-climax if the murderer was a proud Highlander insulted the night before by a runtish Englishman. People have been killed for less.

'You need to work out the timetable for all this,' Dave went on. 'It's all planned to hit the headlines when?'

'On the morning of the leader of the opposition's speech at the party conference next week. That usually takes place on the last day, doesn't it? That doesn't give me much time- a week's gone by already.'

'It seems to me you have no choice but to find out who the real killer is and pip everyone to the post with the big story.'

'That's one option,' I agreed. 'Another is to bust Patrick out of there ASAP on the grounds that they won't dare come after him with blue lights and sirens because the whole thing's not only a scam but a secret until the big day. They need the time to gather as much evidence, real or phoney, as possible. I didn't mention this but they haven't rounded up a nobody with a dodgy history: we're talking about a fairly senior army officer with a high-profile job at the Army Staff College. It would be worthwhile busting him out and *then* going public.'

'Don't look at me if you're thinking of recruiting a hit-squad.'

'I'm not. This is something to be achieved by cunning, not by utilising an armed gang.'

'And even if you did get him out they'd send real pros, undercover people, after him.'

'In that case; a) they wouldn't stand a chance and, b) it would all get very messy.'

Dave's eyebrows rose in polite disbelief. 'And is your Paddy as white as white as far as this drowning is concerned?'

'I don't know,' I admitted quietly. 'But I love him. Now tell me about the Garrochmuir Hotel - every last thing you can remember.'

I needed to write nothing down as Dave, highly articulate like all his countrymen, was a born storyteller. His account was therefore easy to remember and as I have a good memory too I wrote it all down at a later date. It emerged that he had made notes about the other hotel guests after Somerton's death as he had wondered if there had been foul play and was worried his connection with the deceased - with whose methods he had come openly and strongly to disagree before he left the police - would be discovered. When the verdict of the Coroner was reported he had destroyed them.

The Garrochmuir Hotel, he told me, was not large and had some ten letting bedrooms, seven doubles and three singles. Of the double rooms, two were unoccupied during that week-end - one on account of a man and his wife having left the day before Somerton arrived - three of the remaining ones had been used by couples, two retired and on walking and bird-watching holidays, the Rawsteads and the Fullers, and the third, in their twenties and of foreign origin, had been on honeymoon. Dave had not been able to decipher their names in the register. Somerton and the Reverend Archways had had the two remaining double rooms. The singles had been given over to Dave himself, a Captain Dupont, who was elderly and also on a walking - or rather tottering as Dave laughingly put it - holiday, and another man who had called himself Hall and whose description fitted that of Tim Shandy.

Only two had left the morning after Somerton's death, the clergyman and Shandy.

This information narrowed down the likely suspects but was not particularly promising. The folk on walking and bird-watching holidays sounded harmless but then again Patrick and I have adopted this ploy on several occasions and it is a valuable one as you then have a very good excuse to lurk in the bushes hung about with binoculars and cameras. Those in this category had all risen early on the morning of Somerton's death, collected packed lunches and gone off for the day. The young couple on honeymoon were probably innocent of everything other than staying in bed until lunchtime but the fact that Dave had not been able to read their name in the register was interesting. And of course it would be nigh-on impossible to trace all these people after such a long time.

It all seemed rather hopeless.

Dave was watching me sadly. 'It's not really a lot of use to you, is it?'

'Did the local police interview everyone?' I asked. It was important to remain positive, push the distracting Reverend Archways firmly to the back of my mind and refuse to enter paths of enquiry that showed every sign of becoming dead-ends.

'Only with a view to establishing a timetable of events. The boat belonged to the hotel and no one else wanted it that day so Somerton wasn't actually missed until dinner. It was later that night - it stays light hellishly late in Scotland in summer as you know - when an old guy who lives nearby found the body when he was taking his dog for a walk.'

'Surely the fact that the body had come ashore aroused suspicion.'

'No, apparently not. I think it was assumed that he'd tried to swim, almost made it and then become exhausted and drowned. His life jacket was only partly inflated. I know reports said the body was on the shore but it was actually in about a foot of water.'

'And the rook?'

'Oh, that was just the old man and his omens and curses and the stupid things he said to the press. It was a bit higher up, on the shingle. Bloody thing had most likely been there for days.'

'You saw it?'

'What's so important about it? No, and he left it there. Said the same curse would hit him if he moved it. That bird probably kept the old fool in beer for a week.'

'It doesn't appear that there was any suspicion of foul play.'

'I wouldn't say so. The cop who spoke to me said there were rotting trees in the water near the islands that had caused boats rowed by the unwary to capsize in the past. Naturally, they took the body off for a post mortem.'

'Could you give me your own timetable of events? When did you arrive?'

'The hotel has a weekend break offer that runs from Friday lunchtime until Monday breakfast for two hundred quid. That sounds a lot but it includes a return rail ticket from London, all meals, including a bottle of bubbly on the first evening and wine with dinner and there's a sail on the loch in someone's boat thrown in on the Saturday morning and a shopping trip to Inverness in the afternoon for those who want them. Not all the guests were there for the whole week-end but Keith was. Julia had said that he would arrive late on the Friday morning. He travelled overnight by train but I was driving and planned to stay the night with my parents in Shropshire on the way. When I got to the hotel lunch was already over - I'd got held up by an RTA - but they rustled something up for me, which I appreciated as I was bloody starving. I didn't actually bump into Keith until everyone mustered for dinner. It was all rather formal but I'd taken a tie with me - I'm a t-shirt and trainers bloke myself but realise you have to dress up a bit sometimes. There were these two biddies with their blue-rinses and rows of pearls and their husbands crammed into suits that didn't fit them anymore and I thought what the hell have I got myself into. There was the young couple too, although they were too wrapped up in one another to bother with the rest of us. I got chatting to the bloke called Tim Hall. He didn't say much about himself but was kind of upper-crust and might have been in the services. The best part of the evening was the look on Keith's face when he saw me and from then on, as I said just now, he ignored me. But believe me, I planned to have a little chat with him before the weekend was out. I'd already caught a glimpse of him talking to Jamie outside the main hotel entrance.'

'What about the argument he had with the Reverend Archways?'

'Oh, yes. Forgot about that for a moment. That took place immediately after dinner somewhere out the back. A few of them had their coffee in the conservatory and I gather the Rev and Keith went through the outside door of that into the garden. I wasn't there so I didn't hear what was said.'

I could picture in my mind's eye a tall, dark-haired man who could so easily have been Patrick grabbing Somerton by the scruff of the neck and hauling him some distance away before giving him a piece of his mind. Or telling him that he was going to kill him?

'Everyone seemed to go to bed early that night,' Dave went on. 'Either that or they went up to their rooms to watch television. I found I had the place almost to myself so decided to go for a short walk in the twilight, down to the loch shore before having a nightcap. Came straight back though after a zillion midges set upon me as soon as I put my nose outside.'

'Did you see anyone?'

'Just the old guy who found Keith's body the next day. He had a little terrier with him so I reckon he walks it at around that time every night. The midges didn't seem to go for him, which is not surprising as I don't think he mixes with soap and water all that often.' Dave paused to refresh his thirst and then, wiping the froth from his lip with the back of his hand, continued, 'I only saw Keith twice after that, once in the corridor as I came down to breakfast and then again afterwards when he was on his way out for the fishing trip with all his rods and stuff. Both times he looked through me as though I wasn't there. I just rehearsed what I was going to say during our little chat later that day. Julia had said I could tell him she was going to divorce him and I planned to add a few comments of my own.'

'What about the other guests? Did any of them behave suspiciously on that Saturday morning?'

'No, not that I could see all that went on. And you must be aware that nothing had happened then so there was no reason to pay attention and watch people. In fact I'd decided to enjoy myself- no point in going all that way and spending money and not do so. The guy Hall had gone off somewhere: I noticed his car had gone. The retired couples, the Rawsteads and the Fullers, and Captain Dupont- he was a silly old sod so was probably the captain of a river ferry, or something like that- set off for a day's birdwatching or whatever. I didn't see the honeymooners at all that morning so one must assume they were still doing what comes naturally.'

I was about to ask him if he could swim and then whether he had seen the Reverend Archways that morning and for a full description of him when out of the corner of my eye I saw something that caused me to look again. A man wearing black leathers was approaching us, several others in ordinary clothes fanning out. I didn't stop to pass the time of day with them, just grabbed my rucksack and ran.

One of them was obviously a sprinter and was right behind me immediately. I stopped dead and when he almost cannoned into me, off-balance, I tipped him over in the infallible way that Patrick taught me. He ended up diving not so gracefully into one of the groups of shrubs with which the beer garden was surrounded, in this case purple-leaved berberis well-endowed with wicked-looking spines. I ran on, judging by a crash and the tinkle of breaking glass that Dave had tipped over the picnic bench in the path of some of the others. There was no need to look round to know that at least one man was still behind me. He was not puffing and blowing either, here was someone fit.

It was madness to head back for the open heath and I didn't, running instead towards the shops in the high street. Heads were turning, people stopping to stare, one man even started to come in my direction as though to head me off but changed his mind. Car horns hooted, someone jeered at me through a car window.

I was getting out of breath and the man behind me was gaining. I had an idea it was the black man I had noticed with the group, a towering athletic-looking individual. On impulse I jinked down a narrow alleyway at the side of a supermarket, jumped some empty cardboard boxes, dodged around some rubbish bins and then turned sharp left and shot through an open door at the rear of what appeared to be a Chinese restaurant, slamming it behind me. There were a couple of bolts and I shot them across, turning the key in the lock for good measure.

Face to face with mops, buckets and brooms in a dark passageway I stood quite still for several moments, breathing hard. No one tried the door but I was not fool enough to kid myself that I had got away. There was no innocence to be protested if I was apprehended for the gun, plus ammunition, was in my rucksack. I had no intention of using it and now questioned the wisdom of carrying around a weapon I was no longer officially permitted to be in possession of. I had assumed that Patrick's only reason for still having it was purely that no one had ever asked him for it back. I found myself wondering if our names were still on several terrorist groups' hit lists and that was the reality behind the permission for its continued presence, Patrick having not wanted to worry me. In that case I could not be charged with being in possession of a firearm. I had no real desire to test the theory though and made my way across the room towards a door on the far side.

A door that was being opened very hesitantly towards me.

I hauled on the handle on my side and in hurtled a terrified Chinese man, finishing up in my arms. I modified the choreography of this slightly so that I had a two-handed hold of his shirt-front instead and we stood eyeball to eyeball, he probably on tip-toe.

'Illegal immigrant?' I hissed.

He shook his head but sweat was pouring down his face.

I kept it simple in case his English was limited. 'I am. Police outside. You hide me?'

Gibbering with terror he bundled me into a cold store, then with remarkable presence of mind tossed in someone's dirty anorak. I was telling myself that at least there was a light inside when it was switched off and I was left in the dark. It was very cold and I dared not put on the coat in case I knocked something off the shelves, loaded to the point of collapse. And no, I firmly told myself, what I had caught a glimpse of hanging from a rail in the ceiling with several dead ducks just before the light went out could not possibly be a large mummified octopus.

Whatever it was - seaweed, surely - I hid behind its distinctly fishy presence when the sound of footsteps went to and fro on the other side of the door. This went on for quite a while and then there was a long silence. I sank down on to the floor, the anorak around my shoulders and tried to convince myself that I was not going to die of cold.

At last, after what seemed like several hours had elapsed, the light came on without warning and the door opened. My friend parted the seaweed fronds or octopus tentacles and gazed down at me, his fear unabated.

'Go!' he said hoarsely. 'Gone now.'

Stiffly, for I was frozen to the marrow, I took a ten pound note from my purse, regained my feet and pressed it into his hand. He looked at it for a moment and then held it out to me, shaking his head.

'Have it,' I told him. 'Please.'

Had he been expecting a visit from the Triad?

Moments later I was out in the alley. It seemed inconceivable that the search had been called off but I could see no one and walked slowly and warily back the way I had come. The air seemed furnace-hot after the cold store and smelt dusty and stale, a gust of blue diesel fumes blowing into my face as a van moved off in the main road. I felt oddly naked as I emerged from the alley and paused to get my bearings.

Before me was a panorama of a busy urban summer afternoon; traffic, shoppers, mothers hurrying to collect their children from school, people taking dogs for walks. I knew what to look for and carefully scrutinised all the parked cars and men hanging around for no apparent reason or gazing in shop windows. I could see nothing suspicious although there was a black man on the opposite side of the road standing with his back to me talking to someone else. He did not seem tall or slim enough to be my pursuer so I discounted him and, after a quick look behind me, back down the alley, I concentrated on the cars.

There were three cars of various kinds in my line of vision but sloping windscreens and rear windows tend to merely reflect the sky or nearby buildings so it was anyone's guess who was watching for me from farther down the street. Then a huge articulated lorry slowed down and stopped at a pedestrian crossing as the lights went to red, blocking all view of me so I went through the side entrance of a Boots chemist and then immediately out through the main door which was slightly round the corner in the next street. From there I could see The Running Deer and part of the beer garden. There was no sign of Dave and I wondered if he had been arrested. I hoped not, not by policeman who are operating without giving the required warnings and producing warrant cards. Anyone who has protected a woman from what he thought was a bunch of muggers could hardly be charged with obstructing the law.

It was possible that the whole purpose of the exercise had not been to apprehend me for questioning - I had no objection to answering questions but the fear was that I would not be released again afterwards - but again to frighten me into staying at home. If they had succeeded in getting hold of me a slight roughing-up might have been on the agenda perhaps? A ride blindfold in a car and dumping in the middle of nowhere? Ten minutes alone with the one in the leather romper suit?

As I re-crossed the road to a phone box I was shivering a little and this time it wasn't from cold.

There are not many people in the world who are prepared to drop everything and apply themselves to bizarre requests for help made by their friends. Patrick's mother Elspeth is one of them, James Carrick another. I knew instinctively when he answered the phone at Manvers Street police station, Bath, that he was frantically busy; his quiet voice, with just a trace of a Scottish accent, was clipped, like Patrick's when he is in overdrive, against a background of phones ringing, people urgently talking, doors slamming, footsteps pounding up and down. He was in the main CID office, obviously, probably about to give a briefing. It was quite likely that I had caught him in the aftermath of a major incident.

Absolutely the last thing I was going to do was remind him that Patrick had once saved his life. As with Commander Brinkley I was concise and to the point, doing everything in my power to keep my tone matter-of-fact, jokey even.

'Let me get this perfectly clear,' James said when I had finished speaking. 'You're in Roehampton, Patrick has been arrested in connection with the death of that scunner you ran into in Wales, Special Branch heavies are trying to stop you interfering and you want to get to Scotland without bumping into them again.'

'That's it to perfection,' I told him.

'Stay right where you are. Are you calling from a phone box?'

'Yes, I'm not sure if mobiles can be traced.'

'Where exactly is it?'

I told him.

'Stay close by. In around ten minutes time a police car will stop nearby and one of the crew will come to you and ask you the time. Answer five thirty whatever it really is. They'll take you somewhere safe until I arrive.'

Appalled, I had just recollected that he might be called to give evidence if the case came to court and said so. His response was a snort of impatience and then he apologised for being in a tearing hurry and rang off.

James, of course, had served for a number of years in the Met. It was obvious that he still had contacts. Not only contacts, it appeared, but clout. What arrived just over seven minutes later was actually an ARV, an armed response vehicle, and I was swiftly conveyed northwards in the direction of Barnes. I had thought I might be taken to a police station or safe-house but we arrived at a lodge-style cottage surrounded by trees in Barnes Green and the front door was opened by a very attractive woman who was doing her level best not to look annoyed on account of having been in the shower when the phone had rung, her hair still up in a towel.

My escort, definitely of the strong and very silent variety, departed.

'I'm Avril,' said the lady of the house. 'An old friend of James's. He said you were having a bit of trouble.'

Yes, well I suppose he could hardly have told her that bloodhounds were on my trail. I gave her my name, adding, 'And I'm not an old friend in the sense you might think I am. James and my husband worked together on a case.'

Avril looked relieved. 'Oh, is he in the job too?'

I shook my head. 'No, it was when Patrick worked for MI5.'

'Exciting stuff, eh? Come through into the conservatory while I dry my hair. Would you like a drink?'

Instinct told me she meant something alcoholic and, boringly, right then I could have really done with a cup of tea. 'No, I'm fine, thanks.'

The phone played *Knees up Mother Brown* and Avril uttered a peal of silvery laughter. 'I only got it to do that yesterday. I think it's a real hoot, don't you?' She shook a fine head of long black hair out of the towel and went away to answer it.

I made my way slowly towards the back of the extremely stylish interior of the house thinking that as I had been invited to the conservatory it would not be ill-mannered to endeavour to locate it. In the end I just followed the scent of jasmine.

'That was James again,' said Avril, finding me admiring her cymbidium orchids. 'He asked me to tell you that he'll get the six thirty train from Bath and be here latish, after dinner. Then in the morning he'll hire a car.'

'This is the most awful imposition !' I exclaimed.

She laughed again. 'Don't give it a thought. It'll be a real treat to have him under my roof after all these years. Old flames don't always get snuffed right out, do they?' With that she went away to finish drying her hair.

I fervently hoped that as James was now happily married to Joanna no embers would be rekindled on my account.

Carrick was very late indeed, arriving at a little after midnight. By this time Avril and I were well into our second bottle of wine. The conservatory was still warm after the day's sunshine. It was illuminated by several very large church candles in wrought-iron holders and smaller ones in a chandelier hanging from the roof, the scent of the jasmine growing on the house wall almost as intoxicating as what we were drinking.

'You can't sleep on an empty stomach,' Avril was scolding when she returned from letting him in. She was actually addressing him from the kitchen where she had gone to fetch him a beer.

James - in his early thirties, tall, very fair, bleak Nordic good looks, blue eyes - came forward and we knew one another well enough by now for him to kiss my cheek as we clasped both hands. He looked very tired and flopped into one of Avril's cane chairs making it creak alarmingly.

'I fixed up the car tonight as I decided to drive from Bath,' he said. 'Didn't think it would be a good idea to use mine under the circumstances.'

'I'll pay,' I said quickly.

'You won't. No one should have to pay a Scotsman to go

home even if it's only for a short time.' He gazed at me soberly. 'I can't stay - you do understand that, don't you? The work is bottomless at home and I simply can't get too deeply involved with this at this stage. If I have to give evidence...'

'Of course I understand. You can't know how grateful I am that...'

Impatiently, he butted in with, 'I've probably put my head on the block as it is but I was so bloody mad after what you told me that I got the info off the central computer and bull-dozed myself with my warrant card into the remand centre where Patrick's being held.' He paused and then went on carefully, 'He's not very well.'

'You mean he's been beaten up again?'

'God, you never even mentioned it had happened the first time. Possibly not but I'd say he has a chest infection. Terrible cough.'

'Isn't something being done about it?' I asked, trying, with-out success, to keep my voice steady.

'You know him. He said he's okay, it's on the mend and he doesn't need to see a doc. Trouble was I had an idea the room might be bugged and there was a warder on the other side of a glass screen so I couldn't ask too many questions. Couldn't say too much at all really as every time he spoke it set him coughing again.'

'Did he say anything that seemed a bit strange to you? Anything that might mean something to me - one of our coded phrases?'

Carrick pondered and then said, 'Can't say as he did.'

I felt like tearing my hair out. If only he had rung and told me what he was planning to do I could have given him a coded message that would have informed Patrick that Shandy was alive and hadn't drowned Somerton. Perhaps on the other hand it was just as well that I hadn't as whatever I felt about the legality of what was taking place the man before me was a Detective Chief Inspector who might have no choice but be a witness for the prosecution. To put his career in jeopardy was unthinkable. However there was nothing wrong in giving him an accurate account of what had happened so far. If he had been angry before he was absolutely furious by the time I had finished.

Avril had tactfully stayed away but now reappeared with a plate of brown bread and butter and smoked salmon for him, rescued the remains of the empty beer can from his fingers - unconsciously he had flattened it utterly while I was speaking - and put the food before him, drawing up a small table. I felt sorry for her, he hardly seemed to recognise her presence.

Carrick must suddenly have realised his omission for he turned and gave her the kind of smile that makes women go weak at the knees whether they are old flames, married to someone else, or whatever. I wondered what he was like in bed. Probably a breathtaking combination of velvet and dynamite.

You're drunk, I told myself miserably. Drunk and thinking about another man while-

'Not being nosy, Ingrid, but did James have bad news for you?' Avril asked sympathetically, breaking into my thoughts.

Before I could answer Carrick said, 'I've just remembered. Patrick said he'd had a postcard from Devon. I assumed it was from you - I mean, who else knows where he is?'

'I didn't send it,' I said.

'He had it in his top pocket and showed it to me. Just a picture of some tors, Great Mis in the foreground, I think it said.'

'What was written on it?' Avril asked, obviously completely in the dark but interested anyway.

'It just said, "Came up here and thought of the good times we had. Asked the wind about you." There was no signature.'

'Another old flame making their presence known, do you think?' Avril enquired with a mischievous grin in my direction.

'No,' I replied, my heart pounding. 'Great Mis Tor is inside a military restricted area on Dartmoor and only at certain times of the year is public access allowed. Someone's having a joke.'

Ye gods, I thought. Shandy. What *had* the wind told him?

Chapter Six

Loch Duncreggan lay like a steel-grey mirror below the forested hills, its smooth perfection only marred near a headland where an occasional breeze ruffled the water. Thin wisps of mist wreathed and wound amongst the treetops, fading as the early morning sun devoured them. I had opened the window and pine-scented air had flowed in like cool water, bringing with it the sounds of sheep bleating in a nearby meadow, the clap of wings as a small flock of pigeons on a nearby roof took fright at the sudden noise, the smell of wood smoke.

I could see the little jetty, the salmon boat moored to it that Keith Somerton had cast off on his last journey, and the islands - a small one nearest the shore, a larger one farther out - that had concealed his death from any idly gazing eyes. They too had trees growing on them; goat willows, hawthorn, silver birch and stunted oaks. About a hundred yards from the jetty along the eastern shore was a boathouse which I had been informed had within it a steam launch that was in the process of being restored by a local retired engineer. It was to this man that the two boys had first reported their gruesome find on the island and he had gone back with them to make sure that their young imaginations had not been playing tricks with them.

The Garrochmuir Hotel - I had been very fortunate to get a room as there had been a cancellation - was a creeper-clad granite house set among a grove of ancient Scots pines. I had learned that it had been a private dwelling until the end of the First World War, the home of the Lairds of Creggan. But the last of the line had perished on the Somme and the distant female cousin who had inherited everything had sold the house, which had been run-down and in need of expensive renovations and modernisation, to a local businessman and his wife. It was their descendants, Philip and Jenny Cranley, who were the present proprietors.

There was no need to ask questions, everyone was falling over themselves to tell newly-arrived visitors about the discovery of the second body, not least the old man who had found Somerton's. It emerged that he worked part-time at the hotel, keeping the gardens tidy, bringing in logs for the fires and doing odd-jobs and had achieved almost celebrity status after his mutterings about curses now that another body had come to light. This promotion had resulted in his seeming permanent presence in the hotel bar in the evenings when tourists and local ghouls listened as his tales got taller and taller.

James Carrick had given the raconteur short shrift the previous night when it had become apparent he thought it time we bought him a dram. The broadside of Scots that Carrick had fired off at him would have sunk Nessie without trace and the storyteller had removed himself rapidly out of range.

'What on earth's a rummlieguts?' I had asked.

'A windbag,' he had answered shortly.

'I think you've really offended him.' As I was fairly convinced that James had in fact called him an old fart this was hardly surprising.

'That's only because he's reached the greetin fou stage, tearfully drunk,' Carrick had asserted. 'Soon he'll be spuin fou and then Heaven help us.'

'You don't have to feel responsible, you know,' I had teased.

He had looked even more annoyed for a second or two and then laughed.

The young proprietors, full of energy and a trifle too eager to please, were still agog at the publicity the area was receiving by the media and were the guilty ones as far as condoning tall stories in the bar was concerned. I found myself hoping that they would not start running Whodunnit Weekends before the wretched Jamie Kirkland's funeral took place.

Unfortunately, Jenny, with a bubbly manner that matched her curly auburn hair, had recognised me soon after I had arrived late the previous afternoon, and immediately put two and two together and made several hundred.

'No, I'm not here to research a book I intend to write about it,' I had assured her, thinking that my using the bit of make-believe this time would be in equally bad taste. 'It's just a coincidence.' Then not wishing to snub her or prevent her giving me any useful information, added, 'But crime writers are always interested in real crime. You can borrow details and change names and not hurt anybody.'

She had been rather crestfallen but at this brightened again. 'It really was spooky having another body found after the death of the other gentleman. I mean I know Jamie was a local man and Mr Somerton a guest but they did know one another and I can't help thinking that there's some kind of connection - not that Jamie came *here*, you understand, he seemed to live in the Creggan Arms. You won't go there, will you? Please don't think I'm interfering,' she had quickly added,'but it's a really dreadful place. It's the only pub in Duncreggan and the police are always being called there.'

I had thanked her for the warning, thinking that the police probably counted themselves lucky that they had all the villains of Duncreggan under one roof and then asked,'How long had Keith Somerton been coming here?'

'Oh, he'd only been here twice before. I think he liked the peace and quiet and to be left alone - he didn't chat and make friends like most people.'

I had to be careful as I was not supposed to know anything about it and did not want to set everyone in the hotel gossiping about me when I had only just arrived.'By that do you mean he was rude?'

'Well, *I* thought he was very rude but Phil always says you get all sorts and I shouldn't worry about it. He was unpleasant certainly, spoke to the staff in a way I didn't like at all. I would have said something to him if it had gone on much longer actually because the people who work here are very loyal and hard-working and we're like a happy family. I'd rather lose a guest than one of them.'

'But you never got the chance as he didn't come back from his fishing trip.'

'No,' Jenny had said thoughtfully. 'I know it sounds awful but I was quite relieved in a way. There was something about him... I was glad I didn't have to confront him after all.'

I was in perfect sympathy with her on this. 'I suppose the police asked a lot of questions.'

'They did and I remembered something afterwards that perhaps I should have told them. I'm surprised that none of the others mentioned it. It was that the boat was found upturned not far from the bigger of the two islands where there's a lot of rotting branches from a couple of trees that fell into the loch a few years ago. I would have thought he would have known about that as he'd been here before. It's the last place you'd look for fish - they don't seem to go there at all.' Jenny had looked at me with a worried expression on her pretty face. 'Do you think I should say something now? It's an awfully long time ago.'

'Yes, I think you should,' I had told her. 'Especially now Jamie's body's been found.'

Jenny had bustled away, shuddering gloriously with yet more spookiness.

The wrong place for fish, eh?

And now, as I gazed out of the window I saw James Carrick, hands in pockets, strolling onto the jetty and looking across the loch. Soon, after this quick glimpse of his homeland - our journey had taken most of the previous day - he would be heading south again. But before he did so he had promised to undertake a little investigating for me.

Just before lunch, far later that he had planned, James returned. I had had no choice but to stay in the hotel or very close by so that he would be able to find me but I had not wasted the time and had done a little sleuthing of my own. Ancipating that on Sundays most businesses would be closed I had, on arrival the previous day, contacted the only two local establishments that hired out scuba-gear, one in Inverness, the other in Fort Augustus. The former did not keep records that went back that far, the other had had only one customer in the two weeks before the date of Somerton's death, a Mr Hall. In other words, Tim Shandy.

'It's like this,' James said without preamble, joining me on a large sofa in the resident's lounge, a strange odour about his clothing that I immediately recognised. He had been to the mortuary. 'All that's left of Kirkland amounts to just rags and bones and enough of his insides for the pathologist to analyse in order to discover he wasn't poisoned or died from a heart attack or stroke. His liver was dodgy though, he drank heavily. Without the length of rope around the neck it would be an open and shut case of death by drowning. It still *might* be death by drowning but, as you know, the presence of the rope suggests someone else had a hand in his death. They sent the rope to an expert in Edinburgh who came up this morning with an amazing amount of info. It was already old, at least twenty years, when it was used and made of jute by a firm in Bridport, Dorset. The method of manufacture suggests it was made for marine use and is similar to the kind used on painters, that is, mooring ropes for small boats. It's not a chunk of the one on the rowing boat though, that's different again. The police intend to check all the boats used on the loch tomorrow but aren't necessarily suspecting anyone connected with watercraft as the knot that had been used was highly unnautical, not Bristol-fashion at all.'

'They let you see the body?' I asked.

'They seemed delighted to share all the evidence with me - probably because they were fresh out of ideas. And in view of the fact that Patrick made me what amounts to a confession with regards to Somerton's death I felt I had every right to see it.' Carrick swallowed hard at this point and then shook his head before continuing, 'You should never speak ill of the dead they say but he must have been an evil-looking little bastard when he was alive. What was left of him reminded me of a long-dead rat. Poor devil. Anyway, although this area is now policed from Inverness I spoke to a retired cop who used to be the local bobby. He still lives in Duncreggan village and knows everything and everyone - a sort of one-man neighbourhood watch. According to him Kirkland was a no-gooder, one of those who's a problem from the age of five. Like most young Scots he left his home village and went south. After knocking around rough in London he joined up and was dishonourably discharged from the army a couple of years later for thieving and generally being a bad boy. Which would fit in with him being Somerton's snout in London.'

'That was only a theory of Dave's,' I reminded him.

'No, it would figure. I ran a check on him on the way back here. He had a record, all right. Mostly of the living off immoral earnings, possession of pornographic literature variety, with a couple of GBHs thrown in for good measure. The local CID know all about that, of course and they're working along the lines that someone in his past has finally caught up with him. We mustn't ignore the fact that if that is the case whoever it was might have decided to take out Somerton as well as he was present and therefore a witness. Which in the circumstances would be bizarre in the extreme.'

'A man like that wouldn't have had many real friends locally,' I pointed out.

'No, you're right although he used to drink with a couple of local men in the Creggan Arms. And the lads in Inverness haven't been slow in interviewing all the local mobsters- only in this neck of the woods that means mostly poachers, housebreakers and people who hang out washing on the Sabbath. Apparently when Kirkland wasn't actually in the pub he was a loner. He used to skulk around with a few local youths years ago before he went south but they've done the same and haven't come back. Kirkland returned just over two years ago - presumably after you closed down Somerton's Brecon scam. He was unemployed for most of the time of course but did a bit of gillie-work when he could get it. Very good at stalking deer, I was told and made money during the season and also out of it when visitors just want good photos.'

I said, 'Tim Shandy said there was no one in the boat with Somerton unless they were lying in the bottom of it.'

'So either there was a change of the arranged plan or Kirkland was already dead by then.'

'There's no concrete evidence to point towards his death occurring anywhere near the time of Somerton's.'

James grinned. 'No, I'm being really unprofessional, aren't I? But like you I'd put money on his dying just before, at the same time or just after Somerton.'

'But why tether the body under water?'

James shrugged. 'He could have been killed that way. That's *meaningful*. Big time revenge. I'm interested that he'd told his wife he was going away. No doubt the police here have spoken to her but you might get more out of her. And as Somerton's wife knew about Kirkland, Kirkland's wife might be able to tell you something useful about Somerton.'

'Jenny Cranley told me that in her view Somerton's boat was found in the wrong part of the loch for fish.'

'Could it have drifted?'

'Possibly, but there are a lot of submerged branches where a couple of trees fell in.'

'Another line of enquiry then.'

'But you have to go back,' I pointed out.

'Just when I'm getting really keen,' he said ruefully.

'I'm so grateful for your help. You will have spent your entire weekend on the road.'

'I've done nothing but be the taxi-driver,' he replied almost bitterly. 'What I really wanted to do was get Patrick out of that bloody place. And now I'm leaving you here on your own. What kind of a friend does that make me?'

'Sometimes we have to play things by the book,' I told him.

But James just shrugged angrily and wrote down in a note-book the name and address of the retired policeman and the address of Kirkland's wife, Jean, who apparently was no longer living with her boyfriend in Inverness and had returned to the village. Tearing out the page he handed it to me and said, 'As far as I'm concerned you haven't mentioned this guy Shandy to me. I've never heard of him.'

I said, 'I just wish he'd seen and heard more, that's all.' I was also wishing I had questioned Tim more closely about his time at the hotel so I could compare it with Dave's account.

'He sent Patrick the card, didn't he?'

I was more than aware that Carrick was a very good detective and was wondering why he thought it important. 'He might have done,' I replied guardedly. Perhaps if he had posted it early on Thursday morning and put a first class stamp on it would have arrived the next day.

As he had done before our journey James gazed at me soberly. 'You will be careful, won't you?'

'Look, this is hardly likely to end up as Brecon did.'

'With you pair anything can happen.'

Perhaps if he had been anyone else I might have pointed out sourly that as Patrick was behind bars we could hardly start a war. I knew he had our welfare at heart so merely kissed his cheek and wished him a safe drive home.

His final question was, 'You wouldn't be carrying a gun by any chance?'

'You don't know about things like that *either*,' I said with a smile. I did not feel amused. With James's help, especially with his capacity to liase with the local CID, I felt I had every chance of getting to the truth. Without it getting Patrick out of prison seemed remote.

James drove me into Inverness so I could hire a car and then left.

I had found the spinner of the tall tales, referred to by everyone as Auld Robbie, muttering as he stumped along a path from the woodstore pushing a wheelbarrow loaded with large logs for the lounge fire, which was lit every night, even in the summer. I forced him to stop by remaining on the path as it was too narrow for the pair of us to pass.

'I'm sorry my friend was so rude to you last night,' I said.

Robbie, as gnarled and bent as a thorn bush and wearing the same weather-stained tweeds as when I had last seen him, was glad to dump down the barrow. Despite what James had said he did not seem to be any the worse for his intake of Scotch the previous night and Dave's comments about him being a stranger to soap and water I judged to be on the harsh side too.

'Och weel,' he sighed. 'Murder's not tae everyone's heart.'

'I'd really like to talk to you about Jamie Kirkland.'

'It was on account of the corbie,' he said, eyeing me narrowly.

'I thought a corbie was a crow. Wasn't what was found on the shore a dead rook?

'Rooks, crows, ravens, they're all corbies to me. Curst. Deil's birds. Ye get one death and then there's anither.'

I spoke in a confiding undertone. 'Look, I'm not really into all this superstitious stuff.'

'No?'

'No, I'm a writer and crimes interest me. I'd like to know whether Jamie Kirkland was Mr Somerton's gillie on the morning he drowned and if not, why not.' I took from my pocket a twenty pound note I had put there for the purpose and pressed it into his ready hand.

'No, he wasna.'

'Why?'

'They'd had an argie-bargie the evening before. Jamie had gone tae him for what was owing. He got not a brass penny.'

'Money owing to him from a previous occasion, you mean?'

Auld Robbie nodded briskly and said with great relish, 'As my Aberdeenshire auntie would have it, Somerton let fung at his lug and geed it a gweed doosht.'

Without Robbie's graphic gestures it was doubtful whether I would have quite got the hang of this. 'He hit him!'

'Aye, and Jamie's feet were awa from under him and before he kenned it he was in the burn!'

'Did Jamie tell you this himself?'

'Aye and spittin' mad he was too. He'd had several drams though. Got a real fright and sobered up fast as he thocht for a moment he was in the loch. No one had ever been able to teach the gowk te swim.'

One less suspect then, for Somerton's murder. 'Somerton's name wasn't actually released to the press. Did Jamie tell you that too?'

'Aye, he did. Worked for him doon sooth.'

'So he was owed money from that.'

'So he said.'

'He'd told his wife he was leaving her but in actual fact she was leaving him. Was that why no one actually missed Jamie until the day his body was found?'

Auld Robbie dislodged his tweed cap a little in order to scratch his scalp and then yanked it back into place. 'Ye ken Jamie wasna a mannie ye *missed*. Ye just thought te yesel that thievin' bastard hasna shown hissel for a coupla days. He'd said he was goin' te clear oot but Jamie was always bletherin on aboot that and when he disappeared everyone thought he'd done it. Jean's well shot of him, fancy man or no.'

Making it sound like a joke, I said, 'So you don't reckon her boyfriend drowned him?'

'That sweetie-wife hairdresser? Never. Jamie would have scairt him oot o' his troosers.'

I supposed I had to take his word for it. 'Jamie must have had quite a few enemies then.'

'Aye, but who wants jile for squashing a loose?'

'D'you reckon Somerton killed him? Jamie might have carried on pestering him for the money.'

But it seemed that Auld Robbie had come to the conclusion that I had had my money's worth for he bent and seized the barrow handles. Then he straightened again and said, 'You're not the police?' He pronounced it po-lice.

116

'No.'

'Jamie told me aboot his thick lug *after* Somerton set off alone for the fishin'. Now I wouldna like to get a man o' the kirk in trouble but there was an English minister staying here just then. He and Somerton had had a real collieshangie oot here the night before. The minister wasna the usual Sunday-faced mannie - ye wouldna tramp on *his* taes.'

'But surely you don't think the minister killed him.'

With a sideways crafty look he said,'I ken he went for a swim in the loch every mornin'.'

'Did you see him?'

'Aye, I did. Looked like a sheetit corpse, he did.'

'And he went swimming that morning as well?'

But Auld Robbie was really off this time and I had no choice but to step off the path out of his way. 'Oh, aye,' he said over his shoulder.

I had pondered over the 'sheetit corpse' and come to the conclusion that the man in question had probably worn a long white robe of some kind over his swimming trunks. Patrick had bought a new white towelling dressing gown for our trip to the States.

It appeared that Jean Kirkland had returned to the house she had shared with Jamie, one of those on a small council scheme situated on raised ground at the edge of the nearby village. It was actually a highly desirable position as all the houses had superb views of the loch and the surrounding mountains. When she opened the door Jean Kirkland's face had the kind of expression that suggested she might just shut it again without even asking the purpose of my visit. But then again she was a sullen-looking woman; a shock of unkempt black hair, a white triangular face, a turned-down mouth that might have had a hare lip when she was a child. She was dressed all in black, as might be expected, but satin tracksuit bottoms, a sweatshirt and trainers would not be many people's idea of mourning.

I introduced myself and then said, 'I'm very sorry about your husband, Mrs Kirkland. I was wondering if I could ask you a few questions about Keith Somerton, the other man who drowned. I understand they knew one another.'

'Are you from the police?' Her voice was softer than I had expected and without any particular accent.

'No. But my husband has been arrested in connection with his death.'

Her features broke out of the sullen mould for a moment. 'I thought it was an accident!'

'It looks as though someone might have tipped him out of the boat.'

'Well, it was good riddance as far as I was concerned. I didn't know him, only that he owed Jamie a lot of money for work he did for him in Wales.'

'You never met him then?'

'No. Look, I must...' She started to close the door.

'And you didn't know he was a policeman?'

'No! That makes it even worse doesn't it? No, I didn't. Jamie never spoke about him so I can't help you.'

Desperately, I said, 'And you've no idea who might have had it in for Jamie and killed him?'

'Go away! I don't want to talk about it any more.'

The door closed.

It was time to go and find the all-knowing retired village bobby.

Like so many Scottish villages Duncreggan consisted of one long high street with shops at varying intervals, the Creggan Arms at one end and a war memorial at the other. There was no actual village centre although a post office roughly halfway along it with a small Spar supermarket next door acted as a kind of hub and was obviously the place where people congregated to talk.

Rauri Macleod, a very tall, angular man with a slight stoop and greying red hair, was in the immaculate garden behind his terraced single-storey cottage at the better, war-memorial end of the village when I called. His wife, who had answered my ring of the doorbell, welcomed me in with the news that she had been just about to put the kettle on and no doubt Rauri was ready for a good blether. I got the impression that blethering was one of his favourite pastimes.

I was wondering if I would need a Scots, or even Gaelic, dictionary but when Rauri greeted me and went on to speak in unaccented English I realised I was talking to someone who had either been sent to boarding school in England or born south of the Border. This was not to say that he did not use the local idiom.

'Come lass and sit you down here,' he said, leading the way to a tiny paved sunny haven among honeysuckle and rambler roses at the end of the garden where there was just enough room for two wooden chairs and a table. 'Your friend James was here earlier. A great one with the Burns. He and I had a good laugh with *Tam O' Shanter*.'

I thought that as the two were hardly likely ever to meet again a small indiscretion on my part, a snippet of real gossip, might get things off to a good start. 'He's actually the illegitimate son of a nephew of one of the Earls of Carrick. His mother, who was from Orkney, changed her name when James's father was swept overboard from a racing yacht and lost at sea.'

Rauri nodded sagely. 'Yes, he has that look to him. Poetry and the sea's in his blood all right and I don't mean just on his father's side. The Orcadians were singing the songs of the deeds of their ancestors while the Lowlanders were still picking the lice from one another's hair.'

I really had to tell James that one when I next saw him.

We settled ourselves in the little arbour and Rauri said,'He said you might come and see me. He also left it to you to tell me as much about yourself as you thought fit.'

It was easy to smile into his kindly face. 'I'd be really interested to know first of all why a man who has obviously had a very good education is only a retired village policeman.'

'Ah, well, like quite a few other lads round here I was a soldier-boy first - there's precious little employment - a junior officer in the Highlanders, as the regiment's called now. Then during training I got a right ding from a Land Rover driven by a Glaswegian who'd left his brains in the kail-yard and that was that. Invalided out. So I decided to live in the place I love best and make do on my pension. But when I read there was a chronic shortage of police here in the Highlands I joined up. I was only in my early thirties and you don't have to be so physically fit in the police as you do for the army - well, you didn't then, anyway. So I did my job and fished and gardened and walked the hills. I still do most of that. There's no finer life on all of God's Earth.'

After giving him a concise account of recent events, mentioning Somerton's activities at Brecon as unemotionally as I was able I said, 'James asked you about Jamie Kirkland and I've been talking to Auld Robbie. It would appear that Kirkland and Somerton had had a row the night before Somerton's death over some money Somerton owed him and Kirkland got his ear clipped. It was the reason he didn't row the boat. He told all this to Robbie *after* Somerton had set off on his fishing trip.'

'You're thinking there's a connection with the deaths?'

'It would be a huge coincidence if there was no connection. They'd known one another for some years and probably died at about the same time.'

'The pathologist can't put any kind of time-scale on Jamie's passing though - the body's too far gone.'

He was the first person to voice my own doubts. And from there, of course, one had no choice but to progress to the viewpoint that I was clutching at straws in linking the two men's deaths in order to find Somerton's killer.

Rauri went on, 'But maybe instinct is telling you that more than one maggot is often found in a bad apple.'

'I've nothing else to go on,' I admitted. 'What can you tell me about the man to whom the boys reported finding the body?'

'Hamish Dunlop? Ah, well now, he was born at a wee scrap of a place called Clootiebrae between here and Inverness. He went on to be a marine engineer, working at Greenock and Clydebank and retired last year. He lives in a house called Loch Head Cottage set away from the village but spends most of his time at the boathouse near the hotel. He's renting it to restore a rust-bucket of a steam-launch or some such thing. Don't ask me about boats though, damned things make me as sick as a dog.'

Patrick suffers terribly from sea-sickness too. 'And gossip?' I asked lightly.

Rauri grinned fiercely at me. 'There's none and I can't see Hamish going within a half mile of Jamie Kirkland. Likes to think of himself as a bit of a gentleman - doesn't mix with the riff-raff.'

'The piece of rope knotted around the neck of the corpse is of marine origin, somewhat historic but not tied by a sailor.'

'And you ken that a naval officer on the engineering side might well not know a three penny piece about knots.' He gazed at me with somewhat grudging admiration. 'Well, I still doubt he's your man. My advice to you is to talk to those with whom Jamie rubbed shoulders and that means going in the public bar of the Creggan Arms. But be warned, it's not a fit place for a lady, not even in the year two thousand and one. I doubt it'll be fit for anything but tinks and cattle-thieves after another thousand years have gone by - that's if the Good Lord doesn't send a thunder-bolt to blast it from the face of the Earth first.'

'So I'm talking to an Elder of the Kirk?' I enquired.

He laughed, his anger evaporating as swiftly as it had come. 'You ken folk, I'll say that for you. But you know what I mean; a dirty lick-spittle sort of place where unemployable little runts nudge each other and snigger as they hatch their plans. There was a drugs-dealer in there last month but I soon got the lads in blue on to him. He must have got rid of the stuff before he was picked up but they sent him back to Glasgow on a rail.'

'I gather then that Jamie just mooched about the place, went to the pub, took people fishing or into the hills in the shooting season and did a few other odd jobs but otherwise was to be found at home. He'd told people he was planning to leave, where would he have gone?'

'Back to London to his underworld cronies, no doubt. With his cooking experience he'd probably have got a job in a low-grade snack bar but now there's these health and safety bods all over the place as common as the bugs they're after who would employ a grubby little tyke like him?'

No one if all employers were of Rauri Macleod's mind. For a fleeting moment I actually felt sorry for Jamie Kirkland.

'There's nothing in the grapevine about Jamie's last known movements?' I said. 'Everyone just thought he'd finally upped and gone and good riddance.'

'That would be about the truth of it,' Rauri agreed after due consideration and with a tinge of regret. 'You must understand that the man was a loner. Outside the pub he preferred his own company.'

'And he had no real enemies.'

Rauri's response echoed Auld Robbie's. 'No one hated him enough to spend the rest of his life in prison for knocking him over the head. At least, not around here. The good Lord knows what vermin came up from down south to settle old scores.'

'Surely though, strangers would stand out a mile.'

'Rats scavenge at night,' he pronounced.

Chapter Seven

Realising that it was very bad practice to rush from questioning one person to another pausing neither for breath nor reflection, I returned to the hotel for something to eat. As I collected my room key I sneaked a look at the register and then went to find some lunch feeling somewhat apprehensive.

Most of the other guests must have taken advantage of the packed lunches available as the place seemed practically deserted. I crossed the main entrance hall - enough plaids, shields, dirks, broadswords and Lochaber axes on the walls to furnish a hefty uprising - and made for the conservatory with my plateful from the modest buffet. I had it all to myself for a while until a group of ramblers arrived- the hotel was open to non-residents - who thoughtfully brought themselves and their muddy boots in through the garden entrance. However, this was where their good-manners ended for they proceeded noisily to take over the entire area, a couple practically knocking me from my seat with their rucksacks. I finished my meal as quickly as possible and escaped the way they had entered. So much for quiet reflection.

The rear garden was formal and surrounded by tall hedges of yew and holly. It was roughly square and had a central path that led past a small round pond with a fountain towards an arbour containing a classical statue at the far end. Watchful, and also looking for a place to sit and write up a few notes, I wandered down the path to the fountain and then turned left onto another path that crossed it at right-angles. Walking though a gap in the immaculately clipped hedge I entered another, smaller garden, again surrounded by hedges and having an arbour, this time with a Lutyens-style seat.

I sat on the warm wood, took out my notebook and, in shorthand, recorded what Dave had told me at Roehampton. Somehow or other I would have to get hold of the full names and addresses of the guests staying at the hotel that weekend. Perhaps I would need to exert charm on a policeman who had worked on the investigation.

Then, when I had almost finished, I heard footsteps and a man wearing black clerical garb strolled into the little garden, to all intents and purposes enjoying the sunshine. But he was familiar; tall and slim with dark hair. And no, my eyes had not been playing tricks with me the last time I had seen him, when he had been running, he moved with a slight limp. He came and sat down next to me, a little smile on his lips.

'Whatever happened to the bike leathers?' I asked, rising and putting just enough distance between us.

'I left them at home with the bike,' he answered shortly.

'And where are all your henchmen or don't expenses run to your minders travelling all this way?'

He moved as if to get to his feet.

'No, you stay right where you are,' I warned. 'I'm really good when it come to kicking people's teeth in.'

He subsided, the smile having vanished.

'So *you're* the Reverend Norman Archways who signed in this morning in the guest register and who had a stand-up row with Keith Somerton the night before he so sadly drowned. Handy that Special Branch was on the scene, wasn't it? And his killer can now, all nice and legally of course, hang the crime around Patrick Gillard's neck and beat him up until he confesses and names his accomplice.'

'It's not like that at all,' he said tautly.

'You had an idea I might be on my way here so just popped up to check. What were you going to do to me if you'd caught me in Roehampton?'

'The same as I'm going to this time. Take you home and tell you to stay there.' Once again, he moved as if to rise.

I kicked him quite hard on the side of the jaw, not enough to knock him or his teeth out but sufficient to ensure a good swollen face-ache the following morning. He curled over, holding his head, swearing.

'If you're going to join the ranks of all the other people who didn't *quite* manage to kill Somerton it's going to have to be pretty convincing,' I told him in friendly fashion. I had stepped a little farther away from him in case he tried anything.

He sat up, understandably not looking at all pleased with me. He was quite good looking if one discounted the arrogant set of his features and the slightly too small and too close together pale blue eyes. I noticed that his dark hair was actually dyed and growing out a kind of greyish blond colour at the roots. Why though did he make my flesh crawl?

'I came here to warn him,' he said, speaking without moving his jaw overmuch. 'A rumour that had originated abroad indicated that his life was in danger.'

'It was necessary to be ordained to have a quiet word?' I remarked scathingly.

'It was thought his would-be killer might be planning on staying here. The disguise was useful, that's all.'

'Yes, I suppose the black leather long-johns Special Branch are issued with these days might be a trifle conspicuous.' Then I really lost my temper and yelled at him, 'You came to our house in Devon and lurked in the background while my husband was arrested. If you were bloody-well here when Somerton drowned you must have already known that Patrick wasn't!'

'But he was.'

'We were in the States.'

'You might have been. You went to see friends in Washington. But he flew home for two or three days and came here. I saw him. He was heavily disguised but nevertheless easily recognisable by a professional like myself.'

'Disguised as a down-and-out kind of person - which you know he's rather good at.'

'That's right.'

'Ah. And this will be what you'll testify under oath in court.'

He gazed at me with amused venom. 'Of course. So you see I don't have to interrogate you at all. I already know all the answers.'

'What about Jamie Kirkland?'

He expressed amazement. 'I'm not interested in that little shit.'

I leaned on a tree: my legs suddenly had the strength of lightly boiled lettuce. 'You *are* only here to remove me. You don't care a toss who really killed these men.'

'I have my brief.'

'But you hadn't a brief to incriminate Patrick *then*. Was his real killer staying here?'

'If he was I saw nothing suspicious. But it's irrelevant now.'

'So what are you going to do? Grab me right now? Carry me kicking and screaming to your car?'

'There's no need for anything unpleasant like that. All you have to do is check out and we'll quietly leave together.'

'Dream on,' I countered grimly.

He must have thought I was about to launch myself at him again for he quickly said, 'Look, I'm just doing my job, that's all. There's nothing personal in it.'

'No? Doesn't it make you feel really big to have a one-time jewel in MI5's crown in your power? I bet you didn't get much job satisfaction there though. He didn't cringe and whine as you'd hoped he would. He's almost certainly already got you in his scratch-and-sniff book of lousy, stinking policemen.' I was throwing all this at him knowing that I was winding him up. I didn't care, right then I could have killed him.

'It's no use your walking away,' he called after me when I was in the process of doing just that. 'You have to sleep sometimes and you can't always be in a public place. By this time tomorrow night you'll be back down south and I'll leave it up to you whether that's at home or in hospital.'

'I should imagine the water of the loch was cold,' I said. 'When you went for your swim.' I wondered why he didn't merely arrest me. Perhaps a game of cat and mouse was preferable to him. Perhaps I would kill him after all.

Hamish Dunlop was sitting on an old oil drum outside the boathouse he was renting, smoking a pipe, and either had his eyes closed or was staring out over the loch - I could not tell which when I first caught sight of him - sandwich-wrappers and an empty drink can on the ground beside him. Tiny wavelets smacked and rippled into the timbers of the boathouse and the nearby jetty, causing the dinghy to bob and tug at its mooring. As I approached he threw the remains of a sandwich into the water and a seagull that had been waiting hopefully on a rock, watching him with its predatory yellow eyes, flew up and then swooped on the titbit, carrying it away trying to gulp it down in mid-air.

Dunlop greeted me with, 'I hear there's a lady writer asking a lot of questions hereabouts.' He was smiling as he spoke. 'Is this for a new book?'

I said hello without responding to the question and sat down on a chunk of driftwood, a section of a tree-stump, leaning my back on the warm boathouse wall. 'Have you lost any pieces of rope lately?'

He removed the pipe from his mouth and stared at me.

'It's not yet generally known that a short length of rope was found around the neck of Jamie Kirkland's body,' I went on. 'The police, whom I understand intend to question boat-owners around the loch, think the body had been tethered to something under the water. Like beneath that jetty, for example. It occurred to me that when the rope rotted and broke the corpse might have drifted around a bit. Does the water get very rough when there's a gale blowing?'

'Aye,' he replied, still surveying me closely. He seemed to be a man of contrasts; well-spoken but with ruddy, somewhat course features. Although rotund of figure this was not to say that he was fat, the overall impression was of brawny strength and his hands were huge, albeit those of a craftsman.

'Then surely it would be possible for it to have travelled before it ended up entangled in tree roots on the island. It was the larger island, wasn't it?'

'Aye,' he said again.

'According to the expert on ropes who was sent a sample the rope was already old when it was used, is made of jute and might have been tied by someone who didn't know a lot about knots.'

'It's no good your looking at me like that, young lady,' he said sternly. 'I didn't kill him.'

I didn't give an inch. 'How well did you know him?'

Dunlop tore his gaze from me and turned his attention to his pipe, which seemed to have gone out. I noticed that his hands were shaking a little. 'I didn't know him at all. To me he was just a no-good who hung around looking for things to filch.'

'You mean you'd caught him hanging around here?'

'Aye, the old boat has a lot of brass fittings and he'd set his sights on them. I sent him on his way a couple of times but there's no point in looking for trouble so I've made the place more secure now. I've also taken a lot of the stuff home - while she's stripped down.'

'Did you see him the day after Auld Robbie found the other body on the shore?'

'Yes, for some reason I did notice him. It was during the morning. He was with some of the other gawpers near where it was found. Nothing better to do.'

'This business of the dead rook that's made Auld Robbie so famous... If it had been placed by the body deliberately someone might have seen the person who put it there. Did you see anyone carrying a dead bird?'

'No, no one.'

'Did you speak to Jamie?'

'No, but I noticed, when he slouched by here, that one side of his face was bruised. But that was nothing unusual, he was often either walking into doors, drunk or had been in a fight at that flea-pit the Creggan Arms.'

'Was that the last time you saw him?'

Dunlop nodded. 'Aye, I think it was - but I hope you appreciate that this all happened a while back. Apparently he'd been saying for a long time he was planning on leaving. He wasn't someone you'd want to stay in the vicinity.'

'What about the day before? Did you see the man who drowned setting off on his fishing trip on the loch?'

'Aye, I did. I'd just got here. I arrive a bit earlier on Saturdays as the wife's at home - she works in a craft shop in Inverness during the week - and gets the place straight. Which means I don't have to do it of course. I gave him a hand, not that he thanked me for it. I'd thought Jamie might have been rowing for him and telling him the best place for fish to be biting - he'd worked for him before but no, he wasn't there. Chap just rowed off and that was the last that was seen of him, alive that is.'

'Did you see anyone else at the time? I understand that one of the hotel guests was in the habit of going for an early morning swim.'

'No, nobody that I noticed.'

'You were probably the last person to see him then - other than his killer.'

Dunlop registered shock. 'Killer? Who's saying anything about killing?'

'Someone's been arrested for his murder.'

'A local?'

'No. I've been told he was disguised as some kind of down-and-out. Perhaps you saw him around the village.'

'No, I didn't see anyone like that. I spend most of my time here.'

'*Did* you have any rope go missing?'

He rose to his feet. 'Come inside.'

I had already noticed that it was quite a large boathouse, bigger than one that might just hold a couple of punts. But somehow I had imagined a vessel described as a steam-launch as huge. The *Laura*, however, was not very big and fitted inside most comfortably. There was not a lot to her at the moment, mostly the wooden hull but even though stripped down she had lovely lines and I could imagine the fine picture she would make when fully restored.

'The hull and most of the upper work's fine,' Dunlop was saying. 'Although she's to be lifted out next month from the jetty and taken off to be treated with anti-fouling paint. When she returns home I've a chap coming to see to the boiler and then I can really get to work and start putting her back together.'

'Do you mean this is her real home?'

'Oh, aye. She belonged to the last laird. His father had her built - and this boathouse to put her in. It was quicker to get yourself around on the water, you see. The roads were little better than cart tracks in those days and you'd freeze to death waiting for coal to arrive.'

'There were plenty of trees though, surely.'

'No, no Forestry Commission then, the mountains and moors weren't smothered with plantations of softwoods. You didn't cut down fine hardwood trees for firewood.' He waved an arm expansively. 'There's plenty of rope though and hardly any of it came from this little beauty.'

Together with carefully stacked and numbered decking and other timbers there were heaps and coils of rope piled at the sides of the building and also stored in a partly boarded loft above our heads. There seemed to be rope in all colours and of every conceivable weave and thickness.

'Some other chap rented this place for a while and used it as a store,' Dunlop explained. 'He must have either planned to get himself a square-rigger or start a mountaineering project. There's all sorts of rope. Then he went off somewhere and hasn't come back. I'd like to get rid of the stuff as it's in the way but it's not mine so I can't.'

I said, 'I'm in mind of a length of a type used for a mooring rope or painter similar but not the same as that on the dinghy. Is there anything like that just handy in here which someone who ran in might have cut a piece off?'

Dunlop gazed past me for a moment, back through the open doorway as if seeking the answer there. Then he said, 'It's not left open for folk to run in and out as they please.'

'Yes, but surely you must go off sometimes for a few minutes,' I said impatiently. 'There's no loo here is there? Do you lock up every time?' I then saw that the mooring rope of the *Laura* herself was extremely short, only just long enough to attach her to a small bollard.

Hamish Dunlop was casting about with every sign of trying to be helpful. I did not mention what I had just seen but promised myself that I would return later and somehow take a small sample.

'No, most of the easy to get at stuff is far too thick to be used for tying up a small boat,' he said, finally. 'I think the police might be barking up the wrong tree. And I've a lot to do so if you've finished with your questions...'

I deliberately relaxed my manner. 'Perhaps, before I go, you'd be good enough to describe exactly what happened when the two boys alerted you to their find on the island.'

Dunlop plumped himself down again, on an old wooden chair this time, and resumed his attentions to his pipe with the blade of a penknife. 'It was the Douglas boys from the village scheme. They're nice lads even though the family's more than slightly on the rough side. They sometimes come and give me a hand and I show them how to use a plane and drive nails in straight and things like that. That's why they came straight to me. The larger island's bigger than it looks from this angle and with the other one partly in the way and there's an old stone building on it. Auld Robbie tells the tourists that it's a one-time witch's den and most of them are fool enough to believe him. The truth is that no one knows why it was built and it was used by the laird as a place to keep things he didn't have an immediate use for but were too good to throw away. He was a thrifty man, apparently. There used to be fishing nets and bits of boats and old boxes and God knows what else over there.'

'You've been over to the island then?'

'Jenny and Phil asked me to have a look round both of them when they took the hotel over from their parents five years ago. But I haven't been since and no doubt all the stuff has fallen to bits by now. It's a grand place for children to play of course. The boys were not supposed to be there at all as the Cranleys don't want anyone hurt on their property but you know what kids are like. That was another reason they came to me, they knew I wouldn't skelp them.

'They were that scared they weren't even sure that what they'd seen in the shallows amongst the tree roots was really a body or just a bundle of sacks and rubbish washed down the river that flows into the loch at the far end. It does happen sometimes. I just took one look and knew. But I didn't touch it, just came back here with them and phoned the police from the hotel.'

'Did it cross your mind that the body could be Jamie's?'

'Aye, it did. I knew no one else round here with teeth like that: his front ones were rather prominent, reminded you of a rat or squirrel. It gave me a really bad turn, I'll tell you. I could see them for days.' He lit the pipe as though he needed the comfort of familiar, homely actions.

On my way out I noticed that the locks and padlocks on the door were substantial and the one window could be securely fastened. But this was a boathouse and if anyone really wanted to enter then surely they could do so by swimming beneath the doors that fronted on to the loch. Unless, that is, there was some kind of wire mesh fitted to them below the waterline that was invisible from above.

No, not Somerton though, like Jamie he had been unable to swim.

For the rest of the afternoon I stayed firmly in the public eye; taking tea in the conservatory and getting into deep conversation with a retired headmistress from Dunoon who was in the area trying to trace her ancestors. Afterwards I went to my room, shifted a chest of drawers across the door just to be on the safe side, showered and, setting my alarm clock, slept for two hours.

A rested mind brought no comfort. Other than now knowing that Jamie Kirkland could not have killed Somerton unless he was waiting for him on the island to attack him in the shallows and ignoring the phoney cleric I had learned nothing, absolutely nothing. Reluctantly, I was inclined to believe the Special Branch man's assertion, early morning swims or no, that he had come to Scotland to warn Somerton of a possible attempt on his life. Where had that particular piece of information originated? Most of the rest of what he had said were lies and there was not a lot I could do about his clear intention, orders, to lie in court with regard to Patrick's presence in Duncreggan at the time of Somerton's death. Airlines keep records of the tickets they sell so how were they going to get round that one? Another point was that if he *had* come to warn Somerton why go to all the bother of disguising himself and why stay so long?

But was I still clutching at straws? The inner nagging voice was insisting that Patrick could well have done the deed, he could even have bivouacked on the island. Would Special Branch get to hear of something that he and Daws had hatched between them? That seemed highly unlikely.

'You're a useless detective,' I told my reflection in the dressing table mirror.

What was needed was action.

After a very leisurely dinner, the dining room gratifyingly crowded, the numbers swelled by a party of local people celebrating someone's birthday, I went back to my room, ostensibly to bed. There had been no sign of the man calling himself Archways - why on Earth choose such a damned-fool name? - and this did not exactly improve my peace of mind even though I had put the chest of drawers back across the door. He was out there, somewhere, nursing a sore chin.

I waited until it was well after midnight and as dark as it was going to be.

I had a waterproof torch but the manufacturer's main intention was probably that it should stay functioning in the rain, not actually under water. No matter, I would have to risk it and hope that it would make my attempted entry into the boathouse less hazardous. The real problem was to avoid detection but I had worked out that as the double boat entrance doors of the building faced the loch, for obvious reasons, all I had to do was swim silently, no splashes, from a point just along the shore where the land jutted out slightly and trees came right down to the water.

As I had not anticipated this kind of activity I had not brought swimming things with me but had deliberately packed stretch underwear designed for athletes that stays put. So pants and bra it would have to be. Over them I put on a dark blue tracksuit I had bought in Inverness and set off.

It was only a short walk from the hotel which I exited via a fire escape easily accessible from a landing window on the service stairs, an escape route I had worked out earlier in the day. I hardly needed the torch for although there was no moon there is always a kind of luminescence in the night sky in Scotland in summer, a faint light that I observed was reflected by pale-coloured flowers and the leaves of some of the trees as I went through the garden. A light dew had already formed on the grass, giving that too a silvery sheen. From the garden I went out through a narrow gate in the boundary hedge and turned left into a lane that encircled the greater part of the lake.

Swimming in inland waters has never been a favourite occupation of mine although during training I was tipped from boats into quite a few, mostly small and not very deep. Most taste foul, reminding one of garden ponds, compost heaps and drains: none of the salty invigoration of the sea. This loch was no exception, I had smelt it already, like a cellar full of rot. I removed the tracksuit, rolled it up and hid it in a clump of ferns and then picked my way towards the water over slippery rocks and squelchy, washed-up vegetation. I was brought to mind of things like cattle coming to drink and dead sheep and swore I would ingest not one drop. And what, in the name of everything holy, happened to the raw sewage from the hotel?

The torch was tucked into a belt around my waist. The belt, which also had a plastic bag tied to it for the specimen of rope, was of necessity rather tight as I didn't want to lose anything. I intended to keep on the pair of old trainers I was wearing as I had caught sight of more than one piece of broken glass on the shore earlier: a badly cut foot would put paid not only to the sortie but to all my endeavours.

Even in the dark you feel a right ninny clad just in your underwear.

The hotel among the trees was a solidly black and strange shape in the gloom, the boathouse almost invisible from where I was standing. There was a thin layer of mist just above the surface of the water which would probably mean that I would not be able to see very well. I walked out into the water finding it more shallow and even colder than I had expected. It crept up me like liquid ice. Then, suddenly, my feet slipped downwards as the bottom suddenly sloped and I went right under, getting a mouthful. It was only my training that prevented total panic and, surfacing, I succeeded in spitting it out.

The cold was the worst thing and I struck out utilising breast-stroke, least splashes, and also needing to keep my head right up to see where I was going because of the mist. I had worked out that the distance I had to cover was about seventy-five yards. After what felt like about a mile my knee hit something quite large and disgustingly slimy and soft and, still haunted by James's graphic description of Jamie Kirkland's body, I almost freaked-out. Then my right hand hit something solid, slippery wood, the underwater supports of the boathouse I realised when I had raked the hair from in front of my eyes.

I discovered I was actually to one side of the boathouse,

beneath a large weeping willow and that my feet could touch bottom. This was gravelly and firm and, avoiding where I thought the nameless soggy bundle was, I pulled myself along towards the doors. The water became deeper again, the wood very slippery with weed and difficult to grasp and in the end I had to swim again. There was a very small gap beneath the doors and the surface of the water and I held on with one hand while I pulled the torch from my belt with the other. When I switched it on only a faint glimmer of light emerged: there was nothing wrong with the torch but the water was very murky, visibility less than a foot, possibly because I had stirred it up. I switched it off again, there was no point in wasting the battery.

Groping, I soon found that there was no wire mesh or any other kind of barrier fixed to the bottom of the doors. Taking a deep breath I pulled myself through the gap and cautiously surfaced. There had been no sign of a light within even though I doubted that Dunlop worked this late, but the actual window was on the side away from me.

All was in darkness and I switched on the torch again, starting nervously as the hull of the *Laura* loomed right in front of me, rearing above my head. My ears cleared and I heard the soft *slap, slap* of water, the launch rocking gently to my own movements. Holding on to her stern rope I hauled myself out and, teeth chattering, made my way along the planking walkway to the bows. My mouth tasted of oil and long-dead fish.

I had not brought a knife with me, reasoning that as every kind of tool had been lying around on a work-bench I should be able to find something with which to take a sample of rope. It appeared though that Dunlop had put most of them away before he went home so had to choose between an old chisel and a battered Stanley knife. The blade of the latter proved to be sharper than it looked and, holding it with an oily rag - no fingerprints are left scattered around by one-time D12 operatives - I carefully sawed an inch-long piece from the

Laura's mooring rope, doing it by feel as I had no spare hand for the torch. I dared not take more, there was little enough as it was. At last, the rope parted and I checked that the cut end was neat and then dirtied it up a little so it would not look clean and be noticed by its owner.

The sample, I knew, would not be acceptable as evidence as it had not been taken in a proper and official forensic procedure. At this stage it was unimportant for, if necessary, the local CID could return to take their own sample. For all I knew they had discovered dozens of bits of rope answering to the description that day already and I was completely wasting my time. They seemed to have overlooked this boathouse though as, surely, Dunlop would have mentioned a visit from the police.

I stood up from where I had crouched down to carefully place the snippet in the polythene bag, knotted it tightly and retied it on my belt. Then, continuing not to flash the torch around widely in case the light was seen through the window, I walked back the way I had come. On the way I did shine the beam quickly over the *Laura*, succumbing to my shame to an old weakness, an attack of the horrors. Dark slimy things, confined cobwebby spaces...

The man who had been playing cat and mouse with me, he of the black leathers, only now soaking wet and wearing swimming trunks, was lying in the bottom of the boat. He looked very dead.

Such was the shock that the torch started to slide from my grasp. I managed to grab it before it fell into the water. Then the corpse sat up, the staring eyes focusing on me, the silent snarl of death transformed into a mocking grin. He laughed out loud at my involuntary shriek of terror.

'That frightened you, didn't it?' he hooted. 'Didn't you find it?' he went on to enquire, switching on a powerful flash lamp of his own, his voice echoing strangely around the virtually empty hull of the launch.

'I... I wasn't looking for anything,' I stuttered.

'Oh, so this was merely perfectly normal after-dark recreation.'

'As you must have seen I took a sample of the mooring rope.'

He stood up and the boat rocked beneath him. 'Still playing detective then?'

'You told me you weren't interested in Jamie Kirkland's death,' I reminded him. Both hands on the gunwales, he was preparing to climb out. If he touched me...

'I'm not.'

'So what I do in connection with that is none of your business.'

Smoothly, like a cat, he attained the walkway. The light from his lamp was like a searchlight and seemed to be concentrated on the lower part of my body. 'Perhaps not. And while I'm not remotely interested in your stupid grubbing around for evidence into the death of a nobody it irks me that you're here at all. The local plods can try to find out who strung him up.'

'How do you know he was hanged?'

'I don't, damn you. It's obvious that if there was a piece of rope around his neck it's quite possible he was killed that way.'

I saw that as well as having a slightly swollen jaw where I had kicked him he was sexually aroused. Also thinking of doing something about it. Not only that, he was younger than me, fitter by far and much stronger. I gripped the torch more tightly. Buying time, I said, 'So why are you here then? You can't possibly have known what I intended to do.'

'I didn't. But women are predictable. You talked to the bloke who rents the place this afternoon and I reasoned you'd want a proper nose round when he'd gone home. I have to say though I thought you'd have a go at the window, not swim across. I want to know what you were really looking for.'

'I've answered you already. Nothing.'

He looked around. 'Not a comfortable place for screwing but it'll have to do. I hope you're going to be a bit more co-operative than you have been so far. Otherwise I might have to hit you quite hard. And there's the matter of the kick on the chin this afternoon too.' Smirking, he began to approach.

Patrick, mindful of certain risks to his working partner, had some years previously initiated me into mens' most secret weaknesses by providing tuition one Saturday afternoon when we had had our entire home to ourselves. I seem to remember that we - or rather he, for I had known nothing about it until it happened and had been blithely contemplating nothing more strenuous than a little gardening - had also chosen a time when our elderly neighbour was visiting her daughter in Torquay, otherwise, fearing murder and mayhem next door, she might have phoned the police. I had emerged from the encounter bruised and exhausted and I hadn't spoken to Patrick for the rest of the day. This was actually the first time I had had cause to utilise what he had taught me and I wasn't at all convinced that what might succeed with a basically caring husband would work when tested in a real situation. It had to be borne in mind, however, that Patrick has never taken any prisoners in matters of training.

I backed off a little, making whimpering noises. This would tend to defuse any anger on his part and make him think of sex first rather than violence. Hopefully he would become over-confident, not be particularly wary while removing any clothing, in this case his swimming trunks, which in order to keep his balance on the uneven boarding, would have to come right off.

He remembered the kick on the jaw and decided to rush me and crowd me into the corner between the door and the window, the plan obviously to disable the victim slightly before stripping for action. I went with him and my back hit the wall and a small shelf loaded with what might have been old hand tools of some kind - I could not see exactly what - crashed to the floor. Then, swinging the torch high to club me with it he temporarily denied himself a source of light and I hit him on the side of the head with mine but then dropped it as one of his hands grabbed my wrist. A little stunned, he released his hold on his too and more by luck than judgement I swiped it with the side of my foot into the water.

Total darkness.

'You cow,' he hissed right in my ear. 'I'll kill you afterwards.'

It has to be said that Patrick hadn't spoken to me for the rest of that day either.

Chapter Eight

I swam back, found my tracksuit, put it on and returned to the hotel the way I had left it. After lying in a hot bath for half an hour I stopped shivering from cold but, oddly, was still inclined to get the shakes with regard to how I had first caught sight of him; like a corpse with staring eyes and gaping, twisted mouth.

He then, had also entered the building beneath the boat doors. What had he wanted that he thought I might also be searching for?

There were a couple of whisky miniatures in a cupboard, *gratis*. In an emergency there's nothing like a stiff tot to put the life back in you. I stretched it slightly with water, pouring it into a glass tumbler from the bathroom. Quite soon I stopped shaking.

Should I go to the police and make a complaint about him? It would be a good way of getting rid of him and I had been about to give them the sample of rope anyway. If I reported him to the police it was a certainty he would be taken in for questioning. But if he was a fairly senior officer in Special Branch, and there was every indication from his arrogant behaviour that he was, then he would be able to pull rank and possibly make things even more difficult for me. He still might for hell hath no fury like a man demasted and then sunk without trace.

So what the hell *was* all this about?

There could only be one answer.

'No, as a matter of fact I've only just got in,' James Carrick said in response to my apology when he answered the phone. 'We raided a house in the London Road looking for drugs and hit the jackpot. How are you getting on?'

'I've just had another run-in with Special Branch,' I told him. 'The man I told you about. He tailed me up here. He

141

fancied a romantic interlude in a boathouse I'd sneaked into and I'm tossing up whether to report him or not.'

Carrick uttered a few exclamations, the real substance of which were obviously not intended for my ears as they were in that rich-in-expletives language, Gaelic. Then he said, 'Are you all right?'

'A bit shaky but otherwise fine. But that wasn't why I rang you. James, this has to be about money. Keith Somerton might have returned to Scotland to collect money that Kirkland, or someone else, had been looking after for him, the illegal proceeds of the scam in Wales. Such large sums could not have been banked in the aftermath of Brecon without risking detection and I know that no money, other than a small amount obviously set aside for everyday expenses, was found when the complex was searched. Kirkland's wife told me that her husband was owed money by Somerton for work he did in Wales so that sum was either genuine wages or a cut in a hoard that had been stashed away somewhere. From what people round here have told me of an argument they had on the evening before Somerton's death, it doesn't look as though Jamie got anything. Others might have been in the know, people who worked at Brecon and who neither I nor the writer of the MI5 report I mentioned to you had knowledge of, cronies of Kirkland's perhaps, people who ran away when events began to turn nasty and before the police arrived.'

'Someone who lives in or near Duncreggan, you mean?'

'It's possible. Someone who stopped Somerton from getting his hands on the money and then Kirkland. I think Special Branch suspect there's some hidden away somewhere too and that's why this character's hanging around. How they intend to use it against Patrick is anyone's guess. Incidentally, he was here at the hotel that weekend Somerton drowned too.'

'This is all getting rather heavyweight, isn't it? Do you want me to come up?'

'No,' I told him firmly. 'You simply can't get involved.'

'What were you doing in the boathouse?'

'Looking for rope that might match the piece around Kirkland's neck,' I replied without giving him further details.

'You ought to go to the police in Inverness and tell them everything. It's really the only option open to you.'

I promised him that I would sleep on it and ring him first thing in the morning. Then, feeling shivery again, I got into bed taking with me the second miniature of whisky. It proved to be quite effective neat too.

I awoke with a start, the phone ringing. Half expecting it to be my adversary of the night before hyping himself up for Round Three I heard James's voice again instead.

'I'm afraid there's bad news, Ingrid,' he began. 'In order to keep you fully in the picture I checked the database this morning to see whether Patrick had been moved to another remand centre. It appears he was suddenly taken ill on Saturday morning and rushed to hospital in Oxford. I'm not surprised as he looked pretty rough when I saw him. But he's disappeared.'

'Disappeared!'

'After what you told me I'm wondering if he's been spirited away from the hospital by Special Branch to somewhere where they can really keep an eye on him. Nothing's being made of it, you see. It's just words on a computer listing, info that comes to us from the prison authorities so we're in the know as to where suspects are being held at any given time.'

'He might have just walked out.'

'He wouldn't have been in any fit state to do that, surely.'

I refrained from commenting that, when driven to it, Patrick is capable of almost anything, speakable or otherwise.

'Wasn't he being guarded?' I asked.

'Yes, by one of the prison officers but not very well it would appear,' was the reply. 'The bloke went off for a pee without arranging any kind of other watch-keeping.'

I had an idea this individual might not possess much in the way of hair or brains north of his eyebrows.

'Sorry to have to depress you even further,' James was saying. 'And, on the other subject, I hope you're going to do as I suggested and go to the police.'

'I am,' I said. 'But not *just* yet.'

'Ingrid...'

'I'm sorry, I know you're worried about me,' I interrupted. 'But I could do with a little more time. If I go to the police with the whole story it'll be the same as if the Special Branch man had carted me back to Devon: I shall have to stop investigating this. That's what he said he was going to do but he's far more interested in something else and, as I said last night, I think it's locating the money that I'm sure is the reason behind the murders.' I thought it best not to mention death threats after rape and things like that or Carrick really would have jumped into his car foaming at the mouth and driven north: when really riled James's temper rivals Patrick's. Well, almost.

'Promise me you'll only give it another twenty-four hours,' he entreated.

This was the first morning of the party conference. After another twenty-four hours it would be almost too late... 'Yes, I promise,' I replied.

Inverness police station looked like a small fortress and had probably even started life as one. I had no trouble in tracking down the Detective Sergeant to whom James had spoken and he seemed delighted to be interrupted in typing out a report. I handed over my sample, explaining that the DCI from Bath was a close friend, had discussed the case with me and as I was a crime writer I had done some investigating of my own in Hamish Dunlop's boathouse.

'Is it a little hobby of yours as well as your profession?' he asked kindly.

I gave him a big smile. 'Sort of.'

He held up the bag, which was still slightly damp and

peered at the scrap of rope within. 'Where was the owner of the boathouse at the time you removed this, madam?'

'Probably in bed,' I said.

He cleared his throat. 'I see. You broke in?'

I laughed in jolly fashion. 'No, of course not. I swam under the boat doors.'

He pondered for a moment and then visibly decided not to throw the book at me. 'Is there something you feel you ought to tell me about Mr Dunlop? Why do you suspect him?'

'I don't suspect him at all. He might have kicked Jamie Kirkland's backside for hanging around looking for something to steal but the man's no murderer. I think it's highly likely though that someone stole a chunk of his boat's mooring rope and he either hasn't noticed, which is unlikely, or is afraid of the person he knows did it. Whatever the truth, he's ignoring it.'

'In that case there would be every reason to change the mooring rope and burn the old one.'

'Not at all. He might be hoping the police *do* find it as he loathes the other person and hopes they're caught without a hint of his own involvement. But you didn't go anywhere near the boathouse yesterday, did you?'

The DS laid the plastic bag down very carefully, almost reverently, as if onto an altar, and stared at it. 'Even if this is the same sort of rope as was around the neck of the body I don't think it could be scientifically proven to come from the same piece. And Kirkland's body was in the water for a long time, he disappeared just over two years ago.'

'He could have genuinely gone away for a while. Keith Somerton owed him money but refused to give it to him. He complained to Auld Robbie who works at the hotel about it the day Somerton drowned but before his body was discovered. Somerton had knocked him into a burn. Kirkland might have left the area in disgust, as he had said he was going to and then returned, secretly, at a later date. Bodies that have been in the water for two years don't necessarily look much different from those immersed for a matter of months. It depends on so many factors; water temperature, time of year, salinity, to what extent fish and other water creatures have devoured it...'

'While it's true that the pathologist can't pinpoint the time of death I don't understand why Kirkland should return secretly.'

'To look for money that might be hidden somewhere in the locality.'

He had begun to look really interested but now gave me another kind smile. 'Any guesses as to where that might be?' he enquired, openly humouring me.

'It might be on one of the islands in the loch,' I said airily. 'Have you searched them?'

'Not yet.'

'Is there any information yet available as to exactly how Kirkland died? It was a policeman actually who yesterday mentioned to me that he could have been strung up.'

'It's inconclusive,' he replied. 'And I can't imagine why anyone should tell you otherwise.'

I was then shown out, equally kindly but he didn't *quite* pat my hand and tell me not to bother my pretty little head with it.

I had thought very hard about the 'Reverend Archway''s morning dips and had concluded that even the island closest to the shore, the smallest, was too far away for even a good swimmer to reach unless they were wearing a wet-suit and flippers. The distance involved was at least a quarter of a mile, the water, as I now knew all too well, very cold. Had he, in fact, attempted it a couple of mornings and been forced to return? There had been nothing to prevent him from hiring the boat though and as he appeared not to have done so there was every chance he had not thought of searching there.

There had been no sign of him at breakfast and the thought crossed my mind that I might have dealt with him more forcibly than I had thought. So it was with slight trepidation that I returned to the hotel but no one rushed to inform me of the latest corpse and there were no ambulances parked outside the boathouse. A short stroll in that direction revealed Hamish Dunlop pottering around happily in the vicinity so I stopped worrying about it.

The next thing on my agenda was to borrow the hotel's rowing boat and visit both islands. This was a problem as I would have no choice but to set off in full view of everyone. It was either that or do it at night, the prospect of which was not only daunting but struck me as silly as the whole object of the exercise was to look for something. Those on land would still be able to see any lights that I carried. Luckily I had managed to find my torch in the boathouse after dropping it, it had rolled into a corner without going out.

It was when I was on my way to my room, thinking vaguely that I ought to have something to eat - I wasn't hungry but knew I had to keep my strength up - that the colossal hopelessness of what I was trying to achieve hit me. I had been used to working as part of a small team, or at least Patrick had been around for most of the time. Now I had no one and it seemed that I was not only clutching at straws but had probably got to the stage where I was deluding myself.

To hell with heroics in a rowing boat: I was too tired, too bruised from the previous night and, it had to be admitted, too scared.

I sat in my room in an armchair and lunchtime came and went. I only knew one thing; that I had failed. Worst of all; I had failed Patrick.

What James had said; that Special Branch could have removed him from the hospital to a place where they could keep a closer eye on him was borne out by the arrogance of the man sent to bring me home. It might have been thought that his illness was a ruse to escape, the first thing that anyone who knew anything about him would suspect.

Every lead that I had followed up had come to nothing and

although I had a fairly clear picture of what had taken place the weekend Keith Somerton drowned I was no nearer to finding out who had murdered him or what had happened to Jamie Kirkland. The piece of rope I had given to the police might be useful but would hardly reveal *his* killer.

So, like being stuck in a time-warp my thoughts continued to go uselessly round and round and when I finally forced myself to leave the room and go to the bar to order a sandwich I was appalled to discover that it was almost four o'clock. Perhaps I had dozed off. That I was suffering from lack of sleep and some kind of delayed shock from the previous night did not occur to me.

What I really needed was some fresh air, I decided once downstairs and standing in the bar entrance, not a couple of hours in this room where I would buy a bottle of wine and try to blot out my almost overwhelming feelings of remorse and failure. Some newly-arrived guests in possession of particularly affected voices and braying laughter were holding court and appeared to have even driven Auld Robbie back to his little dog and his cottage.

'It's going to be a lovely evening,' Jenny Cranley commented as I stepped aside to allow her to pass through. She paused, perhaps sensing that I was less than happy. 'Can I get you anything, Miss Langley?'

It had just occurred to me that I had not taken Rauri Macleod's advice and sought out Kirkland's drinking companions at the Creggan Arms. I said, 'A sandwich of some kind would be welcome. I'm afraid I missed lunch.'

'No problem at all. Chicken, beef, cheese? I think the chef has some freshly cooked crab too.'

I decided on the latter but then detained her from leaving with, 'During the weekend that Mr Somerton was drowned were most of the guests regulars?'

'I'd have to check back through our records,' said Jenny in the manner of one who had better things to do.

I threw in a large carrot. 'I'm curious, that's all. It crossed my mind that one of the other guests might have killed him.'

She glanced over her shoulder as a particularly loud shrieking laugh set the chimes in a nearby grandfather clock vibrating. 'I'll arrange your sandwiches to be brought to the conservatory, shall I? And go and look for the register.' She bustled off.

When she found me in the conservatory - the outside door open and a soft late-afternoon breeze stirring the fronds of a palm - Jenny seated herself and put the book on the table before us but at an angle that prevented me from reading over her shoulder. Her finger was already in the page. 'Now then,' she began. 'Oh, your sandwiches won't be two ticks, Miss Langley. Yes, here we are... The Rawsteads and Fullers have been coming here for years. And I mean *years*. I think, once upon a time, they met on holiday at somewhere like Frinton. Captain Dupont was new to us on that occasion but has been a couple of times since. His wife died about five years ago and I think this is his new-found freedom.' She giggled. 'There was Mr Hall. We hadn't seen him before either. Nor, come to think of it Mr Jones.'

'David Jones?' I asked, without thinking.

Jenny looked up, her ruthlessly plucked eyebrows raised. 'Yes, do you know him?'

I shook my head, forcing a laugh. 'No, just thinking of Davey Jones's locker.'

She giggled so long and hard this time I began to get a little cross with her.

'Then there was the Reverend Archways,' she continued when she had wound down. 'Mr Somerton of course and a Mr and Mrs... ' She peered closer. 'I've got the typed confirmation of booking somewhere. I think it was Zakiyah. They were on honeymoon.'

'From the Middle East?'

'Jordon, I think. We didn't see an awful lot of them.'

Hoping to ward off a further bout of giggles I said quickly, 'Did you see their passports?'

'No. At least, I don't think so. I have an idea Phil dealt with their arrival.'

'Can you remember if they were on a world tour? Scotland is a rather strange place for honeymooners to come to from that part of the world.'

She shook her head. 'No idea. They didn't really say a lot.'

'Did they go out?'

'No, hardly at all.'

'And you would have mentioned it if you'd seen the man go out on the morning Keith Somerton set off in the boat.'

'They might have had breakfast sent up to their room on that morning.'

'But not on the other mornings?'

'Yes, some of them, I think. But I can't really remember.'

My sandwiches arrived and Jenny went away saying she had things to do, taking the register with her. Then she returned and popped her head round the door. 'I've just remembered one thing about Mr Zakiyah - or whatever his name was. He only had three fingers on his left hand. I noticed it because it seemed to be his wedding ring finger that was missing - he wasn't wearing a ring at all. But some men don't these days, do they?'

'Was there a space where it should have been as though he'd lost it in an accident, or do you think he was born that way?'

'I seem to remember there was a gap. And, you know... he had normal sort of knuckles.' And with that Jenny pattered away.

In the cavern at Brecon, the air thick with smoke and fumes from the fire that Patrick had started, I had tripped over something soft and gone headlong. Someone's leg. A hand had grabbed my arm.

'Help me,' Batrun had sobbed. 'Please help me.'

He had been hit at least twice but it was impossible to ascertain how serious his injuries were. There had been no time to do anything else but get him in a fireman's lift and carry him away. I had not stopped to think and if he had not been a slightly built youth, little more than a boy, then my act of mercy would have resulted in both our deaths. I had walked away from the fire, blindly, until I had hit the boarded walls and then groped my way to the entrance doors. My only thought at the time had been that I was almost certainly a widow.

Somehow, I had found the way out and the real shock had been reaching fresh air and sunshine and hearing a thrush singing from a tree. It had been like being re-born.

I had discovered that I was on my knees, unable to breathe, unable to stop coughing. I had laid Batrun down on his side - there had been no question of my being able to carry him any further. His eyes had been closed but he had seemed to be breathing. There had been a lot of blood on his shirt and on his left hand and when I had looked more closely I had seen that one of his fingers was missing. The third finger.

If the man supposedly on honeymoon at the hotel had been Batrun it was too much of a coincidence to be just by chance. Had he killed Keith Somerton in revenge for the murder of his uncle, The Greek?

This was no time to sit back and relax: the investigation was far from over and there was still the matter of hard evidence. What I still needed more than anything were witnesses.

As Jenny had promised it was fine and warm and I decided to walk to the Creggan Arms. It was only about a mile. Hamish Dunlop was locking up his boathouse as I went by and waved. My thoughts still buzzing with my latest discovery - if indeed the man had been Batrun - I wondered what Dunlop really knew, what the inhabitants of Duncreggan whispered behind closed doors, whether answers to the questions posed by Somerton's and Kirkland's deaths were common knowledge to the entire community but because this was a close-knit Highland village no outsider would ever uncover the whole truth.

While not actually forbidding in appearance the Creggan Arms gave such an impression of insalubrity from the outside that I toyed with the thought that if it had not been built at the far end of the village street the law-abiding inhabitants would have moved it there, stone by stone. Not for this hostelry the pretty hanging baskets and flower-filled window boxes with which public houses usually endeavour to entice visitors: the only movable objects here, other than two dustbins without lids and four metal beer casks, were several filthy collie dogs that bit and scratched at their fleas and snarled at one another. It was only the short lengths of baling twine with which they were tied to various nails hammered into the window ledges, seemingly for the purpose, that prevented all-out war.

As I approached there was a stentorian bellow from within and, moments later, a man built like a Clydesdale horse appeared bearing another, considerably smaller, man before him, using him to batter open the swing door, flinging him into the street where he tottered and almost fell. An incomprehensible burst of Scots then followed in the event of the unfortunate's being unsure of his welcome to return. I postponed seeking out the late Jamie Kirkland's drinking companions and pushed open the door into the lounge bar instead.

The room was like a brown, fly-blown cave, the din of men talking at the tops of their voices deafening, the cigarette smoke a thick blue haze. I shoved my way between groups, mostly crammed between the doors and bar, tripping at one point on the worn and filthy matting that passed for a carpet. The draught horse re-appeared, presumably having quelled the trouble next door to his satisfaction, did a double-take when he saw me, gazed around quickly to see if he could guess whom I was with and then came to the staggering conclusion that I was on my own.

'Yes, Miss?'

Regrettably still in dire need of bracers I ordered a measure of The Macallan, Patrick's favourite whisky when we had last been out together, and he became positively obsequious.

'You're from the *Courier* then,' he asked out of the corner of his mouth. This was not to say that he dropped his voice: if he had I would not have heard a word.

I remembered the newspaper stands in Inverness and nodded with what I hoped was the right degree of journalistic aplomb.

'If it's about Jamie then you need to speak to the likes of Callum and Hugh.' He jerked his massive head in the direction of the public bar which could be glimpsed through a small archway behind him.

'Are they there now?' I shouted.

'Aye, and grab'em soon before they get to follow Neil Crummock into the street.' He then lost interest in me and wiped the greasy bar with a cloth that resembled a small, decomposing mole.

In the crush an anonymous hand travelled across my bottom and I took a quick guess as to the owner of it and delivered a short powerful jab just below the ribs of a shiny-suited smart-arse to my left who was endeavouring to hide his grinning and ugly face in his tankard. There was a most gratifying fountaining of beer from his mouth and nostrils that went all over his leery friends and I left them spluttering and mopping respectively and went through an interconnecting door into the other bar.

Standing just inside the door, actually inhabiting a small niche on one end of the bar, was a small man wearing a Harris tweed jacket and breeches and gaiters, his face walnut brown and lined from a lifetime in the open air. A small terrier lay curled between the legs of his stool.

'Good afternoon,' I said, still having to shout. 'Would you be kind enough to point out Callum and Hugh to me?'

He grinned, revealing very bad teeth. 'There's always well-dressed fowk lookin' for'em. Police, gamekeepers and sich like. What have they done this time?'

'Nothing.' I stared him down and won and he indicated a group playing cards at a long table under the window. 'Callum's the bauldy-heidit one, Hugh's next on his left.'

I thanked him and turned to walk away. Then I said, 'Why was Neil thrown out?'

'He accused yon mannie of cheatin'.'

'Yon mannie' had his back to the window, the light, such as the dirty glass allowed, streaming over his shoulders and onto the cards skimming over the table as he dealt. Other than for Callum, who was quite young but as my informant had said was as bald as a coot, and Hugh, there were two other men, all of them having every appearance of being what my father would have described as 'gallows-fodder'.

I have never been bothered to sit down and learn to understand poker - card games simply do not interest me - but anyone could see that the game had reached a critical point and it would be more than my life was worth to interrupt. There was a tiny table jammed into a space between the card players and the door to the Gents so I sat down on the single chair by it and watched. Every time the door opened it knocked against the table and the stench of stale urine wafted out. I have never been able to understand why British men enjoy drinking beer in disgusting conditions either.

The dealer flicked the final card at the other players with his long delicate-looking fingers, picked up his own cards and leaned back slightly, gazing at them. There was no doubt that *he* was enjoying himself, eyes slitted, partly against the smoke, mostly from concentration. I could imagine that an accusation of cheating would have provoked genuine anger and if the landlord had not rapidly removed the accuser he may well have fared even worse. Neil, I felt, had been rather stupid.

Neil, though, might have resented the fact that he had lost his money - a sizable pile of which, mostly in coins rather then notes as these men were not wealthy, lay on the table - to an Englishman. I was in no doubt about this and it must have been obvious to them too as although not a lot was being said while he had dealt the cards he had sung, quite softly but nevertheless audibly, one verse and the chorus of 'Drink up thee Cider, pronounced 'zoider', a song not normally heard at these latitudes.

My presence had been noted, of course, but nothing was allowed to break the tense silence around the table, not even when the old man to whom I had spoken got up to leave and inadvertently trod on one of his dog's paws, causing it to yelp. Then one of the card players, the man to the left of the one I had been told was Hugh, threw his cards down on the table in disgust, looked at me and shouted, 'I hate being stared at. Bugger off!'

'Don't blame me for your lousy hand,' I retorted.

'Wimmin bring bad luck,' said the man seated nearest to me, darkly.

'Spoken like a true loser,' I said.

'Do you want to start trouble?' asked the man who had dealt the cards, smiling like a shark but not at me, at the cards in his hand.

'Yes, right now I'm really bored,' I told him. 'Some good and noisy trouble would go down a treat.'

'Then go and do it in the *other* bar, there's a good girl,' was the earnest advice.

'Do you really mean that?' I asked.

'Yes.'

I tossed back the remains of my whisky and went back the way I had come.

In the other bar I was dismayed to see that the man from Special Branch was sitting on his own at another small table in a corner by the fireplace. I had not noticed him before so he must have only just arrived. He was wearing his clergyman rig and cradling a glass containing what looked like gin and tonic.

It was stupid to run for he had already noticed me. 'So what do I call you - Norm?' I demanded to know, plonking myself down on a spare chair at his table.

'Norm'll do,' was the disinterested reply. He gave me his full attention. 'You're coming with me. Now.'

It did not seem to me that we were talking of arrest and journeys home. Intuition was screaming at me to hit him over the head with a bottle and run. Instinct, sixth sense, perception, call it what you will, had read the expression in his eyes and it was like looking at my own death in a mirror. This man had his brief but unfortunately the woman he had been sent to keep surveillance on and ultimately return to Devon would now have a nasty accident. This was mostly because she had rejected his offer of rape and tipped him, balls over ears, into cold, oily water.

His hand closed over my left wrist like a manacle. 'No one's paying us any attention,' he said. 'Get up and walk out with me now without making any fuss or I'll knock you cold and carry you out saying you've fainted.'

He was right, no one was paying us the slightest attention, not even the damp ones by the bar who had carried on with their conversation as though such a diversion was an everyday occurrence.

'We've got him, you know,' he informed me with his stock-in-trade smirk. 'Fell into our arms, no problem at all, right outside the hospital. There's absolutely no point in your staying here now. You won't find out anything else and he can't come and help you.' The final few words of the last sentence were uttered in mocking, sing-song tones.

I rose to my feet and he and I went towards the exit; he leading the way pulling me behind him. As we reached an inter-connecting door to the other bar I hurried forward a couple of paces to give myself a little slack, then stepped back and ground a heel heavily down on the toes of a man who was probably a farmer. I was lucky enough to find someone not wearing steel-capped boots and, judging from his reaction, he suffered badly from corns. He yelled out agonisingly,

I clouted my captor on the side of the head with someone's pint tankard of beer in the same spot where I had hit him the previous night with the torch and then, wrenching myself away, I ran through the doorway, ploughed my way through those on the far side of it and then out through a door on the corner of the street.

The baling twine leashes on the dogs were actually looped over hooks on the window ledges and it was the work of a moment to pause and slip them all off. The mother of all dog wars then broke out and I got a hand nipped by one canine enthusiast, so keen was it to get started. My pursuer followed me out - I was running but shot a glance behind me - and as he opened the door two dogs ran inside with their tails between their legs and the rest, all but one, poured in after them. The ensuing din was a bit like a ship falling over in a dry-dock and the last I saw of the man from London he was hopping, lurching around on one foot, with the one remaining collie he had kicked out at determinedly attached to the other.

Chapter Nine

'You must return home at once,' Daws said, laconic and grumpy as always when forced to converse on an open line.

I protested, although I had known that by contacting him I would risk this kind of reaction.

'It's imperative,' he continued. 'And from what you've just told me it looks as though you've succeeded in what you set out to do. Forget Kirkland. He had a murky past and I'm of a mind that someone finally caught up with him.'

'And Patrick?' I asked.

'My advice remains the same. Leave well alone and I've no doubt all will be well. But I shall make enquiries now you've given me this information about the man calling himself Zakiyah and contact you soon - at home.'

Truculently I said, 'I shall only consider leaving here if you confirm that the Special Branch man was telling the truth - that Patrick was immediately re-arrested outside the hospital.'

There was silence on the other end of the line and I began to wonder if we had been cut off. Then Daws said, 'I haven't been briefed about that. What happened?'

I gave him James Carrick's news.

'I can't comment until I've verified this,' was all he said and rang off without another word.

He would never forgive me if I proved his system to be fallible. I was not feeling very proud of myself for having not given him the whole story either. But I felt my deception might bear fruit.

Fearing violent reprisals I had barricaded myself in my room again, aware that the present state of affairs could not be allowed to continue. I was beginning to feel like a ship with no safe port to go to. When the phone rang about twenty minutes later I answered it prepared literally for anything but it was Daws.

'Zakiyah was not his real name but the man you know as Batrun was blown up two months ago by his own explosive device as he was placing it on a bus in Israel,' he reported. 'Unfortunately for you of course he will now be unable to provide any insight into Somerton's death. If your hotel has a fax machine I will arrange for his photograph to be sent so it can be shown to the relevant staff and if there's a positive identification we can go from there.'

'There was a woman with him - either genuinely his wife or pretending to be.'

'That should be comparatively straightforward to check up on. Oh, and it would *appear* that the Lieutenant-Colonel was apprehended although you must appreciate that getting any reliable information in the present circumstances is extremely difficult and no one's saying anything at all. The source of the information cannot be relied upon. Expect a change of plan if he is still at large.'

'Why?'

'If it's realised that there's still insufficient evidence and with the added complication of the bird having flown then it might be thought that more political capital can be made by simply organising a hitman and having the accused taken out. All details of his activities, true or false, then can be subsequently released to the media with no need for a risky trial but very little loss of publicity. Do I make myself perfectly clear?'

'A hitman?' I echoed.

'The best. I've no doubt someone will compose a very convincing account of the incident for the media - along the lines of "armed suspect resisted arrest".'

'You've said "if" and "might". Is this really on the cards?'

There was a silence and then he said, 'I'm afraid there's a very strong possibility that it is. Ingrid, I must *insist* that you return to Devon. I cannot guarantee your safety if you stay in Scotland.'

'If Patrick is free he might have gone home,' I said woodenly.

'No, he hasn't. Not so far anyway. There's a watch been

placed on your house. It would appear that you and the children are not part of this scheme, provided you yourself stay out of the way.'

'They wouldn't want the deaths of the wife and four children to be all over the front pages, would they?' I retorted, adding with bitter sarcasm, 'Will we get police protection from Special Branch?'

'You will be... safe,' Daws replied and for the first time since I had known him I heard a catch in his voice.

'I've got to think,' I muttered.

'Think quickly. There's very little time left.'

I replaced the receiver and walked over to the armchair by the window and sat down. My deception had borne fruit of a deadly nature.

Justin, Victoria, Matthew and Katie. Their names went through my mind, over and over again.

Daws had probably compromised himself just by giving me the information.

Justin, Victoria, Matthew and Katie.

From experience I knew that by a hitman Daws probably did not mean an individual wearing dark glasses and an expensive Italian suit who would toss a hand-grenade into Patrick's car, knife him in the Gents or stab him with the point of an umbrella loaded with poison. A specialist would be assigned to kill him with a silenced handgun or shoot him from some distance away with a sniper's rifle. The specialist in this case would probably be a member of the SAS or a police marksman. All at once it crossed my mind that the specialist might have already arrived and had dyed hair growing out a wishy-washy blond colour at the roots. If so he would have to find Patrick first and so far had not done terribly well.

Then my cat's whiskers intuition really slammed in with the big one.

Working on the stiff upper lip principle I changed into the one formal dress I had brought with me, black with a hint of glitter on the bodice, and went down to dinner. If 'Archways' showed up I would deal with him in the middle of his *Confit of Summer Fruits Enrobed in Puff Pastry and Garlanded with Raspberry Coulis*, one of the soggy mainstays of the rather boring dessert trolley. Bloody-mindedly, I amused myself with the idea of everything concluding Jane Eyre-style: 'Reader, I shot him'.

I was wrestling with my *Rack of Scottish Lamb, Stuffed with dawn-fresh Mushrooms, Served with a Panache of Baby Vegetables and Enrobed in Red Wine Sauce With a Hint of Mint*, the meat as tough as a camel's backside, the vegetables tasting liked tinned ones, the sauce merely lumpy gravy, when Jenny approached.

'Please forgive me for interrupting your meal, Miss Langley...'

'Sit down,' I invited, glad to give my jaws a rest. Obviously, more 'spookiness' had transpired.

'We've had something really strange happen, a fax has come about Mr Zakiyah. A photograph. I'm not quite sure how I ought to deal with it.'

'Would you like me to give you a hand?'

Her face flooded with relief. 'Would you?'

Lightly, I remarked, 'The Reverend Archways doesn't seem to have come down to dinner.'

'No, that was another funny thing. He was bitten by a dog late this afternoon at the Creggan Arms. There was an affray there after someone's dogs attacked some others and then their owners got in a fight and the police were called... The usual kind of trouble. I can't think what the minister was doing there.' Quickly, as if fearing I might think she was blackening his character, she added, 'Only I expect he was out for a walk and just passing, don't you?'

'No doubt,' I said dryly.

'Anyway, he was taken off to hospital to have it looked at.' She got to her feet. 'Please don't rush your dinner. I'm sure the fax can wait for a bit.'

I worked my way through *Chocolate Supremes aux Fines Praline Caressed with Spun Sugar*, a multi-lingual way of saying two very small knobs of ice cream containing bits of fudge huddled, as if for protection, in a case-hardened shell of cooking chocolate, decided against coffee and went to find Jenny.

She was seated in the office that was just to the rear of the reception desk with the door open so it was only necessary for me to draw attention to my presence.

'There,' said Jenny, handing me a sheet of paper. 'It doesn't even say who it's from.'

Batrun's boyish face staring up at me, I said, 'Perhaps the sender isn't the kind of person to put his name and address on communications as he's involved with national security. Is this the man who stayed with you?'

She nodded. 'I'm fairly sure it is.'

I felt strangely sad. He was dead and that was what, sooner or later, happened when you hired yourself out to lunatics. Once I had saved his life and, before that during my captivity, he and Jubeil, little more than children at that time, had risked getting into serious trouble by bringing me food. Even then, terrorists in the making, they had been doomed.

'National security?' Jenny repeated. 'It sounds as though he might be some kind of criminal. How dreadful.'

I gave it back. 'Just send confirmation to the fax number on some of your headed notepaper. It might be a good idea if your husband has a look at it too. Two positive identifications are always better than one.'

I became aware that someone was in the lobby and looked through the open doorway. 'May I borrow that again for a moment? I've just seen someone who was staying here at the same time.' Before Jenny could reply I picked it up and went into the reception area.

The limp was quite pronounced now, a bandage around his right ankle.

'We need to have a little chat,' I said quietly.

The man from Special Branch regarded me with steady loathing. I responded by holding up the fax by its top corners, the photograph towards him.

'A man calling himself Batrun,' I said. 'One-time student at

Brecon who graduated to be a full-time terrorist and paid the ultimate price not so long ago when he was hoist by his own petard. It would appear that he was staying here at the time and I'm pretty sure he killed Keith Somerton in revenge for the shooting of his uncle, a man known only to MI5 as The Greek. Investigations are in progress to trace the woman he was with so she can be questioned. Will you report this back to your Alpha One or shall I?'

He dragged his gaze from me, reluctantly and with a contemptuous curl to his lip but nevertheless studied the photograph carefully.

'Who sent that?'

'It doesn't concern you.'

'Where's your evidence?'

'Where's yours as far as Patrick's concerned? The doctored D12 training film showing him planning the murder with the wrong man, a man who's supposed to be dead but isn't and...'

'Dead but isn't?' he interrupted incredulously.

'No, and he didn't do it anyway because someone got there first. What do you think a court will make of all that? You're going to find yourself sent down for perjury and all for what? In the name of duty or because Somerton was a relative of yours? Brother, was it? Cousin?'

Stiffly, he said, 'Shall we talk in your room or mine?'

'Neither,' I countered, chin probably jutting. 'There's a perfectly good lounge over there.'

I gave the fax back to Jenny. When I followed him into the lounge he seated himself in an armchair by one window, as private as it was possible to be in a public room, the area partly screened by plants. Comfortingly to me, he continued to look exhausted. Other than for a man and women sitting by the fire with coffee things on a nearby table, we were on our own. I seated myself in a chair opposite to him and there was a long silence.

'You're a damned nuisance,' he said, speaking in an undertone but with resentful vehemence.

'Diddums,' I responded. 'What do I really call you? Norm's kind of naff.'

There was another long silence and then he muttered, 'Greg.'

'Somerton?'

'No, but he was my second cousin.'

'It's fascinating,' I told him, meaning it. 'But we simply don't have the time to sit here and exchange whys and wherefores. My husband's in the frame for murder and I'm quite prepared to put a bullet between your eyes if that's what it takes to stop you making any more threatening moves in my direction. I'm not stupid- you had it in your mind to kill me when you grabbed me in the pub. However, I suggest we co-operate.'

'Co-operate!' he exclaimed.

'Keep your voice down. Listen. During that weekend there was a man staying here who used to be in Somerton's team but left in disgust after the project at Brecon was set up - call it a clash of personalities. We now know that Batrun - I don't know his real name - was here. A man calling himself Hall was here. *He* was the one Patrick spoke to outside a pub in Soho and who swam out to the rowing boat when it went from view behind the island only to find Somerton literally dead in the water. You were here and I think I believe you when you say you came because you had been ordered to warn him. Now Batrun might well have swum out to that boat and *also* found only a body. There's every chance that Somerton's killer was already on the island and merely cap- sized the boat amongst the submerged tree roots before fin- ishing him off. I think that someone killed Jamie Kirkland the following day.'

'Too much supposition,' said Greg scornfully.

'It's what comes when you're a crime writer,' I snapped. 'I thought I was talking to a policeman and policemen were interested in motive.'

'Okay - tell me,' he requested loftily.

'I know this is about money, the cash that Somerton somehow got away from Brecon, either with Kirkland who hid it before he was arrested, or with someone else, one of the helpers, who wasn't. My guess is the latter because Kirkland wouldn't have gone off if there was money to look after here. I'm becoming more and more convinced that both of these men were killed to prevent them either having a share in it or, in Somerton's case, making off with the lot. And please don't pretend that you don't know what I'm talking about, you were in that boathouse for a reason too - not that it has anything to do with your official brief.'

Greg, who had been focusing his gaze somewhere behind my left shoulder, sighed. It was the sigh of a man who was fed up with his assignment, whose ankle throbbed and who had run out of lies. 'Despite what you think,' he said. 'I actually hated Keith's guts. I thought he was a bloody disgrace.'

'To the Force?' I enquired sarcastically.

'I knew you wouldn't believe me. He'd bragged to me that he planned to make a bit on the side of the Brecon job. He didn't mention at the time that that included killing all his pupils. When an oafish army bod...' and here Greg fixed me with his far-too-close-together eyes, 'turned up and killed all his pupils instead, I felt that they were as bad as each other.'

I said nothing. This man wasn't anywhere near as senior as I had assumed him to be from his behaviour and I very much doubted now that he was any kind of hitman. My fear had been based on nothing more than sub-conscious knowledge that he resembled Somerton in appearance. I said, 'You do realise though that this is all one huge scam for political purposes.'

He shrugged. 'I don't care what it is. I just do my job.' He winced as he moved his right foot.

'But you're searching for this money.'

'I shall hand it in if I find it. I shall have proved to myself and to anyone who's interested that he was a right bastard.'

'According to several people you had a real row with him in the garden.'

'I'd said my piece and he was bloody rude - really offensive. It would have made anyone see red. I wouldn't have said that we were talking so loudly that others could hear us though.'

'Are you still prepared to lie under oath that you saw Patrick here the weekend he died?'

'If I'm ordered to.'

It was my turn to sigh.

Looking me right in the eye Greg said, 'You've won though. As far as you're concerned, that is. I intend to return to London first thing in the morning so don't think there's any question of co-operation. That bloody dog tore a ligament in my foot - I told them at the hospital I'd get it fixed at home.'

'Before you go you could try searching the larger of the two islands.' I smiled my amusement when he looked utterly astonished and continued, 'Hamish Dunlop said that the last laird, or rather, his father, used an old building of some kind in the middle of the island as a storehouse. Somerton drowned nearby and Kirkland's body was found snared in tree roots there.' I surveyed him gravely. 'Be careful if you decide to go ahead. Take a uniformed man, or two, with you. I haven't been anywhere near it yet but get very bad vibes about the place.'

'Why are you telling me this?'

'Because I'm not remotely interested in finding cash hoards or revenging myself on little shits - only of getting Patrick out of the mess others have got him into.'

Greg struggled to his feet and limped towards the doorway. Over his shoulder he said, 'He's welcome to you. You're a very dangerous woman.'

'Some men prefer their women dangerous,' I whispered to myself.

But I still did not trust him at all and when I went to bed I put the chest of drawers across the door again.

It seemed that Greg's ankle did not prevent him from driving and he was alone in his car when it drew out of the hotel forecourt and disappeared down the drive at eight fifteen the next morning. I had made a point of reading a morning paper in a lounge which one entered through a wide archway and enjoyed a full view of the lobby area. Therefore I saw him pay his bill, pick up his cases and depart. Seeing his luggage gave me an idea. I hurried over to the desk before Jenny could leave.

'Did Mr and Mrs Zakiyah have a lot of luggage with them?'

'Not particularly,' she said slowly. 'Although, as I'm sure you understand, I can't be expected to remember every detail after all this time. But I do remember that one of their cases was pretty heavy. It was more like a trunk really. They said it was presents they'd bought for their families.'

It could well have been diving gear.

I went outside into a perfect late-summer morning. It seemed to me that in this perfection there were many places where a hitman might conceal himself; on the roof of the hotel, plenty of trees in the garden that he might climb and hide in. I scanned the surrounding countryside and saw any amount of opportunities for the trained marksman; hundreds, no, thousands of trees, rocky crags all around, the tower of the village church, a ruined barn...

I wandered down the hotel drive, about fifty yards to the pillared gateway on the main road, in two minds whether to return for the car and drive to Duncreggan when, in the distance, I saw a man walking, through this theatre of hidden warfare as it were, along the virtually straight road towards me. As, subconsciously perhaps, I had thought he might. Even though he was still a good way off I could see that he carried nothing, not even a jacket and I knew he was unshaven, unwashed, and utterly tired. I wondered where he had slept the previous night while I was luxuriating under my warm quilt - in fact I had hardly slept, thinking about him - and what he had eaten, if anything, depending on if he had gone on to lose what he had won at cards. But I knew I had done right in not interfering: he would have to come to me.

I started to run, not caring who saw me. By the time I had gone back for the car he would have arrived.

When he saw me he stopped, surprised perhaps and I wanted to scream at him to keep moving to present a more difficult target. But I was still too far away. I ran faster.

Then commonsense prevailed and I slowed back to a walk when I realised that as Greg had failed to recognise him in the pub - and I didn't think he was clever or subtle enough to have succeeded in hiding that knowledge from me - then it was unlikely that anyone else knew where he was. Not Daws, certainly, and I was still uneasy at having concealed what I knew from him.

Then I ran again. He was close.

The fact that he is an army officer trained to the extent of being virtually pickled in self-control does, thankfully, not intrude into Patrick's private life and he embraced me with a passion that equalled my own. When we finally sundered there were tears in both our eyes.

'I must spoil everything,' I said. 'By telling you that Daws warned me that a sniper might be deployed if you stayed at large. They can still use the situation without risking a court case going against them.'

'Cheer me up again by telling me that that idiot dressed up as a priest got carted away to have his leg off.'

'As good as.'

'Perfect.' Patrick breathed in deeply and glanced around, but not as if looking for snipers, as though admiring the morning. 'Breakfast,' he announced happily.

The irony was that Patrick's Special Branch interrogators had told him I had gone to the Garrochmuir Hotel, taunting him that my every move was being closely monitored. Not knowing that the children and Carrie were elsewhere he had decided to stay well away from Devon for their sakes and had immediately headed north, having thumbed several lifts to get to Scotland.

Once at the hotel and despite his relaxed response to my worries it was obvious he was extremely angry as well as unwell and weak from lack of food - he had been warned off eating in the Creggan Arms by the card players as there had been a recent food poisoning scare rumoured to have started there - exhausted and still heavily bruised from being thrown on to the floor at the remand centre and kicked a few times in the ribs. He disappeared into the en-suite bathroom, leaving a trail of dirty clothes.

The winsome young woman who helped Jenny in reception had been too well-mannered to so much as bat a purple eyelash when I had returned with this slightly malodorous male in tow and booked him in as my husband and if she thought I had picked him up in the pub then gossip would soon bear her out. All I could do was ring down and ask if they would send up a late breakfast for him then race into Inverness to buy him some clothes. When I returned, loaded with carrier bags, I half expected the hotel to be ringed by police but all I found was Patrick fast asleep on the bed wearing my dressing gown. The light-sleeping ex-undercover soldier awoke when I closed the door.

I dropped everything on the floor, not in a particularly good mood myself by now. I knew how the women who had been called upon to do all kinds of exciting jobs during the Second World War felt when their men had come back from the front and they had had to return to the kitchen sink.

'What about this cough then?' I asked. 'You were coughing quite badly earlier when we were walking back.'

'It's just a cough. That's what the docs said but I had a shot or two of antibiotics to be on the safe side. It's better - especially when I drink whisky.' He noted the way I was looking at him for he added, 'That's the truth. I managed to wrench a screw from a wall in the remand centre and cut my tongue with it. When my mouth was full of blood I coughed, spewed it all over the place and then crashed off my chair onto the floor playing dead. In the canteen. It put a terrific lot of folk off

169

their afters.' He grinned at me in the slightly unsettling mad way he sometimes does but for once it didn't work. He said, 'What's the matter, Ingrid?'

'I don't know.'

Patrick sat up. He had managed to cajole some shaving gear from the hotel management and despite the short sleep was very alert and focused. 'Yes, you do.'

A tear rolled down my cheek and I angrily slapped it away. 'I'm all right.'

'Please, tell me,' he persisted softly. Sometimes when he gazes at me in this fashion I feel that he can see into my very soul.

There was an edgy silence.

'I'm sorry,' he said. 'Seeing me in the pub was really great - thanks by the way for playing along and not giving the game away - then you ended up going shopping and this selfish, ungrateful devil didn't even ask you what you'd been up to.'

'It's stupid, isn't it?' I said. 'One moment I'm missing you dreadfully and prepared to do anything to see you again and the next I'm getting really petty.' I kissed him. 'I'm sorry too. Do you think it's safe to behave openly and go down for late coffee or lunch?'

'I am *not* going to start living in wardrobes or ditches - not for all the bloody snipers in the world. We'll go down, eat them out of house and home and then have a good de-briefing.'

He prudently decided against having coffee in the conservatory though.

I had just about completed bringing him up to date with events and the results of my own investigations, Patrick on his third Danish pastry, when he said, 'That character in the pub dressed up as a bish, the bloke who was brought along as general bum-wiper when I was first picked up...'

'Who you as good as ordered me to get rid of,' I replied. 'That was the Reverend Norman Archways.'

'Is that what he was calling himself? You're joking.'

'No. He was sent up here the first time to warn Somerton his life might be in danger. Possibly because he was his second cousin.'

'Why go to those lengths? Why dress up as a clergyman?'

'If he was related to Somerton he had to have a screw loose.'

Soberly, but with a twinkle in his eye - the life was beginning to flow back into him now - Patrick said, 'I shall file that explanation until something more plausible becomes evident.'

I had wanted to tell him about it earlier and had realised that, deep down, it had been the reason for my tears. There was still an overwhelming need to tell all. 'I might just have shot him,' I mumbled.

'Ah. So I take it you tangled with him more than you would have liked. Did it work?' he gently went on to enquire.

'Did what work?'

'Don't beat around the bush. I can tell by the way you're behaving that this guy, to put it politely, tried his luck with you and as your professional trainer I'm interested in whether what I taught you worked.'

Such was his calm I could hardly believe that here was a husband asking his wife if another man had raped her. Therefore I must be calm too. 'Yes, it worked.' I put my hands in my lap when I saw that they were trembling a little. I must not make a scene.

'But?' This on a mere zephyr of breath.

'It's not the same as you and I having a rough work-out,' I whispered. 'Deep down he reminded me of Somerton - I had this dread of him. Since Brecon I'm not brave anymore.'

Patrick picked up my empty coffee cup and re-filled it. 'Would it help you at all if you told me exactly what happened?'

I did and when I had fallen silent he said, 'It would be easy for me to go all gung-ho here and tell you that you not being brave anymore is a load of rubbish and you're braver than most people I know. It happens to be true but that's what men

171

usually say in this kind of situation before they go down to the pub and forget all about it. But to be honest I think that anything else I might say would only sound bloody trite.'

'I don't want you to *do* anything - in revenge, I mean.'

Slowly, watching me, he shook his head.

'Then let's forget it,' I said. 'More than anything I want to forget *him*. Did you find out anything interesting in the pub?'

He was content to go along with my wishes and the complete change of subject but that did not mean that his eyes immediately lost their cold anger or, deep down, that pitiless glitter. He said, 'I take it when you came in the pub you were interested in talking to Callum and Hugh - or anyone, for that matter, who had known Kirkland?'

'That's right.'

'They were all talking about the discovery of his body. Nothing was said though that would actually throw any light on either death except for one thing; a postman by the name of George saw a frogman on the morning Somerton drowned.'

'Was it Tim?'

'It could have been but we mustn't jump to conclusions. No one seemed to know exactly where he saw him. The other thing I found out - and I'd been in the pub for less than two hours when you rolled up - was that Kirkland had been even more of a loner since he returned home, in other words, since Brecon. No one knew what he got up to, not even Hugh and Callum and they'd been chums, or at least gone poaching together, before he went off. Apparently Kirkland had actually come and gone several times since he was a lad so it was nothing strange to the village when he disappeared last time. Someone made a remark that's probably of no importance, out of context really, that he'd come back at about the same time as Billy Douglas - whoever *he* might be.'

'Douglas? Is he a relative of the two boys who found Kirkland's body? I intended to talk to them.'

'It's worth looking into.'

Later, after Patrick had tackled an early lunch without pause from morning coffee, I was told there was a phone call for me and we both went back to our room so I could take it there. It was Daws. Patrick, definitely and belligerently not living in wardrobes or ditches, asked to speak to him and I surmised, listening to one half of the conversation, that, after he had recovered from the surprise, Daws was still very worried on our behalf.

'No, I'm going to see this through,' Patrick told him. 'I'm quite happy to leave someone else to interview Batrun's wife, or whatever she was, but we can tackle the job from this end. As you know I couldn't care a bloody damn about Somerton and although Jamie Kirkland was a spineless, shifty little no-hoper Somerton used him in the same way he used just about everyone who crossed his path and I think he deserves someone putting in a bit more effort. When James Carrick brought Ingrid up here the local CID fell on his neck as they hadn't one idea this side of Caithness. I'm on the spot and Ingrid and I know more about this business than anyone.' Patrick listened for a few moments longer and then said, 'I really appreciate your concern, sir, but I am not going to run and hide and if they send a hitman after me I shall ram his shooter up his backside and pull the trigger.' He then replaced the receiver. 'Jamie also made the best bacon butties I've ever had,' he remarked absently.

'Batrun might have killed him too,' I said.

'And then tethered the corpse somewhere underwater where it wouldn't be found, possibly forever? No, I don't think so. Someone with Batrun's mind-set wouldn't have bothered himself with the cook. We're talking about straightforward eye-for-an-eye stuff here. Besides, he had no axe to grind with Kirkland. All the guy had ever done was cook his meals for him.'

'He was part of Somerton's armed group at the end though,' I reminded him.

'I agree. But Batrun knew as well as we do that everyone

who worked there was scared shitless of the man and did as they were told, or else. No, and I'm coming round to your way of thinking; that Batrun didn't necessarily do the deed and this really could be all about money.'

'Do you intend then to stay on here at the hotel?'

'What do *you* want to do?'

'Go home,' I said. 'See the children, feed the cat, clean the cottage, scrub the loos, paint the barn red, white and blue with a toothbrush. Silly question. No, seriously, all the police have to do is roll up here and re-arrest you.'

'They won't. Daws has fixed it. He's made it plain - acting of course in his capacity of *completely* independent adviser - that if they try I'm armed and will start a small war to hold them off while you get on the phone and tell all to the media. They simply won't dare risk it.' He chuckled cold-bloodedly.

'And this hitman? I'm really thinking of the children here.'

'So am I actually. I don't want them to grow up in a world where this kind of thing can happen to anybody.'

'Noble sentiments don't stop bullets,' I persisted mulishly.

'Okay, I'll go and buy a flak jacket.'

I can read this man of mine like a book and right now he wasn't even remotely interested in strategy, ruses or plot but something far more basic that probably over-rode even the immediate need to stay one step ahead of everyone else. Equally obvious was that he was not at all sure that I would have equal enthusiasm for what he had in mind.

'There's nothing worse than a man who looks randy *and* worried,' I remarked in off-hand fashion.

I was taken in the lightest of embraces. 'I don't think we ought to waste time indulging in this kind of thing. Besides, after what happened to you I can't really ask you to...'

'Don't think,' I said. 'Just kiss me silly.'

'Did Tim Shandy contact you at all - other than by sending the postcard?' I asked much later. After gentle lovemaking we had slept the afternoon away, more mutual healing, and were preparing to go down for dinner, Patrick insistent that it would take the SAS or worse to prevent him from eating another square meal. I had decided to stay and tomorrow we would carry on with our investigation and, with or without permission from the Cranleys, visit the islands.

Patrick shook his head. 'No. But it was wonderful news that he's still alive.'

'The poor man's terribly scarred. I think it was the only thing that stopped him from busting you out of the remand centre.'

'Thank God he didn't. Tim has the alarming habit of going right over the top and would have probably rolled up with a howitzer he'd pinched from the Imperial War Museum and flattened the place. He's only really happy when he's making things go bang.'

'I would have thought that Bosnia would have put him off explosives for life.'

'Want a bet?'

No, I didn't.

Chapter Ten

I waited until after we had eaten before voicing a few more worries. 'Look, sorry to keep banging on about it but if the people behind this are going to make any political capital out of it then they'll have to do it soon. In three days time the Leader of the Opposition will give his speech and on that morning the story of your arrest was due to hit the headlines. Now it looks as though it's intended that the news will be all about your death while resisting arrest. It's all very well to say you'll do some investigating here and we go poking around on a couple of islands but what the hell is all this leading up to?'

After due consideration Patrick said, 'It'll have to be a dead cert, if you'll excuse the pun. They simply won't dare risk putting you in any danger. Now as much as I detest the thought of using you as any kind of shield, no one will be keen on firing off any weapons in my direction, not from long-distance anyway, while we're together. And they can hardly burst in here and shoot me as it's too public. What they need - if this really is going to happen and somehow I very much doubt it, it's too crazy for words - is a nice remote spot where the corpse can be collected without fuss or witnesses and then carted off to where the arrest was supposed to have taken place. Possibly even at home. Now let's consider the options if they get desperate and do go for a long-range job. There are five men in this country - they would have to keep such an assignment in-house - who could be ordered to do it, four in the army and one in the police. I know them all and it was my business to at one time because- well it was my business to.'

I could still hardly believe what we were discussing.

'Trust me,' Patrick said simply.

I had been expecting him to say a lot more in an effort to alleviate my concern. 'I do,' I told him, trying not to sound as desperate as I felt. 'It's everybody else that's suspect.'

He smiled, the big warm grin that had been one of the reasons I had fallen in love with him. 'Later on today, after I've had a word with some of the folk you've already spoken to we set off for the islands. Not from the jetty here though- we do the reverse of what everyone else has done and approach them from the other direction, using them to prevent anyone from seeing us.'

'People will still spot us from the village.'

'No, they won't, at least only when we're a long way away, and that's because we'll change course a couple of times, using *both* islands as screens. I've worked it out on the map. The only risk is that we'll be spotted by an interested party from the road or at a point on the surrounding hillsides. That can't be helped.'

I couldn't think of a more exposed position than to be in a dinghy in the middle of a lake. 'And our transport?' I queried.

'There's a house down the far end of the loch that has a jetty with several boats tied up. I shall exert charm. Yes, and before you remind me, it's a bloody long row if they haven't one with an outboard.'

'Outboards are noisy. It will attract attention.'

He grimaced.'You're right. Just as well I auditioned for *Ben Hur.*'

'Pray for calm seas and a prosperous voyage,' I said, mostly to myself.

'How about you pointing me in the direction of Auld Robbie?'

'Just go in the bar and follow your intuition.'

I went with him. I didn't want to let him out of my sight.

In the event intuition was not required as the bar was only sparsely occupied. Auld Robbie had seemingly only just arrived and was settling himself on a stool in his usual place at one end of the bar beneath a large bossed shield and crossed halberds. A length of plaid material was draped over the halberds and he told anyone who was prepared to listen that it was his clan tartan and that was why he sat there. The group that I had met earlier - I had decided they were on some kind of company 'bonding' exercise - were also in the room, clustered around a table, as noisy as ever, apparently sharing the day's experiences. One of them, a man who appeared to have appointed himself leader, looked up when we entered and also discovered the existence of Auld Robbie. His face expressed amazement.

'Is he supposed to be in here?' he called across to Patrick.

Most people would have probably replied, with icy aloofness, that they were not hotel employees and therefore could hardly be expected to know. Patrick, game for mischief even when beset from all sides, ignored the speaker but stopped dead and turned to me aghast, his eyes glassy, to say in panic-stricken tones, 'I can feel it coming on again!'

Having a good idea what was impending I cried in horror, 'No, not in *here!*'

He started to jerk and quiver, first with just the hands, the shaking and twitching then travelling to every part of him as though an electric current was passing through his body. His eyes rolled upwards, his mouth dropped open and his tongue fell out and hung down onto his chin. He started to shimmy around the room, first over towards the bar and then, with stomach-churning suddenness like a missile homing in on its target, in the direction of the transfixed group, his hands now like claws, making grabbing movements in the air. A ghastly shriek rang out.

It was one of the women who had shrieked. Collectively their nerve broke and they all bolted from the room. The woman who had screamed, who when I had first made their acquaintance had been tipsy and enthusing about the sexual prowess of her live-in lover, dropped her bag and then almost fell over it. She paused, clapping her hands over her mouth as the nightmare approached, scooped the bag from the floor and now, all perfectly normal smiles, held it out to her. She snatched it and tore after the others.

Patrick shrugged his jacket straight and said to Auld Robbie, whose eyes were rather round, 'Hello, you old scoundrel. How's life?'

'Is everything all right in here?' asked Phil anxiously, returning to man the bar carrying an ice bucket. 'I thought I heard a scream.'

'One of the leddies got hersel in a stramash,' the old man reported with relish. Then he started to laugh and although I had seen this particular party-piece before I laughed too. We laughed until the tears ran down our faces. Patrick had to buy us both a drink to help us recover.

'Playin' games up in the heather,' Auld Robbie said contemptuously, but still chuckling. 'That lot. An' with faces like the far awa end of a French fiddle.' He mimed haughty disdain.

'I understand you're the fount of all local knowledge,' Patrick said in hushed tones with a furtive glance over his shoulder.

'Mebbe,' grunted Auld Robbie.

Patrick slid a ten pound note across the bar and then, giving the other a meaningful look, followed it with a second. But he kept a firm forefinger on both for a moment and said, 'I'm not interested in what I believe is referred to round here as a load of haivers.'

Auld Robbie grunted again, with no discernable meaning this time, and was permitted to pocket the money.

Patrick said, 'If I were to need a rook where would I find one?'

'A rook?' the old man said in surprise.

'It *was* a rook, wasn't it? Not a crow or a jackdaw.'

'Aye.'

'So where do you reckon it came from? They're not regarded as vermin these days so folk don't tend to shoot them. *Had* it been shot, by the way or are we talking about death from natural causes?'

I suddenly saw what he was driving at. It was unlikely that someone like Batrun, a foreigner, would be familiar with

British birds or would even be bothered to find the right sort to lay by Somerton's body, even if he gone to the trouble to make such a gesture at all.

'It had been shot,' said Auld Robbie. 'Enough lead in it to sink it.'

'A shotgun then.'

'Aye, but ye wouldna necessarily notice someone blasting off with one though. The Munros run clay-pigeon shootin' courses up at the farm in summer. Ye get used to it.'

'Was the bird freshly dead?'

'It was stiff but it didna stink - no more than a dead corbie usually does.'

'So where do you reckon it could have been shot?'

Auld Robbie shrugged. 'There's a gang o' them in the trees at the kirk, more up at the auld tannery. There's some usually hangin' around the dead elm at Micklestane croft. Any number of 'em if ye ken where to look.'

'What was Kirkland's reaction to Somerton's death? We know he was still alive the morning after the body was discovered because Hamish Dunlop saw him hanging about on the shore.'

'I didna seem him. But Callum did at openin' time - he said he was all of a swither and his eyes were rollin' in his heid until he looked like a one-armed bandit.'

'Does Billy Douglas own a shotgun?' I asked.

The old man seemed to remember my presence. 'Aye. But he would what with working up at the big estate.'

Patrick caught my eye. 'As gamekeeper?'

'Jack of all trades is Billy. He does a bit of loggin' and fencin', gets rid o' the vermin, helps with the shoots- that's if he can walk in a straight line after he's been at the whisky.'

Patrick said, 'I was told he came back to the village at about the same time as Kirkland. Where had he been?'

'The De'il knows. And Billy isn't the kind of man ye *ask*.'

'He has a boat too - the boys were out on the loch in it when they discovered Kirkland's body.'

Auld Robbie pointedly gazed into his empty glass. 'Aye, he does a bit o' fishin' now and then.'

Patrick signalled to Phil when he had finished serving a couple who had just entered.

'But he's no boatman,' Robbie muttered.

'No?'

'He keeps the boat on the shore now since it came adrift from the jetty here a coupla times last year. Isn't that right, Mr Cranley?' he said to Phil, who had just given him another tot. 'Billy's boat sailin' off all by itsel'?'

Phil smiled. 'We had to lend him ours to get it back. He seemed to be useless at securing it properly.'

We left Auld Robbie contentedly sipping his whisky and went into dinner.

The following day our mood had changed and I was reminded of what Tim Shandy had said about the need to cherish and make full use of free moments. Patrick's own thoughts were unfathomable but the previous evening he had chuckled over the menu and ordered a bottle of champagne on the grounds that quite soon it would be our wedding anniversary. The food, albeit filling and probably nourishing, had been irrelevant.

On the hotel steps though, as we set off the next morning, Patrick lightly touched my arm and said, 'By the way, I have no intention of snuffing it today.'

'I'll have that engraved on your headstone,' I told him, not at all in the mood for this kind of humour. 'Where to first?'

Patrick gazed in the direction of the boathouse. 'I feel I ought to learn a lot about the restoration of steam-launches.'

As it happened Hamish Dunlop was engaged on a task that called for two pairs of hands rather than one, the manoeuvring of a heavy piece of wood into the boat, seemingly that had to be affixed to the inside of the hull, without damaging either. While they hefted it into position I sat in the sun and there was silence within but for grunts of effort and the occasional instruction from the boat owner. Then I heard the murmur of voices and guessed they had both sat down for a rest. Judging by the inflexions in Patrick's they were still talking about the launch.

When I entered a couple of minutes later there had been a change of subject though and Hamish was saying, 'You need to talk to those lads. If you hang on here for a wee while...' he glanced at his watch, 'They'll be here to give me a hand in around twenty minutes, perhaps half an hour. I tell them it's no use their saying they'll be along and then stay in bed all morning. Jobs have to be planned carefully.' He waved an arm in the direction of a pile of planks. 'All that decking is getting treated on the underside with wood preservative before it's put back but it's got to be done on a good day like today so it can stand outside to dry. They can do that.' He gazed at Patrick for a moment and then added, 'I pay them when they do what I call real work.' He laughed, a trifle forced. 'I didn't want you to think I was using them as child slave labour.'

I deduced from this that Patrick had switched into his thoroughly unsettling enquiry mode.

'D'you get on with their father all right?' Patrick asked lightly, climbing out of the launch and seating himself on one of the many coils of rope. Hamish was now slightly below him, still perched on the engine housing.

'Don't know the man or anything about him,' said Dunlop gruffly. 'Only that he's rough and tough and can just about read and write. It's one of the reasons I have the boys round here - to give them a different and more worthwhile view of the world than they'll get from him if they stay at home when they've left school; in other words the inside of pubs and betting shops. And prisons, more than likely.'

'He's done time?'

'As I said, I know nothing. But you get feelings about people.'

'Someone said in the pub that he returned to the village, having been away for a while, at about the same time as Jamie

Kirkland. D'you reckon the pair of them had *both* been working where we know Kirkland was employed? Wales, wasn't it?'

'It's no use your asking me,' Dunlop said, getting annoyed. 'All Jamie could do was cook fry-ups and lift other folk's possessions when they weren't looking. As for Billy...' he stopped speaking, lips pursed.

'As for Billy?' Patrick prompted gently.

But the other man just shook his head. Then he got to his feet and snapped, 'I've work to do.'

The touch up until now had been feather-light but now the pressure went up a notch. 'Billy might be employed somewhere dodgy mainly on account of his talent for thuggery and a certain way he has with firearms?'

'Well, if you know so much why ask?'

'Did he walk in here one day and without so much as a by-your-leave hack a length of rope off this boat's mooring line?'

His large hands bunching into fists Dunlop climbed out of the boat with the ease of long practice. But he did not approach Patrick who stayed where he was and although to the casual observer might give every appearance of being vulnerable was nevertheless as unassailable as if a shark-filled moat lay between them, mostly on account of the remorseless stare.

'I'm expecting an answer,' Patrick said, still speaking very quietly, 'because despite some of the things you've said I know you're a sympathetic kind of bloke with a strong sense of fair play. The police will quietly shelve their investigation into Kirkland's murder shortly after his funeral, which I understand is taking place on Saturday - and the file will go into an unmarked drawer and stay there. He wasn't important, in fact he was a nobody and a no-gooder whom everyone was glad to see the back of. But someone killed him as though he was so much vermin. No one deserves that.'

There was a tense silence for a few seconds. Then Dunlop said, a little hoarsely, '*Someone* came and took a length of the mooring rope - when I was standing over there with my back to the door. It was quite a while back and the boat was still being stripped out. I'd carried something heavy out - can't remember exactly what - and was lowering it down to the floor when I heard footsteps behind me. I couldn't turn suddenly, what I was holding was bloody heavy and already halfway to the ground. When I'd put it down and looked round I saw just a rear view of a man hurrying away with a piece of my mooring line. It must have been the first rope he saw and he went for that. It was chucking it down with rain and he had the hood up of his anorak so I can't say it was Billy - it could have been anyone.'

'Did you call after him?'

Dunlop shook his head. 'No.'

'Why not?'

The silence this time seemed to go on for ever.

'Because you had a strong suspicion it was him?'

'Yes,' Dunlop muttered.

'And he wasn't a guy anyone would want to mix with, least of all over a piece of old rope you would probably have to replace anyway. You probably wouldn't bother until the boat was finished in case it got messed up with things like paint. You did leave it exactly how it was though, chopped off short. Why? As a precaution? Hoping that the police would investigate anything Billy Douglas might get up to with it and you'd have the evidence all ready?'

'In a way.'

'That was a terrifically long shot though, wasn't it? I mean, just because you see a bloke steal a chunk of rope it doesn't mean he's going to hang someone with it.'

Hamish Dunlop rubbed his hands over his face, as if trying to rid himself of unpleasant memories and turned his back on Patrick to stare, unseeing, out of the doorway and there was another long silence.

'It was all talk,' Dunlop finally said. 'Billy's like that. Kirkland had helped himself to a pair of good oars from his garage. He has no car but he keeps his dinghy in there during the winter and as he doesn't live far from the water and has a trailer that can be pulled by a man it suits him fine. Anyway, he'd left it unlocked and Jamie made off with the oars and sold them to a man from a village down the loch. Kirkland was a fool. Billy found out about it straight away and threatened to string him up if he saw him near his house again.'

Patrick said, 'You don't frequent the Creggan Arms so how did *you* find out about this?'

'From the boys,' Dunlop answered on a sigh.

'Before Kirkland disappeared, or afterwards?'

'Before.'

'Were you aware, by the way, before Ingrid told you, that Kirkland's body had been found with a length of rope around the neck?'

'No. But I saw it when I went out to the island with the boys.' Louder, he said, 'And here they are, early for once and actually looking as though they've washed their faces this morning. I hope you're feeling energetic, lads, as there's a lot to do. Have you had your breakfast or do I have to go and get you bacon rolls from Mrs Mackie in the hotel kitchen to stop your snivels that you're starving to death before my very eyes?'

This was not for Patrick's and my benefit and the two boys who stepped into our view had the kind of sheepish grins on their faces that intimated this was the kind of teasing they were used to. But when they saw us, they stopped and their smiles vanished. Patrick and I both said hello but it did not break the ice.

'There's nothing to be scared of,' Dunlop told them in rather over-jocular fashion. 'This lady and gentleman want to ask you a few questions, that's all.'

Like deer surprised in a thicket, they bolted.

'Oh dear,' Dunlop lamented. 'I have an idea I did that all wrong. I should have told them you weren't from the police.'

'No matter,' Patrick said, getting up from his makeshift

seat and probably cursing. 'I have an idea they wouldn't have been of much help.'

'So how did you explain your own interest?' I asked Patrick when we were walking back in the direction of the hotel. I had introduced him only by his Christian name and as my husband.

'I told him the truth; that at the time of Somerton's death I was connected with national security and thought there might be a link with Kirkland's. Pity about the boys though.'

'They look like nice lads.'

Patrick chuckled. 'Yes, but if in doubt, run like hell. They're not too far away either - they'll want their bacon rolls and wages.' He surveyed our surroundings with soldierly eye. 'One good observation point is that tree on the slope up there, the one that's half fallen over with branches very close to the ground. It does seem to have a bit more movement about it than the present breeze might suggest.'

'Somewhere where a professional sniper might hide?' I asked, trying not to sound worried.

'Yes, but a professional wouldn't bounce around in it like that.'

Then, as we watched, the branches gave a final flounce and two small figures scurried away, scrambling up the steep slope on all fours to disappear over a ridge.

'A mite *too* scared, wouldn't you say?' Patrick commented. 'No, to hell with it. We wait. I refuse to be beaten by a couple of kids.'

We waited right at the front of the boathouse, sitting as I had done when I had questioned Dunlop the first time, on chunks of driftwood. Within, Dunlop worked away, probably unaware of our presence as occasionally he sang, very off-key, verses of a sad Scottish ballad that I had never heard before but which almost certainly would have everyone in tears at Hogmanay. James, no doubt, would know it well.

The sun grew hot and still Patrick patiently sat there, eyes closed as though dozing. I began to fidget, the wood was very hard. Then, I heard the approach of light footfalls.

We both remained quite still when the youngsters came round the corner of the building. I glanced quickly at Patrick and his eyes remained closed when the boys came to a halt, his face wearing a gently amused expression: quite genuine, I felt.

'There's nothing to be afraid of,' he said softly. 'We're not from the police, who I'm sure have questioned you at length already.' He opened his eyes, surveyed the bright expanse of water for a moment and then his gaze drifted across to them. 'I was told that your names are Robert and Bruce, presumably after Robert the Bruce - you can't get much better than that.'

The two, one fair-haired, the other darker, squirmed. But they were interested.

Patrick said, 'The police seem to think I might have had something to do with the death of the man who drowned a couple of years ago.'

'But ye didna?' asked the fair one - Bruce, Patrick told me afterwards. He had made enquiries about them in the pub.

'No. Did you see me here during that time?'

They shook their heads.

'Did a foreign-looking man who was staying here at the hotel ask you to do anything? Give you any errands?'

Again they shook their heads.

'Did *anyone*?'

'No,' said Bruce.

'Good,' Patrick said peaceably, smiling across the water once more.

'Ye mean - like - uplift their messages?' Bruce floundered.

It was my husband's turn to look puzzled.

This was one I had heard before. 'Carry their shopping home,' I whispered.

Patrick's brow cleared. 'Oh. No, I was wondering if anyone had asked you to chuck a dead bird away somewhere.'

187

'No, but there was one at hame,' Robert, manifestly not quite so quick-witted as his brother, replied eagerly. 'A corbie. Da shot it to hang up to keep them off his peas. But it went - lifted in the night, so Da said.'

'There's simply no telling what people will stoop to,' Patrick said, his expression one of sad regret. 'How long was it actually hanging in the garden before it disappeared?'

'It went that same night,' Bruce said. 'And then next day a corbie was found by the body of the mannie who drowned. So that's what they wanted it for.'

'It might not have been the same bird though.'

'Aye, it was. One of its eyes was gone where the shot had gone right through.'

Patrick crouched down so he was roughly on their level. 'Tell me,' he murmured. 'You seem convinced that the rook was deliberately put by the body and not just tossed down when someone became bored after a silly prank and the man died nearby afterwards. Why?'

'It's what Auld Robbie's bin sayin'. A corbie's a sign of magic or a curse.'

'And it's much more exciting to think of it like that?' The question was kindly put, there was no trace of sarcasm.

Bruce though looked scornful. 'No, but if it was murder the man who kilt him might do that to make it look like...' He sought the word he needed.

'An accident? Fate?' Patrick said. 'The wrath of God?'

'Aye. Those,' said the boy succinctly. 'Only it wasna.'

Patrick had half risen but now gave Bruce his full attention. 'No?'

'I saw him dead. There was no sand or mud under his fin-gernails. If ye'd tried to swim and nearly reached the shore ye'd try to pull yesel up.' His thin hands made dragging movements.

'It could have washed out though if it was a while before he was found.'

'That's what the police said when I told them when they

188

talked to everyone. But you try it. If you're drownin' you're that desperate your nails would be rammed full an' half torn off ye.'

Placing a hand on a young shoulder and giving it a squeeze Patrick said, 'May you live long and your lum forever reek and for Heaven's sake do well at school and go and work for Special Branch. They badly need you.'

'We seem to have a cast-iron suspect,' I said. Inwardly I was chaffing at Patrick's lack of urgency for he had insisted on returning to the hotel for coffee. I could understand a wish on his part to ponder on the latest findings and remain indoors to remove himself from the sights of any concealed marksman but events were developing into a war of nerves, mostly mine. And was it my writers' imagination or had everywhere gone very, *very* quiet?

'Only circumstantial evidence so far though,' Patrick said, coming out of a quiet reverie. 'But basically you're right. We just need to find and talk to Billy Douglas. I presume your friend Rauri will know where he lives.'

I guessed he had not asked Dunlop or the boys for fear they might suffer retaliation from the obviously unpleasant but not necessarily homicidal Douglas. 'Almost certainly,' I replied. 'We already know it's somewhere on the council estate at Duncreggan.'

'Where no doubt it's all very open and there are plenty of old folk looking out of windows as they've not much else to do so we won't be able to break into this garage Douglas has and have a good rummage around. I suggest we check on that when I've had a quick word with the Cranleys. Then we set sail for the islands.' He took another Danish pastry: he seemed to have developed a craze for them. 'Aren't you eating?'

'We've only just had breakfast,' I pointed out.

'You didn't have anything to eat then either.' He looked at me in schoolmaster fashion, as though over half-moon glasses. 'You'll get halfway down the loch and then flake out.'

'I'm not rowing,' I snapped.

'You might have to if someone fills me full of lead.'

I said nothing, keeping at bay the tears that seemed to be permanently waiting in the wings now.

'Look, I know we're not crouched in the heather loaded down with grenades and Gatling guns but we're at war, woman. Eat something.'

War.

I hadn't eaten very much the previous evening either.

Sometimes I do get things horribly out of perspective.

Especially when I don't eat.

'War,' I said dully.

Patrick cut off a small piece of his pastry for me and held it out. 'It's apple. Just the sort of thing you like.'

I suddenly realised that we had returned to the hotel for no other reason than to get some fuel inside *me* and felt rather small. I ate the morsel, forced a smile and said, 'Perhaps I ought to ask for a large bowl of porridge.'

He half rose from his chair. 'Shall I fix it?'

I took a pastry. 'No, but thanks all the same.'

The Cranleys were in the office when I enquired at reception, apparently also having a coffee-break. Jenny, avid for more 'spookiness', invited us in. She immediately got more than she bargained for as Patrick - whom they still no doubt regarded as arriving in strange circumstances - adopted one of his more intimidating personas.

'Is this about Mr Zakiyah?' she asked a trifle nervously.

'No, it's about Keith Andrew Somerton,' Patrick told her and then went on in a flat undertone, weirdly sounding as though he was speaking in a crypt, 'Commander, Anti-Terrorist Branch, Metropolitan Police. In the name of ambition he'd killed, tortured and maimed. In a set-up in Wales, the details of which I need not bore you with, Jamie Kirkland acted as cook. They already knew one another and there's a strong possibility Kirkland had been Somerton's informer when he worked for the Vice Squad. When Somerton came to

190

this hotel the weekend he died it was not just for his health and it seems likely that Kirkland, with or without the help of anyone else, was looking after a large sum of money that represented the proceeds from the scam in Wales. Some time on the evening before he went on his ill-fated fishing trip Somerton was accosted by Kirkland who demanded money, or wages, owing to him. Somerton knocked him into a burn. Are you with me so far?'

They were transfixed.

'Now we know Somerton had a row with someone in the garden some time that evening and it's been assumed that was the man calling himself the Reverend Archways. Archways is actually a cousin of Somerton's and works for Special Branch and had come to Scotland to warn him of a possible attempt on his life. Apparently Somerton was very rude to him and they had words. The origin of the rumour was probably an international grapevine and had nothing to do with Duncreggan. We need not concern ourselves with it now.

'I'm of a mind that the person Somerton had the actual shouting match with outside was not his cousin, as two policemen would not have advertised to all the world what they were talking about, but Kirkland and it probably took place after Somerton had assaulted him. I think that Kirkland, even when very angry, would not just march into the hotel and proceed to search every room for him and he might wait all night if he hung around in the garden in case Somerton put his nose outside. So what I want to know is did Jamie Kirkland come to reception or arrive at the back door here and ask to speak to him?'

Philip Cranley, a thin man with receding hair who definitely did not wear the trousers and to whom I had hardly spoken, giving me the impression he was keeping out of my way, said, 'I don't see why we should answer your questions.'

Patrick gave him a thin smile. 'Ah, so you do have something to hide. Would you rather I involved the police?'

'But we haven't done anything wrong!' Jenny protested.

'*Did* Kirkland come here?' Patrick asked again, not shouting, just giving the impression he was at the absolute end of his patience.

'Yes, he came,' Phil said stiffly, after some hesitation. 'Drunk. Ranting and raving. I sent him packing. But from what you've just said it would appear that Somerton may have already been in the garden and he came upon him there.'

'Before that did you try to find Somerton to tell him Kirkland had arrived and was demanding to see him?'

'No, but only because I was on my own at the time and couldn't just walk away and leave him. He would have followed me.'

'Did you tell the police about all this?'

'Er - no.'

'Why not?'

'It seemed to me to be of no importance.'

'It could be of vital importance. Did you actually have to eject him?'

'Yes, as I said he was ranting and raving. Shouting. I didn't want him to get into the building and upset the guests.' Phil uttered a high-pitched nervous laugh. 'It's one of the worst things when you're in this business - getting a reputation for nutters right on the doorstep.'

I prayed that Patrick's safety valve wouldn't lift.

'But Kirkland wasn't a local nutter, was he? He had a huge grievance against one of your guests who not only owed him what was probably quite a lot of money but who had assaulted him into the bargain. I'm beginning to think you had a go at him too and that's why you don't want to talk about it.'

Silence.

'Only real shits hit a drunk,' Patrick said disgustedly. 'When are all you real shits in this bloody place going to realise that Kirkland was a victim of greed and hatred? What was he ranting and raving about?'

'I wasn't there,' Jenny said in a tiny voice when the furious gaze came to rest upon her for a moment.

'Just drunken ravings,' Phil said. 'I couldn't make most of it out. He just kept demanding to see Somerton. Oh, and something about if he didn't get it he'd see to it that he got the lot. It made no sense to me at the time.'

'Were those the exact words he used - "I'll see to it I get the lot". Not "I'll take the lot"?'

'Yes, that was what he said.'

'What did you hit him with?'

Phil coloured. 'A frying pan.'

'After that he must have been easy prey to whoever killed him.'

And with that Patrick walked out.

I caught up with him near the front entrance. 'Be careful,' I warned, aware that he was angry enough to forget immediate personal danger.

Patrick swung round when he heard my voice and I was surprised to see that his anger had already dissipated. 'You know what that means, don't you?' And without giving me a chance to reply, 'Jamie got reinforcements. He told Billy Douglas the full story. And it looks as though Douglas might have killed the pair of them.'

Chapter Eleven

I felt naked, horribly exposed, as I walked across the open expanse of gravel towards the car. I got in it and drove it right to the bottom of the hotel steps so Patrick took no unnecessary risks.

The house at the far end of the loch, only a couple of miles away, was large and elegant, the kind that had an armillary sundial in the garden. There were also a couple of bronze stags on stone plinths at the entrance to the long drive and, nearer to the house, a glance through an archway in a clipped yew hedge revealed Victorian lantern cloches and hazel obelisks supporting runner beans in an immaculate *potager*.

'They're not going to be the kind of people to lend anyone a boat,' Patrick agonised as we drew up by the portico-framed front entrance.

'So play it for real,' I said. 'Don't pretend anything. Be yourself.'

'So I get a backside full of birdshot as well as a rebuff?' he responded gloomily.

I just looked at him in sufficiently unsympathetic fashion to send him across to ring the doorbell without saying another word.

Whoever opened the door was a mystery for a moment for as soon as there was the merest gap several canine noses appeared in it followed by the rest of them and we were surrounded by gambolling gundogs of various kinds and a gigantic elkhound that tossed a well-chewed slipper at Patrick's feet, inviting him to throw it. Targeting with care he sent it spinning on to the surrounding lawn.

'He's only a puppy too,' said one of the most eminent noblemen in the country.

Fortunately, Patrick has an excellent memory for names

and faces. 'Many apologies for intruding, your Grace,' he said humbly. 'We had absolutely no idea you lived here.'

'I don't,' said the duke. 'I'm actually house and dog sitting for my sister.'

The proper introductions were made and we were almost chivvied indoors, his lordship admitting to chronic boredom and an overwhelming desire to talk to someone. It emerged that he was practically alone and fending for himself, with only a cleaning woman coming in for a couple of hours every day, the other staff, but for the gardeners, on holiday. What with one thing and another, and after we had been given excellent coffee, it was almost an hour before the reason for our visit was mentioned.

'There's no earthly reason why you shouldn't borrow a rowing boat,' said the duke. 'Penelope will be delighted if she's helped an author get a bit of background and atmosphere.' He grinned at me. 'Especially if she gets a signed copy.'

I smiled back. Bless his cotton socks it looked as though I would have to base a book on the whole wretched business after all.

We all went down to the surprisingly rickety wooden jetty, the dogs all tearing round in circles and behaving in the idiotic way that dogs do when their owner is away and they are allowed to get away with blue murder. Patrick did draw the line at the elkhound getting in the small blue dinghy with us though and we drew away from the jetty with it sadly watching our departure. We had promised to be away for no longer than three hours but only so that his lordship did not have to worry about us.

'It's a fair distance,' I commented.

'I told you, bruises or no, I'm a fully paid-up galley-slave.' Patrick said, rowing easily and strongly in perfect conditions, the loch's surface like polished glass, not a breath of wind.

'At least you won't be seasick.' Moving my weight I slightly rocked the boat a couple of times.

'Do that again and you have the oars,' he retorted grimly.

Such was the smoothness of our glide through the water it was as if we were stationary and the banks of the lake and the trees growing on them were travelling slowly past. Occasionally Patrick shipped the oars for a few moments and turned to plot his course, consulting the small compass that is one of the useful gadgets I always have with me. He seemed to be actually enjoying himself.

I wasn't. On the water I felt even more exposed and vulnerable. Even if we stayed in the middle of the loch, which we could not and were in fact at this moment very close to the western bank, we were well within range of a modern snipers' rifle. Patrick's assurances notwithstanding I knew that an experienced marksman could hit him easily without risking my safety at all.

We were actually covering the distance very quickly, the larger of the two islands, which I knew from the map to resemble an hour-glass in shape, close enough after about ten minutes had elapsed for me to be able to pick out the granite single-storey building, screened by trees from every other direction but with what must be an unimpeded view down the loch from this aspect. It did not look like a bothy or cottage and appeared to have stone columns of almost classical design.

'It's a folly,' I said decidedly.

'You can't sort things out by not taking any risks,' said Patrick, looking rather warm by now.

'No, the building's a folly,' I explained. 'A little stone temple.'

'The old laird probably had it built so he and his cronies could slip over for the odd orgy or two.'

'I don't think the Scots go in for those, do they?'

'No, come to think of it, it's usually too bloody cold.' He paused in rowing to look for himself and to have a short rest. There was utter silence but for the croaks of a pair of ravens, high overhead.

'Please don't stop for long,' I whispered.

Just as I spoke a rifle shot cracked out, the sound echoing around the peaks of the mountains.

'You never hear the shot that kills you,' Patrick said casually and recommenced rowing. He gazed at me steadily. 'That was a sporting weapon of some kind and was either fired high or wide or not anywhere in this direction at all. The real thing is a lot quieter.'

Slowly, oh, so slowly, we approached the islands.

Patrick pulled in the direction of the smaller one. It was only about twenty yards in diameter, with just a few trees in the centre. 'We'll rule this one out first. For after all, there are such things as red herrings.' He paused in rowing again. 'What about the submerged branches?'

I said, 'They were only mentioned as being near the larger island.'

'We'll risk it- there are no trees growing near the water at all, not even the remains of any.'

He drove the bows onto the soft sand and we both disembarked, I to keep hold of the mooring rope in case the boat drifted away, Patrick to swiftly explore.

'Nothing,' he reported, returning and shoving the boat off again. 'Unless we're talking about buried treasure.'

We travelled the short distance to the other island.

'The branches must be very close to the shore if they're bits of trees that were blown over into the water,' I said.

'Come and sit in the bow and keep an eye out, would you?'

Changing places was a little hazardous and caused the boat to rock alarmingly and by the time I had settled myself it was tilting forward more than I liked. I could see right down into the clear, limpid water. Tresses of weed moved slightly to the current of our passing and the sun's rays glinted on small fish as they darted for cover.

'This isn't where Somerton's boat tipped over,' I said. 'There are fish here.'

Patrick must have glanced over his shoulder for he said, 'No, and you can see upended tree roots on the shore about twenty yards over there. It looks as though the bank collapsed. We'll beach the boat here - I've no wish to go the same way as he did.'

But we almost did and only a shout from me prevented us hitting head-on a submerged section of tree trunk, slimy with weed, a long curving branch still attached that the dinghy slid along, causing it to cant over alarmingly for a second or two before Patrick got the boat back under control. I leaned over as far as I dared and with me pushing against the branch and Patrick rowing we got back into clear water.

'Odd,' Patrick commented. 'The size and weight of the thing apart it forces you to wonder if it was manoeuvred there on purpose to stop anyone landing here.'

In the end I removed my shoes and stepped out into shallow water, guiding the boat around the obstruction to the shore. Between us we dragged the boat up on to a beach of soft white sand and tiny pebbles and then headed for the cover offered by the nearest trees and bushes.

'Stay here while I do a recce,' Patrick said, taking the Smith and Wesson from his jacket pocket. He went from my side, going out of sight into the thick vegetation and but for the twittering of birds for a few minutes there was absolute silence. Then, with a slight rustle of leaves, a hand appeared and beckoned me forward. I realised when I caught up with him in the next thicket, having crossed an open sandy space, that he was now following a trail of footprints.

'Impossible to tell exactly when these were made,' he said, examining the imprints of a man's shoes in the sand. 'But fairly recently, that's for sure. As you can see the outline's very sharp as no wind or rain has yet occurred to blur the outline. A size eight, I think and made by the kind of shoes that are more rugged than trainers but not proper walking boots either.'

'Poser's shoes?' I asked.

'Someone out in the sticks possibly for the first time and not knowing what you really need to wear? You could be right.

They could also be yachtie shoes - the kind that have non-slip soles.'

'I take it we're alone here.'

The urbane manner beginning to wane under the tension, he said, 'I would have mentioned it if we weren't.'

He back-tracked to the shore and we came to a place where another boat had been drawn up, the sand churned up by the marks made by the keel and a mixture of footprints, including those of someone with larger feet wearing boots, probably Wellingtons. Patrick stood up from closely examining the marks in the sand and set off once again to follow the first footprints. Whoever had made them had paused in the bushes.

'He had a pee,' Patrick announced, indicating a patch of damp soil at the base of a rowan. 'Well, at least we now know it's a bloke - ladies can't pee close to trees.'

'I think it's the only thing I envy men for,' I said. 'Being able to spend a penny without getting virtually undressed.'

A glimmer of humour broke through. 'Don't you think men are enviable in *any* other ways ?'

I made a play of concentrating deeply. 'For being able to squeeze the last bit of toothpaste out of the tube - things like that.'

He uttered a snort, either of amusement or derision, I wasn't sure which. Then he said, 'I think two boats were dragged onto the beach back there. It's a hell of a mess for just one.'

We followed the trail of footprints towards the building that I had described as a folly but which actually defied description. Why struggle to bring stone from the mainland to construct something that could not be seen from the house on the shore given that the trees might not have been planted, or seeded themselves then? The only answer was that the last laird, or more likely his father, had been a recluse.

Patrick's mind was obviously busy with similar thoughts for he said, 'It's a hermitage if ever I saw one. You can almost see him looking out of that window - all long whiskers and hairy tweeds with a dram at his elbow.'

Dryly, I said, 'Sometimes the aristocracy used to enjoy living what they thought was the simple life - commune with nature and rustics and then set off home to roast venison, loads more booze and a roaring log fire.'

'You're a bit of an old cynic, aren't you?'

'No, I'm a realist.'

The building was about twenty feet square and other than for the unglazed windows each side of the door - a wooden affair that had, by the look of it, been kicked in - closely resembled a Greek temple. There were no other openings in the thick walls - Patrick had already done so but we walked all the way round it - and from the outside the interior looked very dark.

'I had a quick look inside,' Patrick reported, switching on the torch. 'There's a hell of a mess.'

As Hamish Dunlop had said, the place was used as a store. Or rather, had been, the floor covered by a thick layer of broken wooden boxes and small crates as though vandals had smashed their way into them looking for anything of value. Some of the damage looked as though it might have been recently done. Stacked against the far wall were a pile of creels and lobster pots and also a couple of small anchors and a few coils of dusty rope.

'Not very classical inside, is it?' Patrick said, standing in the centre of the room, shining the torch this way and that.

'It's not very high,' I remarked. 'There must be a loft of some kind.'

'Yes, but there's no access now,' Patrick murmured, picking his way carefully over to gaze up at an opening in the beamed ceiling. 'Once upon a time there was a ladder. It's fallen down here, over by the wall - all rotten.'

I became aware of a slight sound, a kind of soft creaking. It seemed to come from above. The hairs on my neck prickling, I said, 'Did you hear that noise when you came in just now?'

Patrick had been poking around in a corner. 'What noise?'

'That creaking.'

He listened. 'Can't say as I noticed. But it's difficult under these conditions not to make a bit of noise yourself when you're examining a building for intruders.'

'Look, I wasn't criticizing.' I listened again. 'It sounds like a rope with a heavy weight hanging on it.'

In the gloom his gaze met mine. 'Ingrid, I think your writer's imagination is in overdrive.'

'If there's a ladder hidden in here that isn't rotten...' I began. I shuddered.

Patrick is too well acquainted with my intuition paying dividends to really scoff. 'If there's a ladder in here that isn't rotten there's someone hanged up there?'

I nodded.

'Then, as Tim Shandy would say, for the love of Fred let's find out.'

We found it; carefully concealed under rubbish at the foot of the wall on the opposite side of the room. It was just long enough to enable access to be made to the upper area and looked as though it had been made for the purpose, sturdy and knocked up from rough, unplaned wood. Patrick hefted it into place.

'Take care,' I whispered. There was no need to voice my real fear; that we might not be on our own after all and it was a trap.

He switched off the torch and silently disappeared up into the darkness. Then it was switched on again and the beam swung around quickly a couple of times before going from my view. I heard Patrick exclaim under his breath.

'Well?' I asked impatiently.

'Come up if you want to,' was the muttered reply.

I climbed the ladder.

In Inverness I had bought Patrick a small hunting knife. This could not possess the finesse, supremacy, nor for that matter the sheer illegality of his Italian throwing knife, in the safe at home, but was nevertheless useful and he was using it now. There was a heavy thump as what he was partially supporting fell to the floor. Clouds of dust arose setting us sneezing and coughing.

The torch beam shone for a moment on the livid features of the dead man and then away again, across the overturned chair, as Patrick examined what the rope had been fixed to, a large hook in one of the overhead beams.

'I've probably destroyed valuable forensic evidence,' Patrick said. 'But I've just discovered I have an aversion to just walking away and leaving people hanging by the neck - even when they're extremely dead. Poor bastard. Your Special Branch man. He's been dead for at least twenty-four hours.'

'His name was Greg,' I said. After a long silence I added, 'I suggested he come here.'

'He shouldn't have come on his own.'

It did not make me feel any better when I recollected I had stressed to him to take reinforcements. 'A clumsy and inexpert knot,' Patrick reported, shining the light back onto the corpse. 'Nevertheless, adequate.'

I just gazed dully into space. I felt horribly responsible.

'We go and find out what Billy Douglas looks like,' Patrick said, speaking grimly and in the terse way he does when emotionally upset. 'Now. Right now. McFie was one of the two instructors who survived out of the four at Brecon and he was arrested together with the other, the one you shot in the leg during the final showdown. I never knew his full name but it could be Douglas. They just called him Shorty. I called him lots of names when he strung me up from the ceiling and shoved the electrodes up my backside. This has all his hallmarks. I'm not going to show you but he did other things to this guy before he kicked the chair over.'

'They blindfolded me,' I said quietly.

'Probably because you were allowed limited freedom

and I was banged up in a dungeon. They didn't want you lifting his head off in a fit of pique.' Despite the slanted humour he was still speaking in a very taut, controlled voice.

'I imagined them both still to be in prison,' I said.

Patrick was quickly running his hands over the stonework of the walls. 'For several obvious reasons though there was a conspicuous lack of evidence. All four instructors had previous convictions that would take a month to write down but what could the Welsh police have nailed them with other than being in possession of explosives and firearms, inflicting actual bodily harm and causing a very large underground affray? Precious little.'

In the semi-darkness I felt for the severed end of the rope. 'This is thicker than the *Laura's* mooring rope.'

'It could still have been used to hang Kirkland and then another piece used to tether him underwater somewhere. This is good rope, expensive. He wouldn't want to waste it.' The torch beam flashed upwards for a moment. 'Another lousy knot - I'm surprised that one held. That rather points to Douglas too. Ah!'

This final ejaculation followed the careful easing out of a small block of stone low down in the wall not far from the opening in the floor. We crouched down and by the light of the torch, the battery of which was running low, saw there was a cavity behind it where another stone had been removed to leave a space. It was empty.

'Let's get out of here,' Patrick said. 'He's gone and taken whatever it was - at a guess the money you first suspected was behind the killings - with him.'

'And Greg?' I asked.

'I shall report what we found when we're well away from here.' He paused and then spoke rather sharply. 'His death is very regrettable but obviously he carried on being excessively stupid. If he had acted in a professional manner he would still be alive. You mustn't blame yourself for throwing him what was actually a very good lead - especially after the disgraceful way he behaved towards you.'

The professional soldier speaking.

We emerged into the warm sunshine, Patrick wary, I wondering if Greg's killer had been aware of his relationship to Somerton. It seemed as though the evil created by the man was still in existence even though he was not, still tainting everything and everyone who had known him.

'You're right,' I said. 'Kirkland must have been looking after the money. Perhaps he was the only one Somerton trusted. But when Somerton refused to pay him he told Douglas what had happened. I'm not quite sure why. D'you reckon he wanted Douglas to kill Somerton so they could share the lot?'

'That theory's got a lot going for it,' Patrick said. 'Only Douglas decided he wanted all of it. Kirkland's body might have been left hanging up there for weeks, or even months, until a way was found to dispose of it.'

'Had maggots been at the corpse, do you know?'

'James didn't say,' I said and then walked away for a short distance, feeling sick. Then I heard the sound of a small engine of some kind, possibly an outboard motor. Nothing was in sight, whatever it was was approaching the island from the other side. Without exchanging a word Patrick and I hurried to the rear of the building and then on, in the direction of the shore. When we reached the trees closest to the water we stopped and then moved forward slowly.

'Police,' Patrick said, parting the greenery with one hand to look. 'It looks as though they've decided to re-arrest me after all.'

Even though it was still quite a long way away, not far from the hotel's jetty from which it had obviously set off, I could see it was a small inflatable boat with three men in it. The dark blue uniforms were unmistakable.

'They can't have more than one of those to call upon,' Patrick said, mostly to himself. 'Just pray they don't have a dog with them.'

'What are we going to do?'

'Run up the skull and crossbones. Go back to the dinghy and see if you can get it back into the water. It doesn't really matter if you can't. Wait for me there. If any cops show up keep them chatting. Tell them you've only just arrived and I've gone to have a look round.'

'Patrick...'

But it was as if he had forgotten all about me already, turning to watch the inflatable.

The little dinghy was heavy but I succeeded in turning it round and lugging it back into shallow water, removing my shoes once again and with great difficulty manoeuvring it around the submerged tree. While I had been thus engaged I had deliberately blocked out all thoughts of what might be happening for the boat had arrived by now, the engine had cut out.

Any magic Daws might be able to do in London would not necessarily extend to the Highlands of Scotland.

Climbing aboard the dinghy I unshipped the oars so I could prevent the boat from drifting away from the island. Patrick would just have to get his feet wet.

I could see no movement ashore although occasionally heard a twig snapping and the soft rustle that might be people brushing through vegetation. I could imagine the three policeman fanning out after they had landed, a sergeant and two constables perhaps. At any moment one of them might appear at the water's edge and see me.

No one appeared and the sounds of movement gradually ceased. What seemed like a small eternity went by. Disbelievingly, I stared hard into the greenery trying to detect anyone covertly watching me but could see nothing out of the ordinary. Perhaps all three had gone straight to the folly. We had deliberately left the ladder in place to make the discovery of the body more straightforward but as we had no wish to be suspected of the crime I assumed Patrick hoped to evade them and disable their boat somehow.

Then, loudly and shockingly breaking the calm, the outboard motor roared into life and seemingly seconds later the inflatable came into sight, skimming over the water with its light load of one. It came straight towards me, the engine then cut so that the dinghy was not swamped. I shipped the oars and flung the mooring rope across and it was rapidly secured to a ring in the stern. Then we were off.

Never had that little blue dinghy travelled so fast.

'You're mad!' I exclaimed, almost completely out of breath from pure exhilaration when we were securing both water-craft at our place of departure. 'They'll be on our trail in heli-copters and God knows what else!'

'Only after they've woken up, discovered that their radios are full fathom five and they're marooned and then manage to attract someone's attention on the mainland,' Patrick said.

I stuck to my guns. 'This is the first time you've ever done this: really got the wrong side of the law. Assaulted police-men. Stolen their gear.' I groaned.

'I didn't assault them, just rendered them unconscious very gently. They won't have any after-effects.'

That lightning grip on the neck with those bloody wringing fingers. I had an idea that the officers of the law would not view the event so lightly.

Somewhere up on the hillside near the house several shots rang out in quick succession. We both flung ourselves flat on the decking of the jetty and then rolled over and ran for the cover of a nearby clump of rhododendrons. From where we were, lying on the damp soil beneath it, we could still see the boats. The inflatable was collapsing gently into the water and, as we watched, it sank leaving just a trail of bubbles to mark the spot.

'I'd already stuck the knife in it a few times,' was all Patrick said.

Chapter Twelve

Rauri Macleod did not seem all that surprised to see us. Eyeing Patrick he said, 'You were the one who beggered them at poker.'

'That's right,' said Patrick, unrepentant. After arriving at the hotel he had put what money remained, just over twenty pounds, into a charity box on the bar. I introduced him.

'And a good thing too. What can I do for you?'

Impressed by his tact at refraining from asking awkward questions I said, 'Can you give us Billy Douglas's address?'

'Certainly I can,' came the immediate reply. 'Is he likely to regret my giving it to you?'

'Only if he's guilty of murder,' Patrick said.

'Come in,' said Rauri. 'It's not a thing that can be done on the doorstep.' He closed the door after us and led the way into a sitting room. 'My wife is out shopping where no doubt she will hear the latest developments in the amazing rumour that a police boat went to the larger of the two islands in the loch and then left towing a small dinghy. Both were then tied up at the jetty at Brae House where apparently the police inflatable has sunk- there's an even more amazing rumour that shots were heard just before that happened. A few minutes ago Hamish Dunlop phoned me to say that someone has lit a fire on the island and the Cranleys have contacted the police to ask what is going on.' He paused to remove a thick folder from a bookshelf. 'Did you just want Billy's address or would a glance at the scrapbook I keep with cuttings from the local paper be of any use? There's an article about him when he was had up for burglary soon after he came home.'

We expressed our interest.

I had not expected there would be a photograph of the man and when Rauri had placed the scrapbook before us open at the relevant page I involuntarily gasped with shock. I found myself gripping Patrick's arm. This was the man, among others, who had tortured us.

Rauri was closely surveying us both. 'I take it this answers several questions and that he is well known to you. I've no doubt he's been involved in unsavoury crimes. He lives at number 11, Colliers Row. That's the wee lane that runs to one side of the Post Office.'

'It was his sons who found Jamie's body,' I managed to say.

'Aye, and afterwards they got a leathering for taking his boat without permission.'

Patrick was scanning through the account of the court case. 'The burglary was at the home of an old lady who had a heart attack when she realised there had been a break-in. She died. Douglas was found not guilty.'

'The police presented the case very badly,' Rauri said. 'On top of that an important witness said she couldn't be sure it was Billy she'd seen coming out of the house after all. There were whispers that she'd been intimidated. It wouldn't surprise me.' He cleared his throat. 'I admit I phoned the police myself just now - mostly because rumours of the fictional variety have to be quashed before they do damage. I hope the lads on the island have come to no harm.'

'None whatsoever,' Patrick assured him gravely.

'I have to say that you don't *necessarily* look like a man who could take on most of the front row of the local rugby team single-handed...'

'You don't play rugby by stealth.'

Rauri smiled. 'Well, I expect you would prefer to be on your way. If anyone asks I shall say I haven't seen you. That is, until you contact me and tell me that all is well and this horrible business is over.'

'I shall phone,' Patrick promised. 'Or if I'm unable to for any reason, Ingrid will.'

Ingrid was actually still feeling a little quivery after the business of the shots hitting the inflatable, only a matter of feet from us at the time. Understandably, I felt, I had raised the matter as I was driving us to Rauri's, that is, I had yelled at Patrick that I had had enough. My fear and anger had not been placated by the big, sunny smile he had given me and the way he had then gone on to point out that it were inches that mattered, not feet.

'Patrick, I mean it!' I had shouted, pounding the wheel with both fists, further rattled by my only just missing a cyclist who had shot out of a side street without first looking to see if it was safe to do so. Then we had arrived at Rauri's and any discussion had had to be postponed.

Now we were heading back to the car again and by this time I was shaking so much I couldn't get the key into the ignition. But I had to drive: Patrick, with a man-made right foot with no sensation in it finds driving conventional cars difficult, except for Land Rovers, which have big pedals - his Range Rover has been specially adapted.

I tried to take a grip on myself. '11, Colliers Row?'

'Just put me down at the Post Office. On foot's quieter.'

'I don't suppose he's at home though, do you?'

'Intuition tells me that he isn't. But someone might know where he is. Ingrid...'

'I'm sorry. Seeing that photograph brought it all back to me. And as I told you, since Brecon my nerve's not what it was.' I gave him what was probably a sickly smile.

'I think some of your fears are unfounded. The police have a murder inquiry to set up which will almost certainly soak up all available personnel. The corpse is over a day old so we can hardly be prime suspects even if they were on their way over to grab me again. For all we know the same hands-off policy is in operation as those in power know what we're trying to achieve and might still be banking on Plan B, the hitman, working. But Plan B isn't going to work - that has been admirably demonstrated already. So courage, my dear.'

He knows it aggravates me no end when he calls me 'my dear'. I said, 'Just shut up and give me a bloody good kiss.'

He leaned over and obliged and a couple of children who I

was suddenly aware of peeping at us through one of the rear windows hooted with laughter and ran off.

Finally, and it had been a bloody good kiss, I said, '*What* has been admirably demonstrated already?'

It seemed to have done Patrick good too. 'From where those shots were fired it was probably more difficult to hit the boat than me. But we mustn't kid ourselves that that's the end of it. He's under orders - which can't be disobeyed.'

I gazed into the vibrant grey eyes. 'I think you're trying to tell me that somehow or other you now know exactly who he is and he hates your guts and he's going to play a waiting game, getting a little more accurate every time.'

'Yes, no, yes and yes,' Patrick answered placidly.

I started the engine.

'Trust me,' he said, not for the first time.

Glad that we had not asked the Cranleys for permission to search the islands and had not been visible to anyone from this side of it we returned to the hotel and - my heart remaining in my mouth - checked out. The fire was still burning on the island, little more than a bonfire actually, a beacon, we knew, to attract attention. Jenny told us that the police were on their way in a borrowed launch of some kind as the boats in the immediate locality were either too small or temporarily unavailable. She was unaware of course that a murder inquiry would have to be set up as soon as contact was made with those marooned, taking for granted, that is, that the body had been discovered. One hoped so for Patrick had decided that to report our find was now unnecessary. As he said, 'If they haven't found it by now then Heaven help everyone round here!'

I had no real problem in finding somewhere to park in the high street but we ended up a couple of hundred yards from the Post Office. Patrick made no move to get out of the car though and sat still, obviously thinking.

'How far do we go?' he said after a few moments had

elapsed. 'Perhaps I've made a mistake here. Do I risk being clapped in irons again and report everything we've discovered so far to the police? There's been another murder now and if Douglas is guilty of all three then the long arm of the law has to eventually prevail, my being stitched up for Somerton's or no. What do you think? Do we take that risk? At least you could go home to the children. Where are they, by the way? Where did Carrie plan to take them?'

I decided it was easiest to answer the last question first. 'We thought it was better if I didn't know the exact location - and anyway she was planning to tour around. Obviously, she has my mobile number and I have hers. But I asked her only to use it in an emergency as I'm still not sure if calls from mobiles can be tapped.'

'The answer to that is probably yes, they can.'

'As to the rest I think we ought to make the decision after we've visited Colliers Row.'

'I agree.' He opened the car door. 'There's no need for you to come though.'

I got out. 'I'm coming.'

'If he's at home and as guilty as we think he is things might get rough.'

'I'll ring the doorbell, you go round the back.'

'Truly,' Patrick said absently, when we were making our way down the narrow street, 'Truly, when this is all over I shall heap you with jewels and spices from the East.'

'Some plants for the conservatory would be nice - orchids and palms and one of those wonderful scented climbers - a Stephanotis.'

'You shall have your very own jungle. We'll be able to lose Justin in it for weeks.'

'I miss the children too,' I said wistfully.

Patrick stopped dead. 'Do we turn round and go home then?'

Several seconds ticked by.

'No,' I whispered. 'We go and see if this murderer is at

home and if he is we'll take him to the police - after you've made him confess.'

Did I really want revenge that badly?

Yes, I did.

As the houses were terraced Patrick had to go to the far end of the street where we assumed there was some kind of access to the gardens at the rear. Assuming anything did not make for good planning though and I waited, fretting for his safety and pretending to read the small ads in the somewhat sooty window of a newsagents - the entire area tended to live up to its name - until I saw Patrick wave an affirmative. I counted slowly up to fifty and then walked the short distance along to Number 11 and rang the bell. There were no front gardens, the doors opened directly onto the pavement and I had already worked out evasive action if Douglas recognised me, turned nasty and tried to drag me inside.

No one came and I rang again.

Then I heard quiet footfalls inside and the door opened. It was Patrick.

'I don't think anyone's at home,' he said, gun in hand and already a third of the way up the stairs. But someone was coming down, a thin woman, pale and weak-looking, clutching the banister rail as though afraid she might fall. Patrick immediately stopped and lowered the weapon.

'It's all right,' he assured her. 'We won't hurt you.'

'I'm hurt enough,' she replied wearily, not appearing to have noticed the Smith and Wesson. 'I take it you want Billy. He's gone. Look where you want to if you don't believe me.'

'I'd believe you in any other circumstance,' Patrick said. 'More to the point is that I believe he'd threaten you to make you protect him.' He went past her and on upstairs.

'I do so hope the boys are with Hamish at his boatshed,' said the woman, slowly recommencing her downward journey. 'And haven't met their father anywhere in the village. He might just take them with him to spite me.'

I went up a few stairs and offered a hand. 'Are you really hurt? Did he hurt you?'

She wanly smiled her thanks but still kept a tight grip on the rail. 'No more than usual. And I pray to God it was the last I shall see of him. He said it was and they were the best words I've heard for a very long time.'

I had realised with a shock that this woman was not, as I had first assumed from her haggard appearance, Douglas's mother but his wife. 'Please let me make you a cup of tea.'

She reached the bottom of the stairs and gazed about her own hallway vaguely, as if not knowing quite where she was. 'That's really kind of you dear, but I shall be all right. I'll just sit down for a little while.'

I could not see a phone in the hall but did not want to leave her side to look for one in case she fell. At a snail's pace I guided her into the living room and settled her into one of the two battered armchairs. Everything was threadbare and worn but very, very clean: just like her.

'Gone,' Patrick reported, returning. 'Drawers and wardrobes showing every sign of having been ransacked for hasty packing.'

'This lady needs an ambulance,' I told him quietly. 'I think at the very least she's had a blow on the head and is concussed.'

'I'll do it.' He left the room again.

'Try the kitchen,' I called after him. I had decided against the tea: Mrs Douglas was in a worse state than I had first thought.

I drew up one of the dining chairs and sat at her side. 'Do you know where he's gone?'

'To hide, my dear.'

'So you know...'

'That he's made off with the money poor Jamie was looking after? He told me that much.' She was silent for perhaps half a minute and then said, 'He'd always hoped for what he called The Big One and he said that when that happened he'd

213

be off to sun himself on the other side of the world. It was one of the worst days of my life when he came back from Wales. I'd thought that was his Big One, whatever it was. We were just starting to get our lives back together, the boys and I and then back he came.' Alarming me greatly, she then suddenly sank back in the chair, eyes closed.

'Mrs Douglas?' I grasped a thin shoulder. 'Mrs Douglas!'

'I'm all right,' she murmured. 'Really all right. Happy too. He's gone and I shall never see him again.'

Feeling very guilty badgering her with questions I nevertheless asked, 'Will you be able to give the police any idea where he might head for? Only they'll be watching at airports.'

Her eyes opened wide. 'I don't want them to find him! Let him go to South America or wherever. And stay there.'

Patrick had re-entered the room while she was saying this. Softly, he said, 'I'm afraid they won't look at it like that. But he'll go to prison for a very long time.'

'What, for just taking some money ?'

Out of her view I shook my head emphatically at Patrick. There was no point in adding to her trauma by mentioning murder.

'I'm afraid the money was the proceeds of serious crime,' he simply said.

'Well, that wouldn't surprise me at all,' Mrs Douglas said. 'The Wales thing no doubt was involved with crime. He enjoyed that, I could tell. He *said* he had been helping at some kind of adventure centre and the boys were really interested but he wouldn't tell them any more. Billy has always enjoyed the mountains. And caves. He said there was a big cave there. That's why he liked it so much. He actually said he'd always wanted to live in a cave.' Her eyes closed again, her voice slurring. 'Perhaps that's where he's gone, may God curse his black soul - back to his wretched cave.'

It was then, staring at her, that I knew we would have to return to Brecon.

In a split second everything had changed. The emphasis of our investigation had already shifted, of course, for we were no longer engaged on an investigation but a manhunt. And, as Patrick said to me later, it was now a lot more personal.

'I have a particular yearning,' he confided when we had returned to the car, leaving Mrs Douglas in the care of a friend, her neighbour.

'For what?' I asked.

'My Range Rover. Where did you say you left it?'

'In Kensington. With my friend Trudy. Or rather, I left it in her drive and put a note through the door.'

'Assuming that she hadn't moved since you'd last been in touch with her do you reckon it's still there?'

This banter was being achieved on auto: his brain was really engaged on tactics, probably, if I was honest, of the violent variety.

'Possibly not if Special Branch caught up with it. I deliberately left it there so I could, as far as they were concerned, disappear. Only, as you know, I failed.'

'They must have been right on your heels if they caught up with you at Roehampton.'

'It crossed my mind that Mrs Somerton's phone might have been tapped.'

'Um.' He rested his head back, still weaving strategy.

An ambulance came speeding down the high street and turned into Colliers Row.

'Where to?' I asked, hating just sitting there, a sitting duck. 'Kensington?'

'No, I suggest we get rid of this car and fly down. Ingrid...'

'Let's discuss plans when we're moving,' I interrupted, hand on the key in the ignition.

'No!' The command was like the crack of a whip.

'Sorry,' I murmured.

Patrick was gazing around warily. He even opened the window and carefully eyed the pavement and gutter on his side of the car. 'Don't apologise. It's my fault. Here we are parked outside a derelict garage and the two cottages on the other side of the road are empty. I've been appallingly careless.'

'You said you thought you'd be safe as long as we're together,' I said, skin crawling.

'With such high stakes, who knows?' he murmured.

Without moving overmuch he reached with a long arm and took my rucksack from the back seat and then the small bag I had bought for him, the former of which he handed to me. 'When I give the word leave the car gently and without shutting the door and run like hell away from the town. Take cover somewhere and don't come out until I tell you it's safe to do so.'

I never question this kind of order. But I did say, 'I hope you'll be doing something similar.'

He ignored the remark. 'Okay. Off you go.'

I went. What had he seen?

Behind me though, I was expecting to hear a very large bang.

Did one yell at people to take cover? No point, there was hardly anyone in sight.

I sprinted for about fifty yards and then saw a narrow alleyway between two rows of cottages on the opposite side of the road and ducked into it. I stopped and turned to peer back along the street, one side of my face pressed to the edge of the wall; cold, comfortingly solid Scottish granite.

Absolutely nothing happened. A few people were going about their business, the church clock struck the half hour, a black and white cat streaked across the road: it was slightly surreal, like the song about a Lowry painting; *matchstick men and matchstick cats and dogs*.

A woman came out of the front door of the nearest cottage and walked towards me, away from the town centre. As she passed me she said, 'You all right, hen?'

'Fine,' I told her.

I began to wonder if this was some kind of ruse on Patrick's part to get rid of me for my own sake and safety and he intended to drive away without me. But the car remained where it was and I couldn't see if anyone was sitting in it.

'Sod this for a game of soldiers,' I muttered and cautiously stepped out of my place of refuge. From this new position I could see that two feet were sticking out from beneath the car. They then went from sight, a head emerged, still at ground level, and some kind of utterance must have issued from it as a man who had been loafing nearby swiftly removed himself.

We *were* talking about a bomb-scare then.

Five more minutes ticked by.

At last, Patrick stood up on the pavement side and appeared to be dusting himself off. Then he rapidly went from view again. I rather got the impression he had thrown himself flat. I ran back and as I reached the car a shot ricocheted off it with an angry buzzing sound. After also throwing myself down I shouted under the car, 'Is this thing safe?'

'I hadn't quite finished checking,' was the reply from the pavement side, not shouting. 'There might be some kind of tilt mechanism device in the boot.'

'You look, I'll stop him firing.'

'Ingrid ...!'

I stood up and, stepping over the worst of the litter, walked across the forecourt of the derelict filling-station buildings from where I was convinced the shot had come. I zig-zagged, my heart pounding in my chest. Nearest to me was the heavily vandalised kiosk, the windows smashed, broken glass crunching and tinkling under my feet as I approached. I knew instinctively that no one was inside it: there was no cover whatsoever and I had seen no movement within.

A shot banged into a metal advertising sign concreted into the ground a couple of feet from me, one of those that revolve, setting it whirring around. Automatically, I ducked and then ran towards a building at the rear that had probably been a small car showroom. There was a crash from inside and then a shot smashed a security light, high up on the roof.

It had been fired from a weapon of much smaller calibre somewhere behind me.

I went to earth behind a couple of battered oil drums that were amongst a pile of dumped rubbish and broken pallets, realised who else had entered the fray and got out fast, running back towards the car. There was no real expectation on my part that I would be shot in the back but a string of faded plastic bunting descended on me as I went beneath it, like a red, white and blue snake, slithered down my back, tried to trip me up and was then left behind. Before me, the road was empty, both of traffic and the hired car, the first phenomenon by coincidence, the second because Patrick had driven it away for short distance. I flung myself behind the wheel and then noticed the blood.

'Drive!' Patrick said. 'It's only a scratch.'

When we were a couple of miles in the direction of Inverness I tersely said, 'That's what they always say when they're kissing their horse goodbye while decoratively bleeding to death into the prairie.' I pulled into a lay-by. 'Is it a plaster then or a life-support machine?'

'Probably something in between,' he replied, trying to assess the damage in the vanity mirror.

A ricochet had sent a fragment of stone slicing across his neck, about an inch from his jugular vein. The small wound had bled quite a lot, as injuries to the head always do, soaking the collar of his shirt. I cleaned it up with tissues and lotion from the first-aid kit that was in my bag and applied a dollop of antiseptic ointment and a dressing.

At least, I told myself as we continued on our journey to the airport, no one could shoot as well as that on purpose.

'There *could* have been a bomb on board,' I ventured after a long reflective silence. 'You were quite right to take precautions.'

'Yes, but it wouldn't have fitted the pattern,' Patrick said. 'Unfortunately, what followed did. You rattled him though with your crazy bravado. Did you hear the crash? I reckon he tripped over something as he got the hell out of there.'

'So I get a gong as well as plants for the conservatory?'

'If you like. One of those you bang when dinner's ready.'

We grinned at one another.

I did not ask if he would have taken a risk and not checked the car over if I had not been with him, observing instead, 'A little closer this time.'

'Orders are orders. And if he's put under such pressure from above that...' He broke off and shrugged. 'The sooner we get rid of this vehicle the better.' He was keeping practically constant surveillance in his side mirror for anyone following us. 'You heard what Mrs Douglas said. There's every chance he's literally gone to ground.'

'He doesn't have a car,' I reminded him.

'He soon will have though. He's got the cash so he'll pick up something that's roadworthy as soon as he reaches a place where he's not known. I'm guessing but I reckon he'll take the train to Glasgow and then get himself some wheels.'

'It's possible he can't drive.'

'Yes, he can. I'm almost a hundred percent sure the bastard was driving the Land Rover when we were first picked up.'

'It would probably exorcise all our ghosts if we went back,' I remarked.

He gave me a wry smile. 'Are they *our* ghosts?'

'Nameless fears then.'

'Daws always said that one of your most valuable assets was perception.' Patrick's attention returned to the side mirror. 'Here comes the ambulance with Mrs Douglas. She must be bad, it's the full flashing blue lights and siren scenario.'

'I'm sure I saw that one go down the high street when I was waiting for you to finish checking out the car.'

We had reached a long straight stretch of road, a modern section that Jenny had told me had replaced an accident black spot and only been recently opened. I wished I was really on holiday and able to enjoy the sunshine and walk on a mountain and smell the cool, green scents of the pine forest.

The ambulance was swiftly gaining on us and for some reason I speeded up.

'Better let it go by,' Patrick said.

Yes, perhaps I was now getting the heebie-jeebies about absolutely everything. Obediently I slowed slightly and pulled right over to the left-hand side of the road. Moments later the other vehicle howled passed. Moments later again it had braked hard right in front of us. The back of it loomed dead ahead and I slammed on the brakes.

'It's a military ambulance!' Patrick yelled. 'Go! Go! Go!'

I accelerated again, pulling round to the right but men in combat gear and balaclavas had already poured from the rear doors and someone flung a Stinger across the road. The car ploughed straight into it and we were both thrown forward as all four tyres punctured. All the air left my lungs as the seat-belt did what it was supposed to do so I had no breath to do anything when the driver's door was yanked open, the seat-belt deftly released and I was hauled out. With an arm like an iron bar across my throat I was manhandled towards the ambulance.

They had unwisely utilised a one-to-one tactic with Patrick too and he had felled his attacker using methods that demonstrated the extent of his anger. The next one had a stun gun of some kind and used it and Patrick went down as though pole-axed. It was pointless to wonder why he hadn't drawn the gun: these were soldiers.

Bundled effortlessly aboard I sat where plonked down and a man who had already been inside the vehicle pushed up my sleeve while someone else held my arm still. He had really lovely green eyes, I found myself thinking as the needle slid painlessly in.

Chapter Thirteen

Consciousness returned with three words going round and round in my head; escape and evade, escape and evade. Special forces training when I had first started to work for D12 had been strong on those aspects and the softly spoken Marine with a fondness for pink marshmallows who had shown me how to cut people's throats had emphasized the importance of my apparently admired perception and the awareness of one's surroundings.

'Some folk notice nothing,' he had said. 'You can start a small war under their noses and it simply doesn't register.'

I thought how Duncreggan had gone about its everyday business under those very circumstances.

'Learn to really use your eyes and ears,' he had gone on to say. 'And nose.' He had then clamped two large hands over my ears and ordered me to close my eyes. 'What can you smell now?'

We had actually been sitting in the mess at the time.

'Chips,' I had told him. 'And tomcats.'

'You're right. There's a stray. The bloody thing gets in all the time.' He had then bellowed with laughter.

My eyes were covered and I could smell something now. It was not pleasant; an all-pervading staleness, like a long-closed cupboard containing old mops and floor cloths. I lay still, using my training. I appeared to be lying on a bed, or rather *in* bed, I was covered by something, and in the distance could hear the ceaseless hum of traffic. It was impossible to detect whether I was alone in the room, certainly there were no sounds close by that would suggest I had company, such as someone else's breathing.

My limbs felt heavy, as though weighted down - I had already tried to move a hand slightly and surreptitiously under the covers. It could be physical weakness brought on by the drug they had used. I decided that nothing could be gained by just lying there, extricated my right arm from the covers and touched what was over my eyes. At least, that had been the plan, in the event I clouted myself heavily on the face with my own hand, now a weirdly limp object that nevertheless had a life of its own. But I managed to get hold of what was over the upper part of my face and pulled it off. It was not tied in place and seemed to be one corner of a sheet.

Light burst blindingly and painfully into my eyes and I left the hand where it was and managed to shift it a little so as to shield them slightly. Then, after a few minutes and during which time I tried to programme everything in advance, I made a huge effort to sit up. It was a mistake, I only succeed in flopping over and ended up folded into a kind of C-shape, my head over the side of the bed.

'Shit,' I muttered, squinting at grubby carpet tiles.

I remembered an occasion when I had taken Pirate to the vet and she had had to be sedated for an X-Ray. Afterwards, for a while, she had been just like this. After an exhausting struggle I got back roughly into the position I had been before, my right hand again shielding my eyes. I would just have to be patient.

After what seemed like hours my eyes were still not yet getting used to the light, the bright light of a sunny day and my insides were telling me that it was not the same day as the one when the needle had gone into my vein. I was actually very hungry indeed and my mouth was so dry my tongue felt like leather.

Gradually, I began to see my surroundings, firstly through my fingers and then more clearly when I had achieved dragging my right hand out of the way with the left, which seemed for some reason to have more going for it. I saw a rectangle of window; metal-framed, limp green curtains on either side that looked as though they were never drawn. The view through the dirty glass was no more inspiring, sky and what appeared to be top of a brick wall.

On regaining consciousness I had hoped that Patrick would be nearby but now, struggling to lift my head, I was able to see that the room was small and I was alone. I had to admit that it was not the right kind of place to safely confine an ex-special operations soldier. In other words there were no bars on the windows, steel rings bolted to the walls or even locks on the bedroom door.

The room was however at least a hundred feet above the ground. I made this discovery some time later - my watch had been removed so I had no idea of the time - after I must have become unconscious again, or slept, for a while. My limbs were returning to normal quickly now and after considerable effort I succeeded in sitting up on the edge of the bed, discovering in the process that I was fully dressed, and then lurched, leaning on the wall for support and thus making a somewhat roundabout journey, to the window.

I was somewhere near the top of a high-rise block of flats. What I had thought was the top of a brick wall, before my eyes had focused properly, was actually a utilities building or lift-housing structure on the roof of the next block, round to the right. In all directions, as far as the eye could see, stretched a city. It could be anywhere as there were no landmarks I recognised.

The door of the room actually led into another, a sitting room with a tiny kitchen off at one side, a bathroom at the other. All the furniture was utilitarian, similar, now I came to think of it, to that in the remand centre at Oxford. Which all pointed to this flat being a Special Branch safe house. Or prison, depending on the circumstances.

I went into the bathroom and had a carefully rationed drink of water. Horrible side-effects can manifest themselves if you fill yourself up with liquids when you have been drugged. I then stripped and washed as best I could in cold water - there was no hot - using the hard fragment of soap on offer that looked as though it had been around since the Boer War. The towel had the same kind of provenance and I wrapped it around myself- it was just long enough - and went back into the bedroom to see if my rucksack, containing clean underwear, was there. It wasn't. I got dressed again.

The kitchen was not very clean and seemed to be the source of the smell. I hunted around and soon ascertained that the drawers contained no cutlery except for one anciently sticky plastic teaspoon wearing fluff so I would have to abandon, or at least postpone, my first project; trying to pick the lock on the outside door. There were, however, and more immediately practical, stale digestive biscuits and an opened pot of jam in one wall cupboard, tea, coffee, sugar and three mugs in another and, in a tiny fridge that I had only just noticed behind the door, some milk that was only thinking of going off and part of a sliced white loaf with just one green furry blob on it.

A feast then, despite the lack of a kettle.

I carried out an in-depth raid on the remaining mostly empty cupboards and was rewarded by finding the cause of most of the smell, a dead mouse - it had probably starved to death and I flushed it down the loo with all due sympathy - several old newspapers, some *Playboy* magazines, a battered saucepan and an American paperback entitled *Feng Shui for the Terminally Ill*. I tossed back everything but the saucepan and soon had some water boiling on the two-ring electric cooker.

It was important to continue being careful and I consumed just one slice of bread with jam spooned on to it - the spoon had only reluctantly yielded up its cargo under a running tap - and I took a mug of tea into the sitting room - spilling some, my co-ordination was still bad - to sip the rest of it slowly, sitting in one of the uncomfortable armchairs.

I could no longer stave off the misery.

We had failed. Abysmally.

Not only that - I was convinced that the deadline had now passed, or as good as, and the political scandal had been resurrected with Patrick back in prison accused of murder. That

224

the Scottish police might now collect enough evidence against Billy Douglas for the case to be dropped or Patrick would be tried and found not guilty was immaterial, the conspiracy had succeeded. This was not something about which I would be permitted to write a book.

There was every chance too, I told myself grimly, that Patrick was dead and that Plan B had been put into operation. I sat and thought about it for a long time and my tea got cold.

One hour blurred into the next and it was getting dark, around ten thirty perhaps, when I heard a key in the lock of the outside door. I was still sitting in the chair but had had another couple of slices of bread and jam and made myself some fresh tea. Huddled in one of the thin blankets from the bed - the flat had a chill all of its own after countless unheated winters and I couldn't open any of the windows to let in fresh, warm air - I stayed quite still.

The living room door opened and the light was switched on.

The man; late twenties, dark, spiked-up hair, scruffy clothes, said nothing, noted in passing that I was still alive, dropped a couple of newspapers on a low table and placed on top of them a small paper carrier-bag. He then rapidly walked from room to room, checking that all was as it should be and then went away again, slamming the outside door. I heard him whistling tunelessly, the sound echoing, as, pre-sumably, he waited for the lift and then, but for the endless hum of traffic, there was silence. I found myself thinking how odd it was to have this all-pervading silence in such a place. Was the block otherwise empty and awaiting demolition and I would be demolished with it?

There were large photographs of Patrick on the front pages of both the papers, *The Guardian* and *The Daily Telegraph*. I dragged my gaze from them for a moment and looked at the publication dates; Thursday 17th August. I had been uncon-scious for getting on for forty-eight hours and no doubt had been topped-up with the drug during that time.

The first paper had a picture of Patrick in handcuffs, looking a strange mixture of sozzled, no doubt due to being doped, and downright dangerous, the headline; TOP ARMY OFFI-CER ON MURDER CHARGE, the other had an official picture of him in uniform taken when he had started his most recent post; CO-ORDINATOR OF DEFENCE STUDIES ARRESTED.

He was alive then. I cried and went on reading when I was able.

Both papers had similar brief accounts; obviously cribbed from an official handout. He had been taken into custody while on holiday in Scotland, no mention of wife or family, following a police chase of several miles as he had resisted arrest. A member of the arresting team had been injured, in view of which the decision had been made to hold the suspect in the garrison town of Colchester. The arrest had been the result of months of painstaking investigation into the death of an officer in the Anti-Terrorist Branch, Commander Keith Somerton, who had drowned while on holiday...

I stopped reading. I could have made a much better job of writing the articles myself, lies included. They were even trying to hang Jamie Kirkland's murder around his neck as well and were vaguely hinting that the discovery of his body had provided some kind of turning point in the police inquiry.

All this had relegated the Leader of the Opposition's conference speech to Page 4 of *The Guardian* and the bottom of the front page of the *Daily Telegraph*. Both papers ran other long articles about the previous Home Secretary's plans for covert police powers, *The Guardian* reporting that the opposition was in disarray. The politicians of that party who were prepared to be interviewed, who included the Shadow Defence Minister, said that the whole thing was cooked-up and absolutely preposterous. No one seemed to believe them.

But at least Patrick was alive. Was it intended that he should remain so?

I suddenly remembered and investigated the carrier bag,

the smells emanating from which were telling me that that it contained a carry-out - Chinese and tepid by now. Ravenous, I decided to ignore my inner warnings that it might be doctored in some way and ate the lot. Doctored or not I fell asleep very suddenly afterwards and when I awoke it was the next morning and the front door was again being unlocked. I peered sleepily and no doubt sullenly at my visitor from my blanket nest, surrounded by the detritus of my late-night meal.

A different man; ginger, balding, short, fat, reeking of sweat, dropped my rucksack on the floor, followed it with what looked like my car keys, smiled in a patronising way that made my blood seethe and said, 'I should scarper while there's still wheels on the motor, darlin'. It's not the kind of place to leave a shiny runner like that around.'

For a moment I actually contemplated killing him thereby adding his malodorous presence to that of the unfortunate mouse. This might have been reflected in my expression for when I threw the blanket aside and rose to my feet he took a couple of steps backwards.

'Relax, you idiot,' I said crossly. 'And tell me where I am.' But I had already guessed correctly from his East End accent and he confirmed it. London.

It took me twenty seconds to find my hairbrush and use it on my tangled locks, gather my things together and make my exit, leaving whoever he was to do the housekeeping. I could still smell him in the lift on the way down. My mobile phone had not been confiscated and I rang Carrie's number, keeping an eye on the Range Rover, which as far as I could see only had one small scratch on the near side.

We exchanged fulsome greetings and after establishing that everything was all right and the children safe and well and they were all staying on a farm near the sea in Cornwall I asked Carrie if she had seen the newspapers that morning.

'It's all over the telly too and I'm really gutted about it,' she replied. 'But they've got it all wrong, haven't they? I mean, you weren't *both* in Scotland - Patrick had already been arrested.'

'It's all a load of rubbish,' I said, not wanting her to air too many doubts as I had a good idea there were eavesdroppers. 'I'm on my way home. I don't want to miss Katie's birthday in two day's time.'

'And then of course it's Justin's the week after,' she said after only the slightest pause. 'Katie wants a Mother Clanger.'

'A mother *what*?'

'Clanger. Don't you remember *The Clangers*, that children's series on TV? You can get soft toys now and when you press their tummies they make a lovely hooting noise. There's Major Clanger too. I almost bought Patrick one before all this terrible business started but didn't quite dare to.' She giggled, I chuckled too and we took our leave of one another in girlie fashion.

Carrie had not felt like giggling, was and still is, an actress. The children think she's wonderful for when she reads to them she takes the part of all the characters in the book, giving them different voices. She can also think on her feet and we have made her a party to the Gillard codes. Therefore she had realised that something was still going on and it was the reason why I wasn't immediately going home - Katie's birthday is really in March - and had responded in kind to tell me she understood: Justin's is in December.

The interior of the car smelt of cigarette smoke that did not quite mask the sweaty odour of the man who had just driven it and I opened the windows wide and switched the fan on. Glancing up at the block of flats I could see that there were hardly any curtains at the windows. If I had been left to die there no one would have known.

With a heavy heart I put the key in the ignition. But I did not turn it, bloody-mindedly getting out of the vehicle again to slide beneath it and meticulously check everything in the way I had been taught. I checked everything, fore and aft.

Right now though I was in a frame of mind that could have calmly faced being blown to smithereens. There did not seem to be much of a future.

I was going to Wales.

It was the only thing left that I could do. Perhaps I was only really undertaking the trip to ease my conscience, so that I could tell myself in the future that there was nothing else I could have done. Commonsense was shouting at me that my real responsibility lay with the children and I was being stupid, if not downright pathetic, to even contemplate carrying on.

I desperately needed someone of his calibre but had to continue not involving James Carrick, not now that a court case was even more likely. Terry Meadows, a one-time member of the D12 team, was now a family man with four-month-old Hannah, which ruled him out. Steve, who had also worked for the department for a while, I knew to be in the States. I did not know anyone else whom I could ask for support.

As I drove away the inner coward comforted me with the thought that if I went back to the area I knew so well near Bryn Glas, a hill at the southernmost boundary of the Brecon Beacons National Park, and had a look round I would not necessarily be committing myself to a proper search for Billy Douglas. Yes, I would go there but not to get involved with underground workings, deep tunnels with slime-hung walls and, overhead, gobbets of spiders' eggs. There were subterranean echoes I had heard there that had been like the voices of the forgotten long-dead.

At least though I could drive in a westerly direction for quite a long way without having to make any decisions. I had discovered that that I was not far from Ealing so headed for Reading. After Newbury I would have to go in the direction of Salisbury for home, or Swindon for Bristol and the Severn Bridge.

Still I hesitated, pulling off to top up with fuel when I did not really need to, killing time by stopping for lunch even though I was not hungry. Then, finally, I could delay no longer and, sick at heart, turned off for Bristol.

Patrick, I love you.

Morlais Hill, not far from Merthyr Tydfil, has the stumpy ruins of a castle on its summit and, as Patrick had remarked when he had first seen it, had been a good strategic position ever since people had first started throwing rocks at one another. Those at the school for terrorists, housed within the workings and out-buildings of the disused mine, had set up an observation post concealed beneath camouflage netting in the lee of the one remaining tower, only about thirty feet of which was still standing. It was from there that we had been spotted as we explored a ruined farmhouse on the slopes of Bryn Glas, situated to the north across a valley. We had not intended to be captured.

I had already made up my mind that I would stay right away from all the pubs in the area as I had not the slightest desire to bump into Billy Douglas by accident, assuming that he had come to Wales at all. It was just about the only resolution I had made: I had no plans or strategy, nothing could be decided until I actually arrived. That was what I was telling myself anyway, in fact I hadn't the first idea of what I was going to do.

So with Morlais Hill on the horizon I drove on.

Ten minutes or so later my mobile rang and I stopped in the next lay-by to answer it.

'I know when your children's birthdays are,' said Daws' voice.

'There was always this nagging feeling that someone was listening in,' I informed him coolly.

'It wasn't me. I've just merely rung your home to try to discover your whereabouts and a young lady informed me that you, the nanny and the children were all on your way there as it was Katie's birthday in a couple of day's time. Not so.'

I supposed I owed him some kind of explanation. 'That

must have been Babs. She helps with the housework. Carrie must have rung her - they're staying on a farm - to tell her they were on their way home and she assumed that meant me as well. Either that or Carrie deliberately told her that in case other people start asking questions. Carrie's aware that I'm not going straight home and the birthday story was how I made that known to her. I still don't know if someone's over-hearing so I'm not going to tell you where I'm going either.'

There were a few seconds dead silence while he processed all this. Then he said, 'I'll have a check done and ring you back.' The line went dead.

Damn you, I thought. I'm still not going to meekly divulge any plans I might make.

Patrick and I had once stopped for refreshment at the Brecon Mountain Railway Centre and it seemed a good venue for decision time. I was just locking up the vehicle when my phone rang for the second time and I got back in it to take the call. It was Daws again.

'The good news is that no one's listening, but there's a tag-ging device on your car,' he reported.

I'm afraid I swore.

'It's probably been put there for your own safety.'

'Balls.'

'I saw the Lieutenant-Colonel this morning,' he went on hurriedly. It always rattles him slightly when women swear. 'He's well considering the circumstances. He thinks you ought to go home too.'

'He's a better liar than you are,' I retorted. 'And I seem to remember that you said you could act when you were hand-ed some reliable evidence. The Inverness police might be in possession of some now Somerton's cousin's body's been dis-covered. Why don't you ask them?'

'You mean with regard to someone called Billy Douglas your husband mentioned? A warrant has been made out for his arrest in connection with an assault carried out on his wife. She's in hospital with a hair-line fracture of the skull. It would appear he travelled by train to Glasgow. Enquiries have revealed he then bought a second-hand car.'

'You've just confirmed what Patrick had guessed already. Do you have a description and the number of the car?'

'No. Ingrid, you simply *mustn't* go after this man. Rest assured that the police are on to him. You have my word that this stupid piece of publicity will go no further if there is found to be a case against him in connection with the Somerton murder.'

'Resignations?' I demanded to know. 'Exposure of the shabby character assassination of Patrick in order to secure political gain? Full public apologies? Somehow, I doubt it.'

'You have my word,' he said again.

I was silent for a few seconds and then said, 'You wouldn't understand but sometimes ghosts have to be laid.'

I rang off and then searched the car in all the places I hadn't already looked for explosive devices until I found the minute piece of electronic wizardry. I stamped it flat and put the remains in a nearby litter bin.

Later, I drove up to the dam at Pontsticill reservoir and paused to gaze north, over the water. To my right, behind me, was the peak of Twynau Gwynion, to the left Bryn Glas, in the distance the Beacons themselves, the three largest; Pen y Fan, Cribyn, Corn Du, towering from the blue haze of late afternoon. Somerton had used all this area as a training ground and it had provided good cover in more ways than one. Local people and visitors seeing his 'pupils' would have assumed them to be a *bona fide* military unit or police under training.

I had sat in the restaurant at the railway centre and thought it all through.

Perception then. I drove all the way around the reservoir and stopped and got out a few times, feeling the need to let the atmosphere of the place sink into me. Then I left the car altogether and climbed a small hill with twin peaks that looked like the knees of Bryn Glas if the hill had been a figure of a person sitting down with feet drawn up. Perhaps Tim was right and you had to listen to the wind. I found myself thinking about him.

At the top of the southernmost hill - they were both around one hundred feet high - I stood and looked around. Mountains, lakes and forest lay before me like a gigantic patchwork quilt. A kite hovered on the light breeze and the air was so clear I could easily see the way its forked tail twitched as it steadied itself in the gentle movements of the air.

If I had expected some kind of spiritual revival I was disappointed. I resolved that if I ever met Tim Shandy again I would tell him that all I got when I asked the wind what I should do was an inexplicable and sudden boredom with the view and an impatient desire to get on with what I had set out to do.

Several years had elapsed since my previous visit and I got lost in the maze of winding country lanes to the south of the summit of Bryn Glas. Things had changed; trees had been cut down, the roads had been improved in places. In the end I followed my nose and at last found myself turning into that narrow steep track. There had been a lot of rain and the track was washed out in places with deep ruts. After about ten minutes and a final steep climb I drove into the large flat area in front of the mine entrance. I remembered it as having been a bare kind of place, covered with granite aggregate, like railway ballast.

The ballast was probably still there but nature had gone a long way towards claiming back the area and it was now a sea of wild flowers, rough grass and seedling trees. The house that had been there that Somerton had used for his own living quarters had gone but I had expected that, as enormous damage had been done to the ground floor by an explosion during the final showdown. There were a few reminders; short lengths of police incident tape crushed into the ground, broken glass and a few pieces of splintered wood, something that looked like the remains of a sock.

A long wooden shed directly in front of the mine entrance had also been demolished. It had been used for lectures and for storing equipment and from there, through a false back in one of the built-in cupboards, one had entered a well-lit tunnel. Now it had all gone, razed to the ground, loaded into skips and taken away and a padlocked metal grille placed across the dark cavity. Several notices had been put up: KEEP OUT. DANGEROUS ROCKFACES AND UNDERGROUND WORKINGS.

There were no cars other than mine in sight. To the left of me the open area sloped away gently downhill and there was a view through trees of distant hills, to my right an enormous pile of mine waste. I remembered I had been told that this section of the workings had originally been a coal mine dating back a very long time and the whole complex, which covered a huge area, had been re-opened and extended at some stage to extract good quality slate.

I stayed in the Range Rover, making sure that all the doors were locked. I did not want to get out. It was very quiet, a few birds twittered, the sound of distant flowing water: that was all. I sat still, moving only to open my window a little wider. The biggest problem was that I was now completely unarmed, the Smith and Wesson no longer a companionable weight in my bag.

After Patrick had been taken away Somerton himself had escorted me into the underground complex. He had been wildly elated at our capture - real trophies to display - and right from the start made it plain that Patrick, in his own words, would 'show them a thing or two', *them*, of course being the international terrorists in the making he soon expected to arrive. Somerton had been very proud of the set-up, which had been mostly his idea and he had explained it to me in some detail. The part of my brain that seems to be able to carry on functioning entirely unaffected by emotion or severe shock had taken it all in. Then he had shoved me through a door and locked it behind me. My home, a cell.

I had not seen Patrick for a week except for that same night when he had been brought in and left on the floor of my cell for about ten minutes. He had not known me and was having convulsions. Electric shock torture. I had been told that they would not do *that* again to him if I co-operated. Co-operation entailed lecturing the 'students' on the British security services.

They had arrived and I had lectured them, privately amazed that I knew so much about the subject. I gave them nothing secret or sensitive, nothing that strictly speaking could not have been gleaned from a good library. Over the days that followed I had given them some history; the Burgess and Maclean saga, Suez, even though neither would be of much use to them, following that with the structure and workings of MI6 - remembered mostly from a series of articles in *The Times* - the Peter Wright case, rumblings at GCHQ. From there we had gone on to MI5 and the weapons issued to the various police forces. To pad things out a little I had started to correct their grammar, stemming the complaints, mostly from the Europeans, that if they could not express themselves clearly they would immediately become suspect if they ever worked undercover in the UK. I am still not sure why they accepted this but they did.

Patrick, meanwhile, had been assiduously starved and beaten and when thought to be sufficiently cowed and weak had been given to the students as a servant. He had cleaned their rooms - for everything had been run on oddly military lines and there were inspections - done their washing and ironed their shirts. And subverted them.

The course had been all about subversion, ideal knowledge for the overthrowing of weak governments in unstable countries, especially in Africa, the seizure of power together with land, valuable assets, businesses and any existing criminal organisations. Opposing factions in such countries are often in the market-place, offering rich rewards to those with skills in espionage, sabotage and murder. So Patrick had subverted his masters, befriended them and even though I might be biased it is not many young men- and some of these were little more than boys - who do not find in Patrick something to respect and admire. When the loutish instructors, all criminals of some kind, bullied them, to put it mildly, they went to Patrick with their grievances and he sympathised and offered advice, mostly of the keep your temper variety and soon had virtually the whole lot eating out of his hand.

Less admirable to most people but ideal in this situation is Patrick's ability to out-Herod Herod in matters of one-to-one armed and unarmed combat. Handed over to Adjit, an Egyptian instructor of formidable *mien* and who is most easily described as depraved, as a plaything to provide a bored Somerton with a little light entertainment, Patrick had comprehensively slaughtered him in front of everyone using fairly depraved methods. This still gives me nightmares. Somerton had immediately lost face and had been forced to go along with Patrick's account of their having been partners who had disagreed and he himself had suffered Somerton's revenge. Somerton had had no choice but to 'reinstate' him.

From then on the Anti-Terrorist Branch Commander's bid for heady career advancement had been doomed.

It was now mid-afternoon and I realised I had been living with my memories for the best part of an hour. I started the car and drove right up to the entrance to the mine, got out leaving the door open and inspected the grille, which was actually a hinged gate. There was yet another large KEEP OUT sign attached to it. I peered into the darkness beyond. The sound of running water was actually emanating from the tunnel, something quite new to me, and I wondered if some of the old workings were flooded. Both chain and padlock were in good condition and it might have been my imagination in the poor light close to the rock-face but the padlock looked as though it had been recently oiled. It was securely fastened although there was plenty of room between the metal bars for someone to put their arms through and unlock it from the other side.

I would have to buy some boots, bolt-cutters and a much better flashlight.

And another knife.

Chapter Fourteen

I dared not delay. The tracking device had to be courtesy of Special Branch and if they decided to act on what they now knew; that I was in Wales, then every minute was precious. It was dusk when I returned, on foot this time and from a slightly different direction approaching roughly from the south without using the main track at all. As I wished to travel as inconspicuously as possible I had left the car at a cottage about a mile away where I had booked in to stay bed and breakfast. Being without it made me feel even more vulnerable but so far I was succeeding quite well in shoving all matters concerning personal safety right to the back of my mind. Otherwise I would simply get in the car and leave the area, never to return.

All seemed the same as earlier that afternoon. The chain on the metal grille gate was exactly as I had found and left it. Thankfully it was not very thick and the bolt-cutters, which were heavy and had been expensive, made short work of it. I concealed them in a space between tumbled boulders, opened the gate praying that the hinges would not squeak, which they did, loudly, and went in. I re-arranged the chain and padlock so to the casual eye they would appear undisturbed, switched on my new flash lamp and with extreme caution went down the entrance passage.

I knew I should not be doing this alone: if I slipped and broke a leg I would probably be dead before anyone found me. All I had with me in the way of extra equipment was my torch as a spare source of illumination and the knife I had bought, the latter really only as a morale booster.

Almost immediately and sooner than I expected the tunnel widened considerably and I arrived at what had been a control point, a booth where Somerton had mounted a round-the-clock guard. It appeared to be much as I remembered, even the electrical control panel was still in situ, the rows of switches now all in the off-position. The labels were all there too, although some had started to curl and peel off in the damp. Curious, I shone my lamp full on the panel and flicked down a row of three marked LOBBY. Two overhead lights some twenty feet apart came on, another did not.

I switched off my torch. In front of me were the three tunnels that had been known as Areas One, Two and Three, numbered, oddly, from right to left. Area One had contained accommodation, the canteen and other lecture rooms where I had eventually been permitted to move about more or less freely, Area Three on my left, a ghastly dank passageway that gradually sloped deeply underground and I had an idea finally ended up under water, was where Patrick had been locked up and the central Tunnel, Area Two, led to the old slate cavern that had been used for live-firing exercises, one of the best war-games set-ups I had ever encountered, presumably paid for by British tax-payers.

Why was it possible after all this time to switch on the power? I checked the panel again but other than the ones I had just used all the switches *were* in the off-position. Torch batteries do not last very long when in constant use so if Billy Douglas was here it seemed unlikely that he would rely solely on them. Surely then, right now no one else was in the workings. I discovered that I had been holding my breath and let it go slowly.

I studied the panel again and chose a switch marked A1-C hoping it stood for Area One Corridor and clicked it down. Light immediately emanated from that tunnel and, as it curved, I went a little closer to look into the opening. Four lights had come on and illumination coming from around the bend suggested there were others. I would explore this area first.

Even though the cables were inside metal conduit it was to be wondered at that the lights worked at all. Water dripped everywhere and trickled down the walls to form slimy pools or flow wherever the sloping ground took it. There was a dank smell, like rotting wood. The sound of running water seemed to be coming from the left-hand tunnel suggesting that at one time pumps had been used which were now switched off. I hoped it was too flooded for anyone conceivably to be down there so I could ignore it.

I switched off the lights above my head as these could probably be seen from outside and set off down the tunnel. At the time of our imprisonment I had questioned the reasons behind the existence of all these rooms in what had once been an old coal mine and had wondered if they had been constructed within it during World War Two and the place had been used as some kind of HQ or bomb stores. Everything, now I came to think of it, had a forties look about it.

I tried to walk as quietly as possible but even the slight noise my feet made echoed. Sometimes it sounded as though a person was moving ahead of me in the tunnel, otherwise I thought I was being followed. Ruthlessly, I quelled my imagination and images of Douglas leaping at me from one of the darkened doorways.

Most of the doors were open and I looked into each room quickly, switching on the light as I did so. Some worked, most did not but I had my flashlight. All the rooms were roughly the same; small with just enough space for a single bed and perhaps a chest of drawers, plus a curtained-off recess with toilet and hand-basin. Then I entered a room I recognised, the walls still showing the flaking remains of the peach-coloured emulsion paint with which they had been painted. The apple-green furnishings had gone, the matching curtain to the toilet recess - including a shower - torn down and tossed into a corner. This had been my 'home' for almost two weeks. I lingered for a few moments longer and then left, closing the door, as I had found it. Perhaps this room had been thus decorated to be used by the person in charge. Somerton had preferred to be above ground and had requisitioned the top floor of the house.

There were no tell-tale signs of present or even recent occupation of any of the rooms and I took comfort from this even though my quest was to find Billy Douglas. I just didn't want to run into him *yet*.

The room at the end of the tunnel had been the canteen. The real shock upon struggling to push open the double doors, the bottoms of which grated on dust and tiny pieces of rubble, was that it had ceased to exist, completely buried beneath a rock fall. I looked carefully but could see no way around or over it where someone might hide or gain access to the storerooms I knew to have been situated off the galley.

I returned to the checkpoint and, thankfully, turned off Area One's lights.

It seemed logical to go from there to the central tunnel. I went for the switches marked A2-C but this time only two lights were working. This did not matter insofar as this tunnel was broader and straighter than the others and one was in no danger of hitting one's head either as it was also considerably higher. There were doors on either side, again some open, some closed; offices, stores, a long room with around a dozen bunks in it, two bathrooms. All were thick with dust, presumably from the roof-fall and the only footprints in them were those I made.

There were footprints in the dust in the corridor though, enough to suggest a modest to-ing and fro-ing. What really threw me was that they appeared to have been made by two different people, one wearing walking boots, the other what I guessed were smaller-sized Wellingtons. I suddenly remembered the footprints in the sand on the island, the ones which had not been made by Greg. They looked the same to me.

There were no clues as to the time-scale of all this, the prints were muddled together and I was not clever enough at this kind of thing to be able to glean any more information from them. An advisor to the police who had also helped D12 had been able to narrow down these kinds of footprints into certain makes of boot.

I pushed open the last door on the left - this end of the corridor was in semi-darkness where the lights failed to work - and froze.

Despite advice to the contrary from Patrick during a few minutes we had been permitted to spend together I had refused to give Somerton the information he wanted about D12. Patrick had not known what he himself had revealed as they had given him a shot of truth drug which makes you very confused. He had urged me to tell Somerton everything he wanted to know. I had thought this purely because Patrick had not been able to bear the thought of me suffering as he had done and this was partly true. I had subsequently discovered that Patrick had been working on a strategy that would have resulted in Somerton's death - dead men tell no tales - a plan he abandoned when the situation changed.

The person to be interrogated was stripped naked and positioned with scientific precision; a metal bar or thin but strong beam of wood placed behind the knees, the person then forced to crouch, arms placed around the beam and then tied at the wrists in front and to the ankles. The beam was then raised so that the victim was suspended, trussed like a chicken, the electrodes placed according to the interrogator's whim.

I had told them everything Somerton wanted to know.

This was the room. I had not been able to recollect its exact location. This was the room. It echoed with silent screams.

I was shaking and held on to a pipe for support. The crude but horribly effective apparatus was still on the wall, the wires with the electrodes that had been inserted into my body looped over the top. They had not stopped sending the shocks into me - and although blindfolded I had been aware of men coming and going in and out of the room, avidly gazing at my nakedness, guffawing with laughter, sexually aroused - even after I had talked and it had carried on until I lost consciousness. I had been burned and was so traumatised by the experience I had not fully noticed until we finally got home.

I had not told Patrick all of this but I'm sure he guessed and it had a lot to do with the thorough and almost ritual slaughter of the Egyptian instructor, Adjit.

It did not seem to me now that any personal ghosts had been laid, or old fears faced and scoffed at, rather it had made everything worse and I was shaking, weak and on the verge of tears when I shut the door of the room behind me. I still do not know why I did not run and keep on running until I was a hundred miles from that ghastly place. But I did not, I thought of the sun on the mountains and the breeze that had blown through my hair as I stood on one of the twin hills at the foot of Bryn Glas and pushed open the double doors that led into the cavern.

One was like an ant in a cauldron of stone. I had not forgotten the cold draught of air that was the first thing you encountered when you entered this place; the adjoining slate mine. It blew through an adit constructed in the mountain side above to provide ventilation for the miners who had endlessly toiled, their only light in the very early days provided by candles. I gazed up for there was a little light, and with a shock found myself staring at what looked like a hazy, dead eye that stared down at me. My imagination was in overdrive again; I was merely looking at daylight shining onto the rock face through the mouth of the out-of-sight adit.

I had switched on my flash lamp and quickly, panicking at the prospect of this enormous yawning blackness before me, searched for light switches: the cavern had been lit by dozens of spot lamps. Fingers scrabbling, heart pounding, I found some and banged most of them down. Nothing happened. I tried the rest. Nothing.

Fear really can destroy you.

I stayed right by the doors, took deep breaths and shone my flash lamp around to convince myself that I was alone. I *was* alone, the cavern was quite empty, the reason for the lights having failed to come on quite obvious; they had been removed along with all the other stuff. After a while, I calmed down.

The roof was at least fifty feet above my head and even my powerful light got lost among the stalactites and slate vaulting. The other end of the cavern lay about a hundred feet ahead of me and it was just over seventy five feet wide, the sides lined up to a height of fifteen feet with baffles after people had been injured by ricochets during early trials. Somerton himself had given me this information, confidingly, almost as though we were on a professional par. In a way we had been: I should have guessed he was a policeman.

Even where bullets had raked into the wooden baffles the interior was all-over black from the fire. It had been a very smoky, smouldering affair due to the dampness of almost everything and very little smoke had escaped through the roof due to the strong down-draught. The fire brigade had arrived before it had spread.

I remembered how flat-packed sections of mock-up buildings had been stored at the sides of the area. For training purposes a section of a street or the inside of a building could effectively be re-created to rehearse any kind of attack, kidnapping, bombing, murder, bank-raid, anything. Piled on the other side had been units made of block-board that slotted together like giant Lego. With these towers or cliffs or any kind of obstacle that had to be scaled could be constructed, the sides of the cavern itself having ironically been deemed too dangerous.

Patrick, 'reinstated', and with the help of The Greek, had planned the final day's training, the scenario of the exercise the assassination of the British Prime Minister. Despite the desperate circumstances there had been touches of humour completely lost on most of those of foreign nationality; three make-shift and seemingly on the point of collapse market stalls constructed out of trestle-tables erected in what was supposed to be part of the eastern end of highly fashionable Kensington High Street. One stall had been loaded with battered saucepans borrowed from the galley, the second just with a few rotten-looking potatoes and a very old cabbage from the same source, the third had been, in effect, a gibbet and hanging from it by their feet had been three not-at-all-freshly-dead rooks.

Operation Rookshoot.

Somerton, distracted with his plans to kill just about everyone now the project had gone so disastrously wrong for him, completely missed the implications of the dead birds; that someone had either been outside to 'borrow' them from a gamekeeper's cottage, or they had been brought in. The latter had occurred for after a message had been sent to them Terry and Steve had made contact with Patrick through the adit and had abseiled down to help set everything up. The Greek, who thanks to subversion and Somerton's incompetence, had written him off as useless and was highly amused by what was going on, already had the key to the weapon stores. The 'market stalls' were loaded with explosives and incendiary devices and the rest is history.

I walked forward for a short distance. As outside, everything had been removed but again there were a few *mementos mori*, bloodstains, visible despite the soot and grime on the floor, a broken chair, several items of discarded clothing. There were no echoes in here, just a kind of deadness, like a grave. It smelt like a grave, a whiff of putrefaction.

I left, nauseated, and quickly went back to where the couple of lights were functioning near the beginning of the tunnel. I had had more than enough.

For my conscience's sake I clicked down the light switches for Area Three and went down to the tunnel entrance. No lights, just an inky blackness. I shone the beam of the flashlight down the small and narrow opening: a borehole into the underworld, a sewer into Hell. It seemed impossible that with all the comparatively safer and drier places to hide that Douglas would choose to come down here. I had expected to come across him in the cavern until it had become clear that the spot lamps had been removed.

The light reflected off the sheen of water running down the tunnel walls and there were strange, white, alien-looking growths of some kind of fungus or algae. When I walked down the tunnel for a few paces my feet slipped on the slimy floor and I almost fell. I retreated but something still kept me standing there.

'Are you there, Billy Douglas?' I yelled. 'This is the police and you're under arrest!'

A hundred echoes boomed in my ears and then careered away to be lost in the passageways.

'Come out now or we send in the dogs!'

Silly, I suppose, but I wanted to check an inconsistency, a quirk. It happened again; an echo that wasn't, a banging noise coming from well down the tunnel.

He had recognised my voice then and was sitting tight, mocking me. I took out my hunting knife, removed the sheath and set off down the tunnel. Immediately the slope of the floor became steeper and I remembered that when I had been taken down here to see Patrick it had become even more precipitous before the man I was with had counted three doors along in a group of five and shoved me into the cell-like room. I seemed to recollect that the journey had taken at least five minutes from the checkpoint.

Twenty yards farther on my feet went from under me and I slithered for a short distance before hitting the right hand wall. The flash lamp had a wrist strap but the knife did not and it went skittering away from me and out of sight. Desperately, I struggled to my feet and went after it. This was the really steep bit. I slipped for a second time and started to slide faster and faster. Then the tunnel curved and I crashed full tilt into the wall again. Everything went fuzzy.

The banging started up again. Or was it my heart pounding in my ears?

I realised after some time had elapsed that I had knocked

myself out for a couple of minutes and was still stunned. My head and left shoulder hurt. But I still had the flash lamp and it was still working and my knife was close to my right foot on the edge of a gutter created by the endlessly flowing water. The underground river, or whatever it was, could not be far away now.

Dizzy, I slowly regained my feet, hanging on to a protrusion of rock for support, and then shone the light around the bend. The tunnel continued just as steeply down for a short distance and then appeared to level out. I was approaching the area where Patrick had been locked up. In the end it was easier to sit down and slide down the rest of the slope. I had achieved this without further mishap when it occurred to me that it would be virtually impossible to get back again.

Upon reaching the relatively level area I saw that, some ten yards ahead of me, water was pouring through a fissure in the rock at one side of the roof, in effect turning the tunnel into a drain pipe. Perhaps this feature was connected with the roof fall in what had been the canteen. The first two of the five doors were on my side of the flood, the others hidden by water and spray.

Nervously, I turned to direct the torch beam behind me: there was the ongoing fear that Billy Douglas was not too far away. With bravado I did not feel I banged loudly on the first door with the haft of my knife and then tried the handle. It was either jammed or locked.

There were answering bangs, sounding as though they might be coming from somewhere on the other side of the waterfall.

Half my mind was wondering about the feasibility of freakish echo conditions that could produce such a phenomena, the rest was rehearsing the rush with which I would overpower Douglas. I only realised how desperate I was when I found myself worrying how I would get his body out when I'd killed him. The problem was he now knew I was on my way.

I reached the second door, banged on that too and then endeavoured to barge in but this one was locked as well. The third, the cell where Patrick had been held, I could just see to one side of the waterfall and I got very wet reaching it. This close the noise of it was deafening and I could hear nothing else as I virtually hurled myself at the door handle to avoid being washed away. Locked, jammed. I think I screamed in frustration.

There was a key on the outside though and it turned and I stood back a little and then, not thinking about the implications of this, plunged in, knife in one hand, flash lamp ready to dazzle in the other. There was a light already on in the room and I came to a slithering halt in the two or three inches of water sluicing across the floor.

After a long, long moment I put my arms around him, torch, knife and all. Words were superfluous but in the end I did say, 'I went up a hill and asked the wind and the wind told me to bloody-well get on with it.'

'Difficult to die of thirst round here,' Tim Shandy observed with a weak smile.

After he had eaten the two Mars Bars I had brought with me there had been a unanimous decision to postpone all de-briefings and explanations until later and we made our way back up the tunnel. Despite now having a very weak from hunger man with me I gained enormous strength from his company and, as I knew already, Tim was not a person to feel sorry for himself. So as we both slid and slithered, fighting our way hand in hand up the slope and he provided a sarcastic but tongue-in-cheek running commentary on his own clumsy efforts, I actually laughed. When I took a tumble and could have ended up being washed away altogether he succeeded in keeping hold of me and gradually inched the pair of us to higher and safer ground.

'Dear, God, fresh air,' he murmured as we approached the entrance tunnel, still holding hands. 'Was that a knife I saw you with just now? Would you be kind enough to lend it to this old warhorse so he can carve that bastard Scot into shards should we happen upon him on the way out?'

I handed it over and he gazed at it appraisingly with his one eye before shaking his head sadly. 'Well, perhaps we can whittle away at him for a bit instead.'

We emerged into bright moonlight and there was no sign of anyone.

'Is Billy Douglas living in the mine?' I asked when we were walking back the way I had come earlier. If Tim had not kept hold of me back there I would probably have died, swept away to drown deep underground.

'So that's his name. He was bivouacked in the big cave when I came upon him. Camping stove and light - the lot. The amazing little shit had a shotgun, if you'll forgive the word. There used to be a Scottish regiment nicknamed The Poison Dwarves and it was full of men like him. Effective all right. Some of them would have boiled down their mothers for glue for the price of a fag. Well, before I knew it he had rammed the thing in my ribs, relieved me of my knapsack and shoved me in the slammer.'

'To die.'

'Too right.'

'Tim, what were you *doing* here?'

'Oh, you know...' He found the energy to smile at me. 'You gave me all that tantalising info about the place - the cave where the war games were played. I felt I just had to come and have a look.'

'He must have known you weren't just any old backpacker who'd wandered in though.'

'No. Blasted and eradicated fissog or not he recognised me.'

'Recognised you!'

'I was staying at the hotel when Somerton's number came up, wasn't I? And as I said to you in Devon, my memory's not all it used to be. But as soon as I saw him I remembered like hell. After I found Somerton's body submerged in the loch I went back to the bigger of the two islands - just curious again, I suppose. I left the water and walked along the shore for a short distance and there was this bod messing around with a rowing boat. Him. I played it cool and asked him about the drifting dinghy. He played it cool too and said he hadn't seen it and he'd go and take a look. Said he was a water-bailiff. He's our man?'

Tucking an arm through his, for he was shambling with exhaustion, I gave him the full story. When I had finished he was very quiet. Then he said, 'Alas, if poor Yorrick hadn't got his memory in a mess, or reported what he'd seen to the fuzz at the time none of Patrick's troubles would have happened.'

I snorted. 'And if my Great-great-Aunt Sally's knicker elastic hadn't broken causing her to trip over them as she took the rice pudding out of the oven and dropped it, her husband might not have divorced her and married a psychopath who cleaved his head open with an axe one night and was duly hanged at the crossroads at Much Gasping on the Heath. Conjecture Tim, is pointless. Billy Douglas obviously kept quiet about you too. He must have thought it was Christmas when you rolled up in the cavern.'

He gazed at me admiringly. 'Did you really have a Great-great-Aunt Sally?'

'No, Sally's my sister.'

Tim reckoned he had been locked up for at least three days. It was only the fact that he had found a light switch and it had been functioning that had kept him sane. That had to be a miracle, given that none of the other lights had seemed to be working.

I took him back to the bed-and-breakfast establishment and had to knock them up as it was so late to explain that I had come upon a hiker who had got lost in a cave for a while before finding the way out, losing his pack with his tent and other possessions in the process. Coming back into the public eye was almost as bad an ordeal for Tim as what had happened to him underground as he was still very conscious of his appearance. But the people were very kind and allowed him to go to a room with a bowl of soup and eat it in privacy while they reheated some casseroled chicken for him. Not only that, when he awoke from a long sleep the next day they provided him with clean clothing.

I tried to relax, waiting for him to recover.

It was the next day, late afternoon, when I was sitting in the garden of the cottage wondering what I was going to do about something to eat that evening, as I could hardly prevail on the owner's hospitality, they not usually providing evening meals, when Tim felt that it was auspicious to emerge from his room.

'Saw you from the window,' he said simply, sitting by my side. 'Many, many thanks for yesterday.'

I said, 'I would never have got out of there alive if it hadn't been for you.'

His expressive hands made a courtly gesture. 'We'll have reunions and mither on about it when we're in our dotage.'

I laughed. 'Meanwhile would you like to give me a list and I'll go into Merthyr tomorrow and buy you a new tent and stuff like that?'

He thought about it, staring at the ground. 'The year's turning and soon it won't be so good sleeping out at night.'

'So you'll go back to London and stay at your club?'

'You mean after we've seized this runt of a murderer?'

'But he's armed, and I don't think you ought to be involved any more.'

'Because I've been shoving my long nose into other people's wars for too long?'

'Tim, I'd never say that.'

He grinned at me, the smile that had been on his face in the photo that Daws had shown me. 'I'm a real child when it comes to war games, you know. You've never given me the full details of how Patrick finally shut down that bloody terrorist factory.'

I told him about the mock-up of Kensington High Street, complete with a 'bank' and 'building society', the facades painted like theatre scenery, and the market stalls and then about the construction of what was supposed to be St Mary Abbots church to the rear of it where the Prime Minister was supposed to be attending a wedding. The tower of the church, constructed of six blocks that slotted together, was to have been our escape route; from the top of it Patrick and I hoped to escape via the adit in the roof.

'I took the part of the PM,' I continued. 'Patrick had split the class into pairs who were to take it in turns to try to 'assassinate' me. My minders were two of the instructors. It didn't get as far as the first round though, as Patrick had expected, because suddenly a group of men came in, some of the general helpers, including - and I'm pretty sure of this now - Jamie Kirkland. They were all armed, mostly with sub-machine guns. Somerton, or Lyndberne, as we knew him as then, prepared to give the signal to open fire. But before he could actually do so Patrick shorted out all the lights.'

'Forgive the interruption,' Tim said. 'Were you both completely unarmed?'

'No, sorry, I'd forgotten that bit. A few minutes previously The Greek had approached me and told me that he'd put Patrick's Smith and Wesson and ammunition in one of the saucepans on the stall. He was still highly amused by it all and obviously had no idea what Somerton had in mind for everyone. I think he wanted to even up the odds a little. In the general confusion of last-minute arrangements I managed to get the weapon and took it over to Patrick. He told me to keep it and do what I could. You must appreciate that Patrick had deliberately not told me what was going to happen other than he planned to start a fire.'

Tim was agog, practically rubbing his hands together. 'And when all the lights went out?'

'Well, as they say in Westerns, the guns blazed. Then what I can only call a *son et lumiere* started. A flare ignited somewhere near the roof, swinging from side to side on the end of a rope. Steve, one of Patrick's colleagues in D12, was doing that from up in the adit. The result was utterly surreal as it threw shadows everywhere and of course the shadows danced from side to side too. It made everyone feel utterly disorientated, if not seasick, me included. Then the stall with the saucepans exploded and pots and pans hurtled everywhere. There was a gunfight going on all through this, mostly a one-sided affair as Somerton tried to finish everyone off. Then the dead rooks exploded one by one, sending rotting guts and feathers everywhere. The smell made you want to throw up too. Shortly after that the large cabbage went off with a huge bang in a ball of flames and started a raging bonfire of the stalls. The trestle tables had been kept in the long shed outside and were tinder-dry. And Somerton and his group were still firing.'

'A massacre as well as pure pantomime then,' Tim commented soberly.

'Yes. I didn't know where Patrick was or even if he was still alive and decided to abandon the church tower escape idea and get out the conventional way before the smoke got me. I tripped over Batrun, who was wounded, on the way out and managed to carry him to safety. When I reached the house I found Patrick, who had concealed himself behind a door. He pulled me behind it just before there was an explosion in the front room. He had booby-trapped a small cannon so that it fired when the TV was switched on. Somerton knew it was there, he had spotted the wiring and told some of the survivors who had escaped with him to use Teletext to find out the times of flights home. The three or four men in the room were blown to smithereens - but as you know, he left the house just before it happened. He was running away when we went outside and Patrick played fair by not shooting him.'

'Kirkland and Douglas and a few others must have got out earlier under cover of the lights going out then.'

'That's right.'

There was a short silence. Then I said, 'I don't think I can do anymore, Tim. This might have to now run its course. The police already have a warrant out for Douglas's arrest for assaulting his wife so all we have to do is tell them where we think he is. Special Branch must already know I'm here because they'd bugged the car.'

Tim did a little phantom knot tying. 'I assume there was no sign of him in the cavern.'

I shook my head. 'No.'

'Did you go right down to the back?'

'No.'

'He had set up camp in a kind of alcove down there. It's not very obvious - you have to go through a gap in the wooden panelling to reach it. There's a store room of some sort in there as well.'

'This is all news to me,' I admitted. 'Frankly, I was too spooked to explore more fully.'

'No one could blame you for that.'

'It's nigh-on impossible to get a man armed with a shotgun out of somewhere like that, especially when you only have a knife.'

Shandy gazed at me kindly in the gathering twilight and I thought of the old saying concerning grandmothers and eggs. 'No, not at all. It's actually quite easy. You just need the facilities. A couple of stun grenades, for example. That would be preferable as I have a feeling that if the police go in there will be injuries. It's a crying shame we need the bastard alive.' He sighed.

'Are you hungry?' I queried, wondering what the thinking had been behind the remark.

'Ravenous.'

'It'll mean going to the kind of pub or restaurant where we won't bump into Douglas should he still be in the area and risk venturing out.' I knew what I was asking of him.

'Crunch time,' Tim muttered. 'I met a few people on my journey here, you know. I thumbed a couple of lifts from truck-drivers or wouldn't have arrived this year. They didn't seem too sickened when they saw me. I think if we went somewhere small and a trifle dim...'

'We could always get a takeaway.' Looking at him though I had my answer. This brigadier did not eat takeaways.

Chapter Fifteen

I did not contact the police. The main reason for this was that I fully expected them to contact me. Nothing happened, no one came knocking and I did not see a single police vehicle when Tim and I went out. We did not even speak of the matter again that night and I think he actually enjoyed our quiet meal together even though the restaurant we found was not all that small or particularly dim. I felt he had something important on his mind that was having the effect of making him temporarily forget his disfigurement.

We were risking approaching the entrance again, ostensibly because I wanted to retrieve the bolt-cutters but privately because I was desperate for ideas and seeking inspiration. And all the while that inner warning voice was saying, 'Go home, you stupid woman, go home'.

'How did you get into the mine, Tim?' I asked. 'As I told you, the gate was chained and padlocked when I got there.'

'There was no padlock,' he replied, loping at my side. 'The chain was just wound around. I think our canny Jock had not long since entered, possibly with provisions and intended to return before long and secure it properly.'

'And was he actually in the cavern when he threatened you with the shotgun? I mean, did you just kind of burst in on him?'

'No, indeed. I'd had time to have a nose about and came upon his little camp before he arrived. I was careless, I know that but the old hearing's not quite what it should be these days either. I've no idea where he was when I was poking about in the other tunnels. You know, I've a mind to go looking for him, Ingrid. The little swine's got just about everything I possess that isn't at home, including my wallet.'

By 'home' I was not quite sure whether he meant his digs at the club in London or the house he had left behind with his family. I did not like to pry.

'You have no stun grenades,' I pointed out, speaking lightly and with a smile to try to nullify his increasing anger as he mulled over his humiliation. This was a situation to which I was no stranger: Patrick, after being sufficiently provoked, can wind himself up until he is capable of doing practically anything. 'Tim,' I continued gently. 'Please be sensible.'

'You don't win wars by being sensible.' He stopped dead in his tracks. 'Ingrid, I don't suppose you'll understand this for one moment but I have to go and find this man. If it's my last war and I fail then so be it. But if I walk away now knowing that after a long and not too disgraceful army career I can't face a civilian armed with a shotgun then I think I'll probably just make like an elephant and wander off to die. I thought about that when I left you on Dartmoor but every morning the sun rose hot and strong and the birds sang and life didn't seem so bad after all. I'm expressing myself very badly but do you get the gist of what I'm trying to say?'

I had learned not to look at him too directly when I spoke to him but now gazed into his good eye and said, 'Of course. I can imagine Patrick feeling exactly the same. But I hope there's nothing along the lines of you frittering away your life for a man like Billy Douglas.'

He actually smiled and then clasped my shoulder briefly. 'No, no frittering. Shandy never fritters.'

We walked the rest of the way in silence and I was very uneasy.

Exercising extreme caution and with an unspoken understanding that we would make no noise we emerged from a grove of stunted birch trees and approached the mine entrance from one side. For a full five minutes we had watched, without even whispering, from the cover of the trees before we made our move. Nothing had been discussed about tactics but I observed that the shortened length of chain had been re-secured with the padlock, removed the bolt-cutters from where I had hidden them and handed them to Tim. He indicated that I should support the chain so that it did not crash to the ground when he cut it again and I did so, all the while looking over my shoulder in case we were surprised.

The severed chain was lowered carefully to the ground. Then I took back the bolt-cutters and gave Tim my flashlight. He made shooing gestures and when I hesitated took one of my arms and made it very clear that he wanted me to leave, not only that but vacate the area altogether. He held up both hands emphatically, palms outwards; I was to wait ten hours before I did anything.

Ten hours?

I wept a little as I walked away, it was like the aftermath of a funeral. I had not really thought, when we had set out to undertake a little surveillance, that he would suddenly make the decision to plunge off underground. This was what he must have been planning, preoccupying him the previous evening, even though he had obviously enjoyed his rare T-bone steak. I was fairly convinced that he had left out a few details about his original explorations. I paused in my walking: yes, that was it, he had been behaving like someone with a secret, a momentous secret.

Ten hours is a very long time to wait and wonder.

I set up my observation post in the birch grove. There was absolutely no question of my going right away, whatever Shandy had said. I was unlikely to go hungry as, just in case I needed them, I had bought more chocolate and a couple of cans of soft drinks and had had a good breakfast. I was fairly confident of remaining undetected unless someone exercising their dog stumbled across me as I was far from any public footpaths and a good distance from the approach-road. If anyone did happen upon me it was none of their business.

The morning was dull and humid. I sat with my back to a tree, a position that gave me a view of the mine entrance - not a completely clear one otherwise I myself would have been visible - and ate some chocolate, really for something to do. Then I had an awful thought; had Tim looped the chain around the gate again so that to the casual eye it appeared securely fastened? The last thing we needed was people out for a walk wandering in. In the end though I stayed put.

Noon came and went, biting insects got to work on me and despite them I dozed. Waking up suddenly after my chin had fallen onto my chest I stood up, stiffly. Everything seemed as before. A jet fighter flew over, very low, frightening a magpie from a nearby tree. The afternoon went back to sleep again. I looked at my watch and was surprised to see that it was two fifteen. What time had Tim gone in? At around nine.

By four I was sitting down again, still fighting sleep. I had not slept much the night before. Seven hours had elapsed and I was desperate to know what was going on. Once, I considered ignoring Tim's request and go in after him. Perhaps he had slipped and fallen and was lying injured. Perhaps Billy Douglas had killed him.

No, I would wait the ten hours. My thoughts drifted.

The aftermath of the shootings and fire had been protracted and exhausting. Patrick and I had had to give long and detailed statements to the police. There were the added complications of the two men who had died while on night exercises, King and Regan, and the complete disappearance of Rhona. Somerton had told The Greek that he had strangled her. As I now knew she had merely managed to run off and he had not wanted to admit it. The worst thing, as far as Patrick and I had been concerned, was that we had, under drugs and extreme duress, divulged all the important names in our department. Telling your colleagues, and especially your boss, that their cover is now blown is not an enviable task, the situation only subsequently mitigated by our discovery that Somerton was a policeman. Fortunately, whatever he had done in other directions, he was no traitor and not remotely interested in the workings of MI5. He had only set out to make us talk to enhance his own standing and ego.

He had got what he deserved.

Now it was ten past six and I was very stiff and getting cold as the weather had deteriorated. Dark clouds started to drift across from the west and a little while later it began to spit with rain. Then, while I was zipping up my anorak a bit more, yawning, I saw movement. A man had just come into view, walking across the open area towards the entrance. He was short and stocky and had a shotgun, broken and crooked across his right arm and was carrying a bag of some kind in the other. It was impossible to tell whether it was Douglas from this distance but purposefully and not at all covertly he went straight to the gate and saw that the chain had been cut through again. Even from where I was standing, hardly daring to breathe, I saw the fury, the way he tore off the chain and hurled it to the ground. Seconds later he had wrenched open the gate and gone inside.

I adjudged, immediately, that the ten hours were now up.

I still had my small torch and had put new batteries in it. One thing in my favour was that Douglas, in his anger, would make more noise than he might otherwise have done and not exercise the usual caution. This would mean he would be less likely to notice anyone following him. However, I must take nothing for granted and was very careful as I left the cover of the trees.

Not only had Douglas, apparently, thrown all caution to the fours winds he was now putting on all the lights. I concealed myself in a tiny alcove just inside the entrance, little more than a hollow in the tunnel wall, and peered around the rock face as the sound of him banging down all the switches reached me. Then footsteps receded into the distance.

It seemed likely that he would head straight for the cavern. Keeping hold of my torch in case the dilapidated electricity supply suddenly failed I warily headed for the checkpoint and was just in time to see that my guess was correct: he was disappearing at a fast walk, almost running, into Area Two. I followed.

The problem with this tunnel, as I had already discovered, was that only two lights out of a total of probably a dozen, were working. I simply dared not switch on my torch for fear that he would see me so had no choice as I got farther and farther into the tunnel but to walk in almost total darkness. Then Douglas switched on a bright hand-held light of some kind and I immediately dived to one side. But I needed not have feared, he was oblivious of everything but where he was going.

Soon, I began to see why. A faint light was ahead, shining through the grimy glass panels of the double doors that led into the cavern. As Douglas shoved his way through them it shone brighter for a moment and then they slapped shut. I ran on silent feet.

Even with the doors closed I could hear him shouting and he was in such a rage when I looked through the glass and beheld him that if I had brought an army with me I do not think he would have noticed. I slipped inside and concealed myself as best I could behind an upright steel girder, one of several that I had not really noticed before that seemed to be supporting other horizontal ones above my head.

It was a magical sight, the entire cave lit with what must have been hundreds of candles. Most were on the floor, quite a proportion on small ledges around the sides or set on the top of the wooden panels, all seemingly held in place by small blobs of wax.

Douglas was still shouting, mostly obscenities, kicking over the candles that were nearest to him on the floor, shining his torch this way and that looking for whoever was responsible. Finally he became calmer and grimly began a proper search. He walked away from me, presumably towards where he had camped at the back, so I was able to relax my vigilance slightly and look about me.

There were two rows of candles in the centre, forming a large ring, making the area look like a stage. Within the ring had been placed two wooden boxes, the larger one on the right hand side, a smaller one on the left. As I watched and while Douglas prowled out of sight, shotgun at the ready, Tim Shandy soundlessly emerged from the gloom, carrying his rucksack, and seated himself on the smaller of the two boxes.

Only seconds later there was a roar of rage from the back of the cave and Douglas ran back into view.

'Your loot's well hidden, old haggis,' said Shandy calmly.

Douglas looked like a man turned to stone, such was the shock.

'So even though I'm unarmed I advise you to lower your weapon. As you're probably aware there were a hell of a lot of old explosives in that store and they're in a highly unstable condition. We don't want any nasty explosions, do we?'

'Bastard!' Douglas yelled. 'How did ye git oot a there?' Then he resumed thinking. 'Were?' he shouted. 'What d'you mean, *were*?'

Shandy waved an arm expansively around. 'They're all in here now. Pretty as can be.'

'I dinna believe ya!' Douglas spat.

'Just shine your light around above the battens then.'

'I'm nay fool - while ye jump me.'

Shandy smiled his horribly twisted smile. 'Be my guest,' he murmured.

The beam jerked round and about the cave. And there, fixed to the tops of the battens, seemingly all the way round were wires and what looked to me like parcels of plastic explosive - although I'm no expert - and sticks of dynamite and fuses and what could have been very large fireworks and...

Douglas sat down hard enough on the other box to suggest that his legs had given way but kept the torch beam full on Shandy.

'Men slaved down here by candlelight,' Shandy continued. 'And they had to pay for them out of their pittance wages. Just think of it; a short brutish life with the risk of crushed limbs and lungs full of dust, killing themselves by inches to keep wife and children alive. And now we have *you* coming in here like some obscene slime and enacting your cruelties for greed and sexual gratification. I don't normally moralise, Billy Douglas, but I have to tell you that I met better Serbs out in Bosnia and they were the scum of the earth.'

Both torch and shotgun were now pointing in Shandy's direction but he sat quite still and went on talking. 'We last met on an island in a loch in Scotland and you had just killed a man. He was returning to the island to collect a large sum of money that he, Keith Somerton - did you know that was his real name? - had given to another man, Jamie Kirkland, to look after for him. Kirkland had hidden it in a folly on the island, a detail of which Somerton was already aware. The previous evening Kirkland had asked for his reward for this and it appears Somerton had told him to go to hell, clouting him when he protested. I'm guessing from what others have told me but I think at that stage Kirkland was so upset that he spoke to you about it. You had worked together here and-'

'He was the bloody cook!' Douglas yelled.

'My apologies. He was the cook and you were the exalted Chief Torturer, Thug-in-Charge and Lord High Everything Else. But you were both *here*. You decided to get rid of both of them, Somerton first when he went to the island to pick up the money and Kirkland afterwards because he knew all about it and you reckoned he was only a whining little rat anyway who had always got under your skin. You disposed of his body by tethering it somewhere underwater by the neck and were not at all pleased when your own sons found it after a considerable time had elapsed, the body having either broken free or the rope severed by the propeller on the outboard motor of a boat.'

'Say away,' Douglas said comfortably. 'While ye can. No one'll listen to ye when ye're deid - that's soon.'

'So I'm right then?'

'Aye, but I'd already kenned Kirkland was lookin' after the money. He'd had his cut and wanted more. Said he'd tell the police if he didna get it. It was Somerton who told me to shut his mooth for'im.' Douglas chuckled. 'He didna know his own'd be full of water before I strung Kirkland up.'

'You hanged him? In the folly?'

'Right close to where he'd hidden away the cash. I got him over to the island because I didna ken where he'd hidden it away. I waved some of it under his nose as he was chokin'. A right bloody laugh, that was.'

'And Somerton?' Tim asked, as though they were discussing cricket scores.

'The stupid bastard could'na swim, no more than Jamie. I just waded out into the shallows and he thought I was going to help him beach the boat. Tipped him out real neat an' held him under having let most of the air out of his life jacket. Then I got him back in the boat and rowed out a little way, tipped his body in again and then swam back to the island. I was dryin' mysel' off when you came along. So later I decided to move the body nearer the mainland shore and away from where ye'd seen me. So I hooked it and towed it behind my own dinghy - it was under the watter so no one could see it - and dropped it off near the beach - to make it look as though he'd almost made it. I couldna resist dumping the corbie on the beach: I had the last laugh there too.'

And with that the box he was sitting on blew up.

It was only a small explosion but sufficient to make me throw myself down and when I next risked looking Douglas was lying near the up-ended, smoking and slightly damaged box and had dropped the shotgun. Shandy had obviously immediately grabbed Douglas, together with his rucksack, by the scruff of his neck, shaking him as might a terrier to deter any struggles. This extraordinary spectacle then headed speedily in my direction.

I stepped from hiding.

'About five minutes, I think,' Shandy said, still on the move. 'But nothing's guaranteed with stuff that old. I suggest you run.'

'Give me the gun and rucksack then,' I said. 'So you have both hands for him.'

'And God help me I might use them!' Shandy raged, bearing Douglas aloft as though he might hurl him into the fastnesses of the cave. Douglas whimpered and found himself travelling at speed but still in a strong grip.

We ran.

'What about the money?' I panted from the rear when we were within sight of daylight. 'From the point of view of evidence, I mean.'

'Inside my shirt.' Tim answered.

We ran straight into the arms of rather a lot of police.

Tim Shandy came to a halt and roared, 'Get back! All of you! It's going to go! It's going to blow! Run, damn you! The whole thing's ABOUT TO GO UP!'

It was a voice to be automatically obeyed, especially as it was being broadcast at them from a matter of inches.

Everyone fled.

I had just reached the clump of birches when I felt the ground literally bounce beneath my feet. Then, when I had flung myself down, facing the mine entrance, someone else thumping down beside me, a vast cloud of smoke and dust belched out and, a split second later came the colossal detonation. Inexplicably, there was a loud clang somewhere skywards. I put my arms over my head as stones and debris pelted down, crashing into the parked police vehicles, breaking windscreens, bouncing off the compacted earth and showering through the leaves and branches above me. After this came a strange humming noise and I glanced up to see the metal grid that had been over the adit high up on the hill plummet down like some terrible, profane harp into the nearby spruce forest.

Once again, when the patterings and thumps had just about ceased, Shandy's voice boomed out. It was he who had been at my side so, despite the blast, I jumped out of my skin. 'All stay where you are!' he yelled. 'Right where you are!

We're not through yet!' He nudged me and whispered. 'I have a notion we can stand up though.'

We stood and I just had time to notice that he was no longer in possession of Billy Douglas when I felt the ground beneath my feet shudder again. Then there was a roaring, rumbling noise from within the smoking tunnel and a lot more dust belched from the opening. The sound diminished like an underground train going into the distance. I knew what it was; the roof had collapsed in the cavern. Judging by the continuing rumbles and crashes the rest of the underground complex followed suit. A large plume of dust hung over the hill above, like an emission from a volcano.

'It was all on a knife-edge,' said Tim gleefully, an ecstatic expression on his face. 'Cracks all over the place, some of the steel supports had fractured. I reckon it would have fallen on its own in time, soon - when perhaps kids had broken in and were messing around in there. Lord, Ingrid, did you see the way that grating come whistling down? Didn't that make your heart sing?'

By way of congratulation I put an arm round him and gave him a hug. 'The roof of what had been the canteen had already fallen. And water never used to gush into the tunnel like that.'

'The canteen? Where Kirkland used to serve up his bangers and mash?'

'Apparently his bacon rolls were without parallel.'

'It's fitting that the place should be buried - with him, in a way.'

'What did you do with Douglas?'

'I tossed him to a passing policeman.'

'Patrick told me that you were only really happy when you were making things go bang.'

Tim chuckled.

We were then both arrested.

I got the distinct impression that nothing quite like it had happened to this particular nick since the last time. Initially, and before a lot of telephone calls had taken place, we were to be charged with terrorism, conspiracy to cause explosions, wilfully damaging police vehicles, affray, trespass and anything else they could think of. Shandy, possibly because he was still on a high and back in an environment where people wore uniform and either issued orders or obeyed them, conducted himself with dignity and confidence. We were both then interviewed separately and at length and that was when the phone calls commenced.

'You again,' had remarked Inspector Jones when she had entered the interview room. Later, having thawed somewhat, she commented, 'The wretched place has been a menace for years. Vandals get in and the County Council, who now own it, say they can't afford to make it safe. It looks as though that chum of yours has done everyone a favour. Is he a *complete* nutter?'

'No,' I replied. 'He's a perfectly ordinary retired senior army officer, a decorated veteran of the Gulf War who was seriously injured fighting for the Croats in Bosnia and who just happens to get a kick out of explosions. If he'd done what he did this morning under war conditions they would have given him *another* medal. I have no idea how all those explosives were in the mine though or how they came to be missed after the intelligence service closed down the school for terrorists that *your* mob had set up in there.' This last remark, I suppose, was a trifle unfair but I desperately wanted an end to it all so I could go home.

She was not forthcoming so I gathered from that that no one else had the first idea about it either.

Finally, events seemed to just peter out. Nobody said very much but eventually, and although asked to stay on the premises, I was released from custody and permitted to go to the canteen, having it practically all to myself. I had been astonished to see when my watch and other possessions were returned to me that it was just under an hour before midnight. Then, Tim came in, obviously looking for me.

'You're free?' I asked in surprise.

He sat down. 'I seem to have saved the local authority about three quarters of a million quid in demolition fees,' he said gloomily but it was a sham and he laughed quietly for quite a while, his broad shoulders shaking. When I returned from fetching him a mug of tea and something to eat he was staring reflectively into space, apparently at peace with himself and the world.

'Bangers and mash!' he exclaimed. 'A feast for a king.'

'You did seem to have them on your mind earlier - besides, it's all there is.' I went away to buy myself another cup of tea and some biscuits, taking my time, letting him unwind as he ate. But when I returned to the table I could contain myself no longer. 'Now please put me out of my misery and tell me where you found all the explosives. Were they in that storeroom you mentioned?'

'That's where I found the candles and boxes - amongst a load of all kinds of rubbish. Most of the interesting stuff was stacked in narrow spaces between the battens and the cavern sides. You actually reached the fairly narrow gap there by going through the storeroom, the door of which I managed to force. The little arsenal was all ready to go and I assure you I left it quite alone.'

'So all the wires and stuff...'

'A few comparatively safe bits and pieces I came across plus a few dummies I knocked up. I didn't bother to wire them into the rest of the big bang, they'd have gone up with everything else anyway. So a timer here and there and a little surprise under one of the boxes... His backside is a bit scorched and full of splinters, by the way.'

I choked on my tea, laughing.

'I discovered it all the first time I went in when I went between the gap in the battens and found where he'd been hiding,' Tim continued. 'I'm surprised it wasn't found earlier but knowing the police they would have put up incident tape everywhere and might even have inadvertently cordoned off the opening. It was very dark and unpleasant down there: a real rat hole. Or in the aftermath of the fire it could have become blocked with rubbish as they looked for bodies. Douglas knew it was there though. I reckon it was Somerton's Plan B.'

'To bury the evidence,' I said. 'I have to say I heard something along those lines at the time. But I thought the idea had been shelved before anything had been done about it.'

'I overheard someone say that Douglas was being taken straight back to Scotland. And something about a piece of rope. That might have been the sample you took from the boatshed. There, I'm forgetting again: there was all of thirty thousand pounds in that bundle I appropriated. He'd shoved it in a cranny in the rock near his sleeping bag. I noticed that a couple of the top notes appeared to have small bloodstains on them... You said Patrick reckoned he'd knifed that Special Branch bod about a bit before he killed him? Perhaps the little bastard waved the money under his nose as he was dying too.'

We were both silent for a moment as we digested the horror of this and then I said, 'They can prove that with DNA testing.'

'And I can testify in court that he admitted he'd killed Somerton too but there's precious little evidence to support it. If he gets a good brief...'

There was another reflective silence which I broke by saying, 'That was really brilliant, in the cave. I don't know how you just sat there knowing all that lot could just go up at any moment.'

'And a lot more jumpy I'd have been too if I'd known you were around,' he scolded. 'I heard him return, of course, and he made a lot of noise about it as he'd found he'd had visitors again. Angry, not careful anymore, downright useless as a soldier, in fact. The first thing he thought about was his loot as he'd dared not carry that kind of sum around in case he was mugged. Straight in to look for the money then. Shock! Gone!

Completely lost temper while the old tiger waits and sets his timers and then goes to sit on the *little* box. Boost a small ego by leaving him a bigger one. Plonk! Sat down. He was done for as soon as he did it.' Tim leaned back with a beatific, if crooked, smile on his face. 'War games,' he went on dreamily. 'Pure theatre. It could have been... '

My mobile phone rang.

'Where are you?' Daws' voice said.

'In the canteen at Merthyr Tydfil police station,' I answered.

'You're still there?'

'We're not in custody, just enjoying their hospitality,' I said sarcastically.

'Is Shandy with you?'

'He is.'

'If you feel up to the drive I'd like you both to come to my place. I'll square it with those in charge at your end.' He rang off.

'He obviously doesn't believe in wasting money on phone bills,' Shandy commented when I had relayed this to him.

'He's still very annoyed with me for not going home when he told me to.'

'Here's one person grateful that you didn't,' Tim said with feeling.

'How are you with castles?' I went on to ask. 'Daws is actually the 14th Earl of Hartwood.'

'You mean living in them or setting sieges?'

I grinned at him. 'I'm asking whether you want to socialise a little, that's all.'

'Crowds though?'

'I very much doubt it. Pamela, his wife, may be there. She's lovely.'

'He's only a bloody colonel for all that, isn't he?' Tim made one of the intricate gestures with his hands that I had come to expect. 'I'm joking. Yes, I think it would be very interesting.'

Chapter Sixteen

Everything turned out to be far more interesting than even I had expected. It started quietly enough with Tim and I; worn-out, creased and crumpled, departing from the back door of the police station to find the Range Rover in the car park. It seemed to have collected only one small dent in a wing to go with the scratch during its journey from the bed and breakfast cottage - having been arrested along with its owner - and otherwise appeared to be unscathed. Tim volunteered to drive but I declined the offer with thanks, fairly convinced that he was uninsured. I had had quite enough of helping policemen with their enquiries for one day.

I drove only as far as a motorway services on the outskirts of Bristol and there slept for three hours. Tim had gone to sleep as though sand-bagged the moment we had started off, reinforcing the wisdom of my not letting him drive. When I woke up it was just getting light, raining hard and I did not feel one whit less tired. A wash and brush up and a cup of strong coffee improved matters slightly and I started off again after buying petrol, Tim still snoring gently by my side. The caffeine really kicked in then and I did the journey to Sussex in less time than was strictly legal.

'You *must* see this,' I said, shaking a limp arm.

As men do he snorted and grunted a few times before everything got switched on. 'Ah, yes,' he merely said sleepily.

I had stopped the car in a lay-by at the end of the valley. At the head of it, a couple of miles away, was Hartwood castle. The sun had just come out from behind cloud and everything sparkled, as though brand-new, freshly created. I had been hoping for a rather more enthusiastic reaction from my passenger.

'We're going to look a right couple of scruffy Herberts,' he lamented.

'Don't worry, I'm sure we'll have the place practically to ourselves and although Daws can be a bit formal he isn't stuffy.' My mind was going no further than our actual arrival and in reality, I had absolutely no idea what to expect.

'Does the place by any chance have an armoury and cannon and stuff like that?'

'A massive armoury,' I assured him. 'One of the best collections of historic weapons outside a museum in the country, including a rare 16th century falconet, if I remember rightly.'

A little farther down the valley Tim said, 'I used to live not far from here myself.'

'You've seen the castle before then.'

'Yes, but it's always been a private house - never open to the public.'

'Tell me about where you used to live - that's if you want to, of course.'

'Oh, nothing terribly special. A bit of ground. Been in the family for quite a while.'

I did not probe further, undeceived by his off-hand manner of speaking. He was missing home terribly.

The castle drive was packed with cars. In the end I drove right round to the back and discovered there was space in a courtyard I knew of, which had a stone cross of ancient origin in its centre. If there had been any doubt in my mind about what was happening on these premises I now became convinced as I positioned the vehicle between two television company vans.

'You can't leave that here, my bird,' said a somewhat pimply youth, poking his head out of the window of the driving cab of one of them.

I told him, having got out and slammed the door, and using regrettable language, that I would be his bird only after Hell froze over and meanwhile he could remove his spotty self from my line of vision. Then I spoke to Tim through the still open window. 'There's obviously a press conference going on. Would you rather stay here?'

Frowning, Shandy undertook a little invisible weaving. 'It's conceited to assume that one will be the centre of attention,' he murmured.

'Hacks are incredibly hard-boiled,' I observed. 'They've seen it all.'

He got out of the car. '*Do* give me a list of all the things that make you run a mile - if there are any.'

'Big woolly spiders,' I said. 'Smaller ones right up close to me. Cobwebs on my face and in my hair make me freak-out completely. People with disgusting teeth or body piercing, monkeys in any shape or form.'

'There are some really good spiders in Sierra Leone, you know,' he said enthusiastically, coming round to my side of the car. 'Huge webs, right across the forest tracks.'

'Please don't tell me about them,' I begged.

I had no intention of politely ringing the front doorbell: this woman was feeling increasingly bloody-minded. But there is always something that stops you storming into someone else's house so I led the way to a rear door that was open due to media paraphernalia that had been left on the doorstep and just inside. I knocked. Almost immediately Jordon appeared.

'I saw you arriving when I was in the front drawing room,' Jordon said to me when we were inside. Then, more formally to Shandy, 'Good afternoon, Brigadier. I am Jordon, his Lordship's butler. He sends his regards and apologies for not greeting you personally. If you do not wish to attend the press conference he has asked me to show you to a guest room where you may rest, shower and change if you so wish. He has taken the liberty of offering to lend you clean clothing should you need it, which I shall also organise for you.'

Again, Shandy swithered.

'Forgive me, but I think you'll find all media interest will mainly be on Miss Langley,' Jordon said quietly. 'Lieutenant-Colonel Gillard's just arrived.'

'Patrick's here?' I gasped.

'I understand that he was released from custody early this morning.'

'Who else is in there?' I asked bullishly.

'Most of the Shadow Cabinet actually.'

'This I must see,' Tim said. 'Politicians - the nobodies who send soldiers out to die.' But he was smiling just a little as he spoke.

'Is Patrick all right?' I asked Jordon under my breath as we made our way down a long corridor watching where we were going on account of the trail of discarded media baggage.

'A little drawn,' was the considered verdict. 'But, otherwise, absolutely splendid.'

To Tim's delight they were holding the press conference in the armoury, a good venue, I thought, if one wished to show political muscle. A long table with chairs behind it at one end of the room - or several smaller ones, I couldn't tell which - was covered with what looked like either a heavy damask cloth or a tapestry. I discovered afterwards that it was a reproduction table carpet that Daws had had made specially to cover a 16th century dining table when it was not in use. Facing the table were chairs, at least a hundred, and they were all occupied. Television cameras, microphones and all the people who went with them filled all the remaining space. I found myself hoping that none of the photographers perched on step-ladders at the sides and back of the room dislodged anything from the fearsome rows of pikes, dirks, daggers and swords on the walls or nudged one of the suits of armour.

Jordon's 'absolutely splendid' no doubt referred to the fact that Patrick was in uniform. Daws was sitting on his left and the Leader of the Opposition on his right. Also seated at the table were the Shadow Home Secretary, another elderly man I had an idea was a retired High Court judge, a Chief Constable and a couple of very serious-looking individuals, at a guess civil servants from the Crown Prosecution Service.

Typically, Patrick carved through all the protocol when he

saw me and waved. He might then have wished he had not for I was immediately blinded by a blaze of flash bulbs and the press surged in my direction. Tim, with an arm around me protectively, shouted, 'Don't knock the lady over or you'll never get the story!'

They fell back.

Daws was beckoning us forward and all at once I saw what was being stage-managed. Depending on the colour of your politics and taste in reading matter the headlines would be along the lines of; GOVERNMENT SHOOTS ITSELF IN FOOT; GILLARD MADE SCAPEGOAT; ACCUSATION 'MISTAKE' SAYS PM; ELECTION SCAM EXPOSED, WHOOPS! SHAME! or even the cringe-making NOVELIST REUNITED WITH HERO HUSBAND.

'Are you ready for this?' I asked Tim grimly.

'No, but it seems to be a bit too late to run,' he responded.

It would be tedious to relate the events of the next hour or so, or calculate the political capital that was being totted up, minute by minute like sums of money on a supermarket till; statements, endless questions, hundreds more photographs. A few details stay indelibly in my memory; the genuine pleasure with which Patrick and Tim greeted one another, Daws soberly but with eyes twinkling asking Shandy if he would prefer him to call him sir, and then at the end, Patrick, egged on by the press, captured highly unprofessionally on film with one arm around me and throwing his hat up in the air. And then everyone from the media was packing up equipment and leaving, the politicians whisked away by aides and we were being ushered through a doorway and up a flight of stairs into Daws' private accommodation.

Patrick and I, in the comparative privacy of being last up the stairs, sneaked a kiss, not sizzling but definitely worth while.

'He really blew up the cavern?' was his whispered question to me as we entered a large sitting room.

'A positively humungous bang,' I told him. 'That grating

over the adit that Terry and Steve forced open had been replaced but it was blown out as a load of rock hit it from inside and it came down like a choral symphony into the forest.'

'I'd give anything to have been there.'

I could see that the two would be swapping yarns for hours.

'Please help yourselves to the refreshments that Jordon has prepared,' Daws said, speaking to the three of us. 'I'm rather hoping that you'll all stay for a small celebratory dinner that Pamela has planned for this evening but we quite understand if you'd prefer to go straight home. Pamela did not feel she ought to be involved with the press conference but will be here directly. There, that's the end of my little speech. Please make yourselves comfortable.' His gaze directly on Patrick he added, 'I'll be delighted to hold a short de-briefing and answer any questions later.'

'It looks as though we'll have to stay,' Patrick said softly as we helped ourselves to sandwiches. 'If only to find out on whose behalf he's been acting.'

'I think I'll just quietly disappear,' Tim said.

I said, 'Can't you stay and then come home with us for a few days?'

He was thinking about this when Jordon knocked, entered and went over to speak quietly to Daws. They then came over and Daws said to Tim, 'It appears there are two lads down-stairs who saw you on a television news-flash a little while ago and say they are your sons, Ivan and Alex. Is this genuine?'

'Do they look like me?' Tim asked faintly.

'Like three peas in a pod, sir,' said Jordon.

'How bloody wonderful,' Tim said, even more faintly.

'Would you prefer to go down or shall I ask them to come up?'

'I'll go down,' Tim decided.

He and Jordon left the room.

Patrick and I looked at one another. 'Ivan the Terrible and Alexander the Great,' we said in perfect unison.

'It was a garbled rumour that Tim's wife, Penny, had gone to live with a horse breeder,' Patrick said later when we were strolling in the grounds before dinner. 'She let the main part of their home - which is apparently an Elizabethan manor house that's been in his family for generations - when her army widow's pension was slow in coming through and she and the boys now live in one of the two lodges. She went into business with this bloke, who is apparently an old friend of the family, to give herself something to do and help make ends meet. They'd spent a small fortune carrying out restoration work on the house, hence the lack of funds.'

The evening was warm and beautiful and I was blithely happy. 'Had she brought the boys over here herself?'

'Yes, and stayed in the car as she didn't care to gatecrash.'

'It's far more likely that she thought he too had made a new life for himself. It must have been a terrific shock, seeing your husband on TV like that when you thought he was dead. I would love to have been a fly on the wall when he went out with the boys and she jumped out of the car and told him she loved him whatever he looked like.'

'You women. Go on, say she ought to write a book about it.'

'He ought to write a book about it.' The reunited family had gone home together but were coming back for dinner.

'There's another little facet of all this that I've discovered; Mr and Mrs Zakiyah were perfectly genuine and really were on honeymoon. He'd lost his finger in a childhood accident.'

'The Cranleys really were hopeless!' I exclaimed. 'Jenny was almost beside herself with the excitement of it all. I suppose I should have been a bit more cautious.'

'Phil wasn't that sure though. One of those who say that all foreigners look alike to...'

There had been a sharp cracking sound and a small branch on a tree directly above us had suddenly broken, dropping literally on Patrick's head. The next moment he had lobbed me unceremoniously into a clump of dogwoods.

'Cornus alba "Elegantissima",' I said. 'Have you completely taken leave of your senses?'

Patrick's voice came from close by. 'Someone's forgotten to call off the sniper.' Leaves rustled as he wriggled closer. 'D'you remember Ken?'

'Hair like a full-blown marigold, the rest like a cross between a scarecrow and Eric Bloodaxe?'

'That's neat. Yes.'

'He was in charge of that assessment and training set-up you used to have to attend. A bit like the war games in the cavern only all electronic. *He's* the sniper?'

'Slowly move backwards without making the plants wave around over-much. There's a tall hedge not too far behind us.'

How the hell do you move backwards when you're wearing a long dress without it going over your head in the process? I had to wait for the answer to my question until we had reached the comparative safety of the hedge, where I wrenched the garment back down where it was supposed to be.

Patrick continued, 'I know it's him from the pattern of the volley of shots he fired at the inflatable. A signature if you like. I told you I knew them all and we agreed on signatures. That was my idea and I'm afraid I only insisted on it to assert a little authority.'

'So what now?' I asked in asperity, really wanting to know.

'Be so good as to go indoors and ask Daws to arrange for someone to ring him up on his mobile and tell him to sod off. I shall stay here and if he shows himself in the meantime I shall tell him so myself.'

'He's under orders though.'

Patrick was stripping off his uniform jacket. 'Look, I'm not just going to stand here like an effing target.'

The beech hedge was a long one and at least eight feet in height. Muddy, I ran like a hare. When I had almost reached the house I heard another shot. I tore on.

'Sniper?' Daws said in bewilderment, staring aghast at the state of me. 'Well, of course he's been stood down!'

'Perhaps he didn't get the message,' I panted.

Daws strode away, saying over his shoulder, 'I'll check. Find Jordon. He'll sponge your dress for you.'

'I'd much rather you lent me a rather good hunting rifle,' I said, matching his speed, stride for stride.

He came to an abrupt halt and I almost cannoned into him. We stood stonily face to face. 'Strictly for self-defence purposes only,' he rapped out.

We marched to a study just off the library where Daws opened a door that revealed the interior of a walk-in cupboard. Within it was a steel cabinet furnished with every kind of lock you could think of. He opened it, using keys on a bunch he took from his pocket. More locks, on a bar across the weapons inside. Unhesitatingly, he then chose a rifle with telescopic sights.

'It's loaded,' he said tersely. 'I can't let you have any more ammunition so don't imagine you can start a war.'

I seemed to have heard similar words from James not so long ago. I took it, turned and ran back the way I had come. Behind me, in the study, I was aware of Daws grabbing the phone.

Carrying a weapon under normal circumstances, or rather *these* circumstances, was an invitation to being shot at. I had met Ken, he of the unruly red hair, and had told myself that men do clown around. Ken clowned but was also a man who had not hesitated to fire live-rounds at people under training. He was, it must be said, a crack-shot. He and Patrick had an on-going competition of some standing and Patrick, who had methodically and persistently demolished whatever set-ups Ken had thrown him into, was winning. The trouble was that, more than once, I had questioned Ken's mental balance.

Using every available leaf and stem of cover I retraced my footsteps back along the path by the long hedge. To the right of me was an herbaceous border at the foot of the brick boundary wall which was of equal height as the hedge. At the end of the path the hedge gave way to low shrubby plants, including the dogwoods, that partly edged a large pond, really a small lake. The wall carried on, it went all the way around the estate. A gazebo that I had not noticed before faced the pond and was framed by larger shrubs, mostly viburnums.

I stopped. I could see Patrick's uniform jacket, or rather the gold braid on it, in the leafy gloom behind the gazebo. There was no question of him being inside it. As I paused another shot, much closer than the others, rang out and the jacket jerked and fell down out of sight. I went forward again, slowly, and reached the end of the hedge. There was nothing to be seen, no movement, anywhere.

Unfortunately the sides of the gazebo were constructed mainly of trellis-work so there was no safety there. There was not much in the way of cover where I was standing either so I dived right, across the path and into the viburnums. Making myself as small as possible I reasoned that as this was where he had aimed for last time I had probably boobed.

Where the hell was Patrick? Surely he had seen me and would make his way over and take the rifle. Then he shouted out, but not to me.

'The battle's over, old son. Haven't they got you on the blower yet?'

It was impossible for me to tell from where I was where his voice was coming from. It sounded near yet far.

The answer was a shot that I distinctly heard go right through both sides of the gazebo only a yard from where I had concealed myself, at Patrick's heart height, I noticed when I carefully peeped and saw a smashed trellis strut.

I thought it through and came to the conclusion that Ken, telescopic sights or no, had not actually clapped eyes on his target since we had both dived for cover. That meant that Patrick had not gone much farther than where I had left him. *That* meant he had probably climbed to the top of the wall, well-concealed by the overhanging branches of the trees growing on the other side of it, and dropped his uniform jacket into the plants below as he walked along the top. And all the while, staring at the evidence before my own eyes, I could hardly believe what was happening. It was crazy, freakish, one man probably ignoring orders and continuing to gun after another who was virtually a colleague.

Something made me straighten up and look, as well as I was able to through the leaves, down the garden. I had a very limited view but within it a man was slowly coming up the grassy slope towards me but on the other side of the pond; dark combat-style clothing, body armour, a balaclava helmet over his head, rifle at the ready. Then, he came to a halt about fifty yards from me and faced the wall and I realised he held something in his left hand and was making sweeping movements with it. A heat-seeking device of some kind. Then he whipped the rifle up to his shoulder and, rather wildly, fired. There was a crash as of a body falling through branches and to my utter horror Patrick dropped from the lowest branch of a tree and toppled over to fall face up onto the grass, writhed for a moment, horribly, then became still.

The blood ran as I bit my lip, watching the man run back, around the far end of the lake and then warily approach. Some yards from his prone victim he stopped and pointed the weapon. I heard him say something and the figure on the ground was galvanised into life. The shot missed but the second could not and Patrick stood still and I could see his expression of incredulity as he faced his executioner.

I had already moved from hiding and stood; coolly, calmly, relaxed, breathing easily as I had been taught and aimed where the eyes would be if I could see them. The weapon kicked hard against my shoulder. When I reached them Patrick had grabbed the fallen rifle and yanked off the hood.

'Oh, God, oh, *God*!' he almost sobbed. 'Even though you've half blown his head off from that range...' He could not say anymore and sat down suddenly on the ground, shaking. I think he was praying too.

Blood, a swarthy pock-marked complexion, a mass of black hair, spilled brains...

I sat down too and we put an arm around one another to stop ourselves shaking to bits.

'Who was he?' I asked tremulously.

'Heaven only knows. As you know, I'm on several international hit-lists . . .'

'And when someone saw you on TV... '

'We'll have to take the kids abroad for a while.' He scrubbed the few tears away with his free hand. 'Oh, God.'

'I'm really glad it wasn't Ken.'

'No, but it was Ken in Scotland. I still thought it was him and that he'd lost his marbles as I'm convinced he will one day so I thought if I played dead I could get the weapon away from him somehow. Then when he spoke...' Resting his head on my shoulder for a moment Patrick said, 'Ken made a good job of missing me. Remind me to buy him a pint some time. Oh, God, Ingrid, you're a bloody fine shot yourself.'

People were running towards us.

Chapter Seventeen

The next morning and against the background of the government floundering towards a general election during a day promising to reverberate with revelation, letters of resignation and parliamentary votes of no confidence, Patrick and I drove home to Devon. He had in his possession several weighty letters of his own; apologies from one quarter, congratulations from many others. Daws had politely refused to tell us on whose behalf he had been acting, saying simply that he had been asked not to. Newspaper accounts described Daws as 'an eminent government adviser' with the power to blow the whistle on what was taking place.

Privately, we had been told that Billy Douglas had been seen by two psychiatrists and was regarded as being mentally ill. He was now suffering from bouts of what was described as delusional insanity interspersed with calmer spells when he bragged how he had finished off all three of his victims, Somerton, Kirkland and the man from Special Branch, Greg Richards. It was the Big One, he kept repeating, the Big One. This meant that he would probably be deemed unfit to plead and would be detained at Her Majesty's pleasure in a secure psychiatric unit.

'He's been dangerously unbalanced for quite a while if you ask me,' Patrick commented. 'Just got worse.'

I said, 'When he saw Tim sitting on the box in the cavern he probably thought it was a ghost. That might have been enough to tip him over the edge.'

I had not been present during the discussion that had taken place between Patrick and Daws the previous evening after dinner as, after I had made the inevitable statement to the police with regard to the shooting, I felt there was nothing else I could contribute. In my mind's eye I could still see that smashed head and I knew it would haunt me for a long time, probably for ever. But by my side was the reason I had pulled the trigger and he was alive and quite well, considering, and resuming his love affair with his new car.

'By the way, the tests they did on that sample of rope you took were inconclusive,' Patrick said. 'It was exactly the same *type* as was found around the neck of Kirkland's body and although the information's useful it couldn't have been used as conclusive evidence. It doesn't matter now though. Douglas is going to be banged up somewhere where he can't hang anyone again.'

'So I got wet for nothing really,' I said.

'Not if you look at it from the point of view of testing my never-fail method of dealing with would-be rapists. Perhaps I ought to give classes - all the ladies in Devon flocking to our door.'

Understandably, he had been in this kind of effervescent mood since breakfast.

'Actually I didn't do a lot of what you taught me - just kicked him in the goolies and then tipped him over backwards into the water.'

'Oh.'

For a short while, while investigations into the still unidentified gunman were continuing - no mention of the attack had been given to the media - we were to have police protection, in my view a thoroughly ironic situation. We had no real wish to flee, as it were, abroad for the children's sakes and I was wondering what the family would think of our pair from the Diplomatic Protection Branch who were, at this moment, riding comfortably in the back.

The children were all waiting for us in the courtyard, having heard the car crunching down the gravel of the drive. I took in that they were tanned and all seemed to have grown at least two inches, especially Justin, and then was enveloped by them all and rendered a little unseeing by tears.

'Carrie bought it for me because it *wasn't* my birthday,' Katie was saying breathlessly to Patrick when I was able to take effective notice of what was going on around me. 'She's Mother Clanger and you squeeze her tummy and she makes a lovely hooting noise and Justin and Vicky have Baby Clangers but Matthew said he was too old for that kind of thing so she bought Major Clanger for you if you want him but she doesn't want you to think she's being silly or rude. And there's lots of flowers for Auntie Ingrid indoors and we're going to have a lovely dinner tonight with a taste of wine if we're good and you say yes and we can stay up a bit later so long as we don't get naughty.'

'Wow!' Patrick said, duly squeezing the middle of the pink, whiffly-nosed soft toy that had been thrust into his hands. Tuneful hoots filled the air. 'I remember the Clangers from years ago - the Soup Dragon and the Iron Chicken and the little planes they had powered by music notes going round and round.'

'You *do*?' I exclaimed disbelievingly.

'Of course. I used to watch it with Justin.'

'But we didn't have any children when it was first on TV.'

He shrugged. 'So?'

Much later when the older children had just gone to bed Patrick went outside to make sure he had locked the car. Police protection or no, I distinctly heard the deep burbly voice of the Soup Dragon.